MW01136066

DEAD OF WINTER

Printed in the United States of America

www.6kpress.com

TABLE OF CONTENTS

TILTING AT WINDMILLS

JT had heard Kansas was supposed to be flat. Yeah right. Then why did they just spend days and days going up and down rolling hills, following the I-70 Interstate? His feet and legs screamed in agony at night when they stopped to bed down. He fell asleep every night with the same wish. That he could get a rub down and some time in a hot tub, like back in his football days.

JT stood on the overpass, rubbing at the prickly growth on his chin. He was supposed to be getting a good look at what was ahead. Instead thoughts competed for space in his head. He contemplated what lied ahead and dwelt on all the things left behind. With a shake of his head and a rub at his eyes with his palms, JT brought himself back to the present.

Looking out into the distance he finally saw what they meant about Kansas. Brown, dead grass stretch unbroken as far as the horizon. Not even an anthill as far as he could see. The only thing breaking up the endless land and sky were the colossal windmills which towered over the landscape. None of them turned. White sentinels of a now dead world. There was one other thing ahead that shattered the almost hypnotic flatness. JT muttered the first words that came to mind after seeing it.

"Holy shit."

There were not tens or hundreds of them. JT estimated there must be thousands of zombies ahead. They milled among the dead machines, a massive wave of flesh. They covered the Interstate like a cancer, crawling across the land and killing the host body, in this case America. Possibly the world. You couldn't even see the road. JT guessed this was probably what it looked like when settlers first came west. Instead of zombies, they saw endless herds of buffalo.

"What in the hell lured them here?"

He had seen his fair share of zombie hordes both big and small by this point. Usually they clumped together because they were attracted by the sound of something living they could munch on. JT wondered if there was some rhyme or reason the zombies grouped together. In the dead of night JT sometimes wondered if they could remember in there undead brains being human and wanted to seek out other humans to be with. If the zombies could think at all. What could have attracted this many to this spot he had no idea.

JT heard a wonder struck whistle off to his right. He looked over at Gus, who stood beside a working truck they had found yesterday. His feet had never been more grateful; even more so his bum knee. Gus was dressed in a hoodie over a long sleeve shirt and blue jeans, just as he was. Winter wasn't here yet but you could feel its cold fingers in the wind.

Linda was behind the driver's wheel of the truck, which was still running. She was looking out through the passenger window, her face grim.

"I don't think I could have said it any better old timer." JT called over.

JT looked to his other side where Hannah stood. She also wore the same outfit as he and Gus. In addition she was wearing a beat up flannel shirt and a baseball cap, to hold her now wildly long hair back from her face.

"What now?" He asked her, wondering what her response could possibly be.

It was hard for him to defer to her even now, weeks after leaving Albright's church. It was hard for him to even admit he wanted control so bad. He had been telling himself he didn't want to be looked at as the leader of the group since they had met up. He didn't want the pressure and the responsibility of being in charge. The way he felt now, well it made a liar of him and all his protests to the contrary.

After the way he had botched things up since The Outbreak began, he thought it was better this way. How many people, how many friends, did he kill along the way? *You have to face it JT. Maybe you weren't cut out for it.* He ran his tongue against the roof of his mouth. He suddenly felt parched. He stopped himself from walking over to the truck. *Not now. Later* JT took a swig of his water bottle instead.

He continued to stare at Hannah, who hadn't answered him. "What now oh fearless leader?" he joked.

She gave him a tight smile. "This does present a problem. Let me think."

"I'd say you got time darlin'," Gus said, sitting down with his back to the concrete barrier of the bridge. "Doesn't look like the zombies are in a big hurry to go anywhere."

JT didn't envy Hannah at a time like this. However, he knew what he would do but he choked down his suggestion. No reason to start a fight now. It would have been a cheap shot and unfair anyway. When Hannah first wanted to head to the mountains, where she thought the trip across Kansas would be safe from zombies and other people. That the land between the church and the mountains would be empty. She couldn't have known they would run into a situation like this.

Everything was still as everyone seemed to get lost in their own world. There were no sounds except for the constant whooshing of the wind and the puttering of the truck. The wind had become a constant companion, blowing day and night.

A sudden, unexpected truck horn blast made Hannah and him jump and take instinctive cover by ducking down. The sound had come from behind him. JT rushed to the other side of the overpass. Barreling down the highway side by side were two dump trucks. Behind them was a semi driving down the center lane line. Its horn sounded again as it drove towards the bridge. JT covered his ears as he ran back to the other side.

JT looked down. As the dump trucks barreled under them, going at what was probably thier top speed, JT could just make out there were people riding in the back part of both trucks. They looked like they were all wearing a uniform, maybe police riot gear. He couldn't be sure, they passed in such a blur.

JT stood and watched with a mixture of awe and disbelief. The trucks smashed like lumbering dinosaurs into the zombie horde. Everything in its way was flattened or dismembered. Little dots sailed out of the back of the dump trucks. Then explosions went off on either side of the trucks, making open pools in the sea of zombies. Body parts flew through the air then rained back down.

"Are they doing what I think they are doing, or have my old eyes shit the bed?" Gus asked.

"No Gus," JT chuckled. "They really are lobbing grenades out of the back of dump trucks into the zombies."

"Let's go," Hannah said abruptly. "JT and Gus, in the back on shotgun duty. They are plowing the road and I intend to follow them."

JT and Gus exchanged looks of raised eyebrows at each other then did as they were told. Hannah joined Linda and Randall, who had also stayed up in the cab of the truck during their little recon. It was a tight squeeze.

JT gave Gus a boost up into the open tailgate and then pulled himself up as well. He grabbed his shotgun and put in the shells while the truck bounced off, accelerating down the exit ramp. JT saw Gus grimace a little bit and grab at his side as his body pushed into the truck bed.

"You okay there old man?"

"Yeah. It's that little present Harold gave me. Seems like it just keeps on givin'. Don't worry, I can still blast the heads off of a few deaders."

The flat land zoomed by as they gained speed. JT laid the barrel of the shotgun up on the bed rail. The sounds of explosions grew louder. In a moment the expansive, flat land was blocked from sight. They had entered the horde. It was almost like they had entered a tunnel. One collapsing around them as they drove on. On either side of them were zombies upon zombies. The undead had been pushed back but were already mere feet from the Interstate shoulder. A glance behind him showed the zombies filling up the space like a zipper being pulled up.

"Instead of the Red Sea, they're parting the zombie sea," Gus yelled over to him.

"Let's hope it doesn't crash down on us," JT yelled back.

A loud bang reverberated his side of the truck bed. Hands, one missing three of its fingers, reached up over the side. JT glanced over, shotgun raised, to see a little boy zombie was pulling himself up and over the side. *Must have been a runner. Let me give you some peace kid.* JT blew its head off. The body did four rolls on the ground before it was swallowed up out of sight.

The blur of dead faces came closer and closer. JT took a moment to glance over the top of the cab. They were almost on the semi's tail. An explosion rocked the truck. JT fell over onto his side. When he sat back up, he saw fragments of reddish orange metal littering the side of the truck. Hearing a strange hissing sound, he leaned over a little farther. He could actually see the back driver side tire deflate in front of his eyes. The hissing sound turned into the flopping sound of a flat tire. The truck swayed this way and that as Hannah struggled to maintain control of the now bucking vehicle.

Gus fired at several zombies that had clamped onto the careening truck. He missed them all as the truck wildly bobbed again. JT leaned across and smashed a zombie in the face with the stock of his shotgun. It fell, leaving behind its hand and half of its arm still attached. JT swung again and knocked it off.

Explosions, smoke, and gunfire were now JT's world. He could feel the tension in his body as he struggled to stay in the truck and keep it cleared. The screech of metal on the road as the tire completely shredded made JT grit his teeth. Gus fired again and again. He glanced over at JT, his eyes worried, as he reloaded.

I don't think Hannah is going to be able to keep control now. I'm amazed she has this long. We have to be at the end of this or we're dead.

JT began to think they would never see the ground again when the horde visibly started to thin. The truck started to lose speed. JT shotgunned a zombie that was hanging onto Hannah's side mirror. It fell under the exposed rim, which cut it to shreds.

Linda opened the sliding window of the truck and hollered back. "Hannah said she almost lost control, she can't drive on. Get ready to jump and run like hell!"

The semi shrank further and further away. It and the dump trucks had left a path of destruction in their wake. JT thought they might have enough time, with the reduced number of zombies now, to get out before the path ahead closed. The truck did a sudden fishtail, throwing Gus against him. The truck stopped with JT and Gus sliding and slamming into the cab.

"Ma'am, I need to see your license and registration. I think you're driving under the influence," Gus yelled up as he straightened himself to a standing position.

JT hopped over the side, wincing a little at his bum knee as he landed. He opened the tailgate and helped Gus step down. They each threw their pack over their shoulders.

"Later officer," Hannah said, jumping out of the driver side. "Everyone grab your gear and let's get going."

They all ran as the two sides of zombies closed back together around them. JT had to shoot a couple survivors of the grenade blasts who shambled close to them. He could see some of the blasted zombies still mindlessly stumbled and crawled after them, even when half of there bodies were gone.

Hannah didn't let up the pace as they cleared the closure. JT's side burned and his breath was ragged. To his left he saw Randall spot a runner. He drew his pistol and took it down with a single clean head shot. All without stopping. JT was once again impressed by Randall's skill.

JT raised a hand to his eyes to block the glaring sun. He looked for the dump trucks and the semi but saw no sign of them. Only the still windmills and the black and grey line of the road, marching off into the horizon. Nothing else broke the flatness ahead.

He turned and jogged backward, looking at where they had escaped from the zombie herd. Already the road and the land was covered from left to right as far as the eye could see. It was like all the destruction hadn't even made a dent in the zombie horde.

It was a marvel they had made it through unharmed. The truck was already covered, the zombies were like insects swarming over some dropped food. Now they were without a vehicle again. JT should have known it wouldn't last long. His leg and knee cramped like they were already protesting the thought of walking again. He turned back around and slowed to a walk. Not for the first time JT thought about what a crazy fucked up world he lived in.

SHELL

The massive water tower in the distance proclaimed this was the city of Goodland. The sun sunk, massive and pink, on the horizon line. Hannah already started to shiver. This was a cold she wasn't use to. She thought it was good luck finding a town like this before dark. They were few and far between in the days they had spent in western Kansas. If they didn't run into any zombies in the town would be a blessing from God.

A sign ahead declared the truck stop they were walking towards was the 24/7 Shell Travel Center. Compared to most of the looted disaster areas they had come across the store looked fairly intact. A few cars were parked at the pumps and in front of the store. Two semi trucks were pulled side by side to the right of the building. She could see no dead bodies, normal or zombie. Usually they were lying everywhere. Still she drew her weapon. She tensed up, shoulders aching, as she got closer.

The five of them huddled at the store entrance. Hannah peeked inside through the glass, hands against either side of her head. She thought the store looked as if aliens had come and scooped up all of the people as they were in the middle of doing their daily routines. Not a thing inside looked touched or out of place.

"Okay," Hannah said, motioning with her hands as she talked. "JT, you and Gus check the back room. Linda you take the restrooms. Randall you check the employees offices and the adjoining restaurant. I'll take the store."

Even though it wasn't completely dark yet it would be dark enough inside. At the last stop, Colby, Gus had the brilliant idea of taking flashlights and taping them onto some hats. Hannah got hers out, turned the light on, and swapped it out with the hat already on her head.

JT and Randall pulled open the glass sliding doors. Everyone came inside and the two pushed them back closed. JT gave her a half smile before going off. Every time JT showed her any attention or affection a wave of guilt passed over her. She brushed the feelings aside. She had a job to do, now was not the time.

She swept through the aisles and behind the checkout counter. Her thoughts wouldn't be so easily swayed though. She began beating herself up again. How could she have been led so astray at the church? How could she have almost been seduced by Reverend Albright? How could she have allowed herself to become an accomplice to the murder of Tyrone?

That last thought always devastated her. She felt the tears come to her eyes again as she relived the moment. Albright put his hand over hers. Together they pushed Tyrone into the cage of zombies. A cage Albright had created. His sick, twisted version of Purgatory for those who defied him.

Did she murder Tyrone though? A part of her always countered back no. But she had to be an accomplice right? There was no doubt she murdered Albright. Was that a sin? She tried to tell herself it was in self defense. It had felt so good to do the deed though. What did that mean for her soul?

She struggled with these questions and more late every night, alone in her sleeping bag, ever since leaving the church. She couldn't remember the last time her sleep was peaceful, unbroken. Hannah prayed all the time but so far she had received no response from God. She read her Bible when they stopped each night but it gave her little relief from the pain she felt.

A bang from the other room broke her train of thought. She ran to the back, where the sound came from. Praying JT and Gus were alright the entire way. The door stood open and two lights bobbled up and down in the near dark.

"You guys okay?" Hannah shouted into the room. A light turned towards her.

"Yeah. Just a little jumpy I guess," said the voice of JT. "Sorry."

"Something moved, saw a dead body. Turned out it was a cat, curled up next to a corpse," said Gus, sounding shaken. "I feel like Indy Jones when he has to put up with snakes. Fucking cats, why did it have to be cats."

The two came back out of the room to join her, proclaiming the back all clear.

"There's a lovely aroma of rotting convenience store food and what I assume to be store clerk back there," JT said with a grimace. "Dinner is served."

No one laughed.

"It was clear out there. No corpses, no zombies," Hannah said. "I wonder why this place looks so untouched."

"Good question miss," Gus said. "Lets go back up front and see if Linda and Randall are done."

The two were standing idle by the front door. Linda was looking out into the parking lot. Randall's mustache twitched as he reported in.

"The restaurant was clear. You wouldn't want to stay over there for long unless you like the smell of spoiled meat and cat piss. There must have been ten of them over there."

Linda turned around. "I found a zombie body over in the women's restroom. I don't know who took care of it, but it's head was missing. No other bodies were around."

"Okay. Sounds like a good place to stay the night," Hannah said, shrugging off her backpack. "Let's see what we can find to eat."

Hannah grabbed a bottle of Pepsi, a can of tuna, and a fold up lawn chair she had found between the magnet display and the row of tiny glass knick knacks on a display case. She glanced wistfully at the microwave ovens as she passed them. She couldn't remember the last warm meal she had. She guessed it had to have been at the church. Now it was back to eating out of cans again. She wasn't much of a meat eater before, but she was craving a steak right about now. Medium, with a baked potato, the steam rising over it as she cut it open. A nice garden salad and some fresh fruit too, since anything fresh had all rotted away by now.

Hannah sighed, she was almost drooling now as she set up her chair over in front of the large row of windows at the front of the store. She looked out in the gloom, watching the sky grow cloudy and attempt to spit down snow. A few pitiful flakes made it to the glass and melted on contact.

JT set up a seat beside her. He opened up his bag of Lays Sour Cream and Chives and his bottle of Mountain Dew. Its hiss seemed as loud as the whines the cats had made when they were chased out of the store. Gus had made some comment about how he knew pussies would take over the world one day. She was glad, not for the first time, that Gus was still with them. He could almost always bring something funny and light to the grim situation they were trapped in.

"This one's not flat and is actually kind of cold," JT said, taking a hesitant sip. He knocked back half the bottle before digging into the chips.

"Chips and soda: dinner of champions." He let out a big belch. "I stuck a six pack of Budweiser outside for later tonight."

Hannah hoped he wouldn't get as drunk as he did in the last city. He must have regaled her with twenty stories of his high school and college football days. He'd rattled off names of people and places she didn't know. Laughed at what must have been inside jokes. She had fallen asleep during his happy ramblings. She didn't know how much longer he had kept talking.

"Sounds delish," Hannah said. "You want to share some of those chips?"

JT tilted the bag to her without a word. He tried to act casual but Hannah could feel the awkwardness between them now. How could there not be, after what had happened.

She grabbed a handful of chips out, thinking now might be a good time to attempt to clear things up again. To see if there could still be anything between the two of them or if the door was closed for good. Maybe she could find some forgiveness as well. If JT could forgive her, then she could possibly begin to forgive herself. Not for the first time, she missed Ashley so bad her heart hurt. If only she was around to talk to. She said a quick silent prayer and then plunged right in.

"When it's quiet like this I miss Alan and Dusty. I also miss Ashley and Tyrone. I miss them the most."

JT froze, his drink hovering in midair for a moment. Then he slammed back the rest of the bottle. "I do too, if you know what I mean."

JT smirked and it broke Hannah's heart. She could feel herself on the verge of breaking down again. She took a few deep breaths before continuing on.

"I know it sounds like a lame excuse but I never wanted anything like that to happen. To hurt Tyrone. To...kill him."

JT put down the bag of chips and turned his chair to face her.

"You know, you didn't kill him. Reverend Albright did."

"Do you believe it? I mean, I am the one who pushed him in."

"You forget Hannah, I was there to see it. I saw him move your hand up, place it on Tyrone's back, and push. I saw you crying, bawling, the entire time."

"I want to believe you."

JT leaned forward, his elbows on his knees.

"He brainwashed you Hannah. Even now it seems like you aren't completely free of it. At first, I'll admit I was pissed at you. I blamed you for your part in it. I've had time to think about it though. It feels like years since we left. Trudging on and on. In time I've come to realize Albright used your faith and your vulnerability with the whole Ashley and Harold thing to manipulate you. That son of a bitch was the definition of silver tongued. He had everyone at that church eating out of his hand."

By the end of his tirade, JT sounded like he was ready to rip someone's head off.

Hannah couldn't help it. Tears came out and she sobbed softly. She put her hands over her face. JT's words should have been a comfort. She couldn't believe in her heart she wasn't guilty.

She heard the shuffling of boots on the floor. Hannah looked behind her. Sheriff Randall had came over sometime during their talk.

"Hannah, you alright?" he asked.

Hannah wiped away her tears with her coat sleeve. She didn't trust herself to talk. She nodded yes.

"Hey JT, you want to come over here with me for a moment?" It was a question that didn't sound like a question.

"Sure, I can. Here Hannah," JT handed the bag of chips to her. "Don't eat them all."

He did a terrible Schwarzenegger impression. "I'll be back."

ANGER DONE

Randall led JT to the door of the storage area at the back of the store. Randall's boots clicked, echoing in the enclosed space.

He took the stance he did back when he had them locked up in jail in Gateway City. One hand on his hip the other on the butt of his holstered gun. Like he was some kind of gunslinger.

"I want to start by saying I'm not one who gets involved in lovers quarrels or enjoys giving out advice but I feel like I owe you, after what went down. I don't like that feeling. So here it goes. Let me tell you something about hot heads like yourself there young man."

JT noticed the rise in Randal's voice

"I used to be an aggressive and quick to anger man. It didn't take much for me to want to knock some mouthy pricks teeth down their throat. Sound familiar? The girl out there, Hannah, she needs you right now. You act like your anger is an entitlement to be a top notch ass hat. This tough guy routine? It's run dry, no place for it anymore."

JT tried not to make any sort of eye contact as he audibly huffed. *Who does this guy think he is? Dusty, version two?* Sheriff Randall still took notice.

"What? Doesn't interest you? Let me rehash a familiar story for you. How about being pinned down in a trench with your best friend bleeding to death at your feet and watching your platoon fall one by one in the rain and the mud and the muck that came from the blood being added to it."

If he was trying to make JT feel ashamed it was working. His face burned in the near dark.

"Here's the thing JT. Like I said, you act like you hate the world, like this is all some plot against you. This Harold character you speak of. My time with you at the jail, when you tried to convince me about the things Albright was up to. I could see it even then. You enjoy your anger. I can see it, like fire in your eyes. Probably the same fire you had burning when you knocked that little girl out of that window."

JT inhaled sharply.

"Yeah I know about what happened. Part of my job is to ask around, when something doesn't seem right to me. Hell she was probably more scared of you than you were of her but you were too damn pissed off to realize what you were doing. I deal with your type all the time, react and attack and THEN think about what you've done."

JT couldn't think of anything to say. He could still feel the anger, the one he thought he was done with, try to rise up at Randall's ambush. JT thought they were done then Randall spoke again.

"You ever seen that movie *Red Dawn*? The good one from the eighties? Not the crappy one with Thor in it." Randal stared intently and awaited a reply.

"Of course I have, who hasn't," JT muttered.

"Good. Glad to see you're paying attention. So you know what I am talking about when I say the two brothers in that movie that lead their little misfit operation of raggedy high schoolers. There they were in the end, the older brother a hot head bent on revenge finally realized he couldn't save the world and held his dying little brother in his arms and realizing how in over his damn head he was. How would you feel if that was you and your girlfriend Hannah? You speak so highly of her."

"I am failing to see your fucking point here Sheriff" JT's intensity grew as he ran his hands through his hair. He wasn't prepared for this onslaught. Dragging Hannah into this was kindling for the fire growing inside him. He didn't want to deal with this anymore. Or any of them. For the moment he didn't want to fight back. He wanted to escape. Go outside, grab his beers, and drink them in the cold, all alone.

"My point is a simple one here JT and the point is this, and I hope you listen closely. You will NOT be punished FOR your anger, BUT you WILL be punished BY your anger. Do you want Hannah to end up like the little brother in the movie? If you still don't know the point I'm trying to make maybe we can go find that town where a little girl is splattered on the sidewalk and ask her for her opinion on the subject."

JT felt his lips begin to tremble as his eyes welled up. "How dare you," JT said spitting each word in a whisper.

"You're a stranger. You're nobody to me. I don't fucking know you and you sure as shit don't know me!"

Randall remained cool in the face of JT's outrage. "You're right. I am. So there is no reason for me to hold back and be concerned about hurting your feelings. I don't really care if we're friends. We're thrown together because of circumstances, that's all. So you can take it to the bank I'm shooting straight with you. Do you want Hannah to be the next tragedy in your life? Think about what I've said." Apparently done, Sheriff Randall walked away.

JT stood still. He needed to collect himself before he went back and joined Hannah. What he wanted to do was nothing more than to slam through the front doors and wreck some shit. He looked across the store at Hannah and like that his anger deflated like a leaky balloon. He still hesitated and took two steps towards the front door before veering back to his seat next to Hannah.

"I left you exactly one chip," Hannah handed the bag back over to JT.

JT looked at her and gave a weak smile. She was still so warm and so upbeat after all she had been through. She was an amazing and beautiful person stuck in an ugly world. He felt a little envious of her ability to keep looking up. If anyone should be raging, it was her. He couldn't take it.

"Nah you keep it. I'm not hungry anymore." He got up before he could say anything else.

JT squeezed his way outside, got his six pack, and sat on the curb. He polished it off in quick fashion, one after the other. He grabbed another pack, not caring about the brand. He stomped back outside. By the time he finished those six, the clouds had blown away and the stars shone fiercely overhead. JT shivered as he stared off, not caring. After awhile he went back inside. Everyone else had gone off to sleep. He crawled into his sleeping bag, feeling a warm welcoming buzz growing and drifted off into blissful nothingness.

DEAD OF WINTER

BATTERY

Hannah decided for the next few days they would stay at the gas station. In a way it reminded her a lot of the first one where her and Ashley had met Gus, Dusty, and Tyrone. She had forgotten what it was called. Boy how different things might have turned out if they had stayed there. She didn't want to stay at this one either. She thought hiding up in the mountains in some small town, so remote that only a couple hundred of people actually lived there before the Outbreak, would be the best idea.

She did want to give her group the time to rest in a spot that seemed safe enough. They could eat up while there was food easily available. This would be a chance for everyone to recharge their batteries. They would need their strength for whatever was ahead. She hadn't expected to find a zombie horde in the middle of nowhere and for sure not one which stretched as far as the eye could see. All bets were off as to what they might come across going forward.

She spent the next few days passing time by read through old magazines or her Bible. She made a request they all ate together at every meal. Idle chit chat passed the time. Randall spent a lot of time pacing, like a tiger in a zoo cage. When he wasn't doing that he was outside, playing lookout. JT spoke to her politely but only when spoken to. Otherwise he disappeared into another part of the store most of the time. Hannah shrugged it off, deciding maybe space was the best thing for JT. She had a full plate keeping herself together.

Hannah spent the third afternoon of their stay looking over maps of Kansas and Colorado. Gus and Randall joined her, adding in their opinions. After analyzing the maps, and a calendar, trying hopelessly to figure out what day or month it was, Hannah decided after two more days in the gas station, they were going to move on. There were many miles to cover, winter was coming, and no guarantee of being able to drive all the way to the mountains.

JT was spending more and more of his time the next two days drinking. Hannah was getting a little worried about it. She thought maybe it had something to do with what he talked with Randall about on their first night at the station. Or he was experiencing some of the same guilt she was carrying around. He wouldn't open up to her about whatever was bothering him, so she decided she wouldn't bother him anymore about it for now. Besides, when they moved on, his chances of drinking anything but water would be slim.

She used the next two days to read the Bible, looking for answers and for solace. She prayed for forgiveness and reflected on what exactly had happened at the church with Albright. She was starting to feel a little better with each passing day. She she was starting to make peace with what had happened and come to some terms with her part in it through Jesus.

It was on the last morning at the gas station that Hannah got up before anyone else. She felt energized with the excitement of moving on. Having so many days without any attacks or any zombies, with time for reflection, had bolstered her spirit.

"Come on JT, you sleepyhead," Hannah said, shaking him.

It felt like shaking a boulder. When he started grumbling, she went to find the rest. Gus was snoring so loudly, she wondered how Linda could sleep. After giving Gus a shove he woke up wide eyed.

"Are zombies here to nibble on my biscuits?" he asked, bones popping as he stretched.

"No, it's still calm outside. I'm really ready to go. Can you get the rest up Gus?"

With that done, Hannah ate some breakfast. The group joined her and afterwords they got ready to go. She rolled up her sleeping bags, filled up her backpack, and put on her heavy coats along with her hat and some gloves. It was overcast outside. The dreariness didn't dampen her spirit.

"I can't help but feel like we are stealing every time we do this," Sheriff Randall said, stuffing bottles of water into his pack.

"I would too," said Gus, "but who are we stealing from? They're all dead or checked out. Money don't mean a thing anymore."

Hannah was ready before any of them. "I'm going to head outside. Don't you worry, JT," she said, when JT opened his mouth. "I'm checking the cars. You'll be able to see me the whole time."

Hannah split off. She had no luck, none of them had keys or anything of worth inside. She joined the rest of the group, who were now huddled outside the station's doors. She told them the bad news.

"We're walking, yes indeed," JT said. "At this rate I'll be back to my High School pants size by the time we get there."

"Linda, why didn't you keep the wheelchair?" Gus joked.

"You thinking I'd push your lazy butt around if I did have it?" Linda shot back.

"No, not all the time. I'm sure I could have talked JT into doing most of it."

Gus gave JT sad, puppy dog eyes. JT laughed and the rest joined in, except for Randall.

"If we're going to go, let's go," Randall said. "This pack isn't getting any lighter standing here."

"And my balls are getting any warmer," Gus added.

"Autobots, let's roll out!" JT yelled. "Ops sorry Hannah, this is your show now."

Hannah rolled her eyes at JT. "Boys will be boys. Anyway Randall's right." Hannah looked right at JT, a smile spreading across her face. "Let's make like a tree and get out of here."

She couldn't help but giggle when JT's jaw dropped. He fell in beside her.

"Be still my beating heart."

Their good mood lasted the first four miles but was worn thin by mile ten. By then they had all stopped talking and shuffled along, heads down. The wind blew constantly across the flat plains. A car broken down here or there were the only breaks in the monotonous scenery. Each time they tried one of them they had no luck in getting them to go.

They stopped for the night on the side of the road. The next morning started out the same as the last as they continued on. Hannah began to see smoke on the horizon. This was something new. Alertness filled her previously slouched body. The smell became stronger and stronger. She wasn't sure what was being burned but it wasn't a pleasant smell. When she could see the source of the smoke she shivered, goosebumps breaking out on her arms.

Along a dirt road running parallel to the highway stood a woman. She wore a floral pattern shirt and dark blue jeans. A straw hat was on her head, but she wore no jacket or coat even though the day was brisk. She stood with her hands on her hips looking at the fire, like she was satisfied with her job. It was a pile of corpses. Hannah guessed maybe forty bodies, mixed with wood and leaves. Some of the bodies still twitched while they burned.

"And there goes my appetite for lunch," Gus said.

Even though she should have heard him, the woman made no move like she had. She never turned to look at them. She stared straight ahead, like a statue. Hannah decided she wouldn't bother the lady. No one else brought up approaching the woman either. That was fine with Hannah, she didn't want anymore run ins with crazy people. She brought her shirt up over her nose on plodded on. She couldn't wait until they cleared the smell.

On they continued. Hours passed. Hannah thought her ears were playing tricks on her when she heard the erratic honking of a horn instead of the ceaseless whistle of the wind.

They all stopped and turned to see a short school bus zooming up on them. The honking continued as it approached and sped by. The bus was painted up in purple and silver. What was once probably a school logo had been painted over with the words ZOMBIE PATROL. Three younger guys hung out the windows as the bus passed, waving and yelling. The bus continued on until it was out of sight.

"Shit, I'm jealous," Gus grunted. "Those people are having a lot more fun in the zombie apocalypse than I am. I'm a party guy, they at least should have stopped and picked me up."

"Just when you think you have seen it all," JT said. "I'd like to get me one of those."

"Come on guys," Hannah said, trying to sound encouraging. "Let's see if we can find someplace to stop for the night. Be nice if we could get inside some building. I'd like a break from the wind."

They didn't find anything except more flat land. When Hannah gave up and called it quits, it had been dark for hours. They found an old Chevy Malibu on the shoulder with a flat tire. Gus spread his sleeping bag out in the back seat and crawled inside. The rest put up their little tents next to it in the grass. Hannah settled down as best she could. JT took first watch of the night. He had been doing first shift since they left the church. He wouldn't listen to anyone else when they tried to give him a break, he just insisted on going first.

The wind howled and Hannah's teeth chattered as she tried to drift off. She thought about how she had taken such simple things as a cozy bed and heated home for granted. Good, hot food available whenever she wanted it. A steaming shower in the morning. She tried to picture herself back in the room she grew up in as a kid. Her four post bed, covered by a thick quilt. Lying on it, snuggled in like a cat, covered up to her chin. She kept this fantasy in her mind until she shivered herself to sleep.

HAMMERED TIME

The next stop was nothing but a pure disaster. JT told Hannah they were running low on fresh water, which wasn't entirely a lie. The real reason he wanted to stop somewhere though was to pick up some liquor. The stronger the better.

Back before the Outbreak he guessed he was a typical drinker. A beer or two a night. Sometimes he went out to party at a bar not unlike the one he was a bouncer at and would get shit faced. Him and his buds. It was all in good fun.

His reasons now for drinking weren't for fun and games. His knee had been hurting him more the further they put the church behind them. He must have twisted it or something bailing from the last truck they had. It made it hard to fall asleep at night, exhausted as he was.

Even more importantly, the other thing the booze numbed more than his knee was his head. He couldn't stop thinking. About Tyrone, about Ashley. Dusty even. In the solar system of the thoughts orbiting around his head they were small, like Mars, compared to Hannah. She was Jupiter, the biggest, the ruler of them all. He blamed himself for most of what had happened to them. Half a bottle of rum or whiskey and all those thoughts were gone. At least until the hangover. Then his head hurt too much to think.

He made sure to hide it. He didn't want to hear about it from Hannah right now. He assumed she would go on a tirade about it. He didn't want Gus to find out either, more because he was embarrassed Gus would think him weak. He, for fuck sakes, didn't want any more lectures from Randall. He always tried to put someone between Randall and him since leaving the last gas station. Randall didn't seem to mind. He didn't talk much to anyone. Not even Gus could pry much out of him. JT wondered if he regretted coming with them out here in the nothingness when he could be at home in Gateway City.

They walked along the shoulder of I-70. Cold wind smelling of winter blew steadily at his shaggy hair. He had a warm feeling in the pit of his stomach, so he didn't notice it much. It was the last of his Jack Daniels. Thoughts about Randall blew out of his mind as if the strong wind had whooshed them away. Instead he was on the lookout to score some more hard stuff before they stopped for the night.

"Hannah," JT called up. She was at the lead of their marching line. "I see a gas station up at the top of the next exit ramp. Let's stop there, I want to pick up some water if there is any to be had." *Whatever small alcohol bottles they have too*, he didn't add outloud.

Hannah gave him a gloved thumbs up. Behind her followed Sheriff Randall, Gus, and Linda. He brought up the rear. They trudged up the exit ramp and a half mile down the road to the little station. Two cars, both sitting on chewed up tires, blocked the one pump. The glass had all been shattered out of the building.

"I don't know JT. Looks like it might have already been hit up," Hannah said.

He was so intent on getting his bottles, he momentarily forgot he was suppose to be the lookout. He peered in through the broken window with the rest of them when a voice yelled out from behind them.

"Drop your packs and your weapons, nice and slow."

JT turned. Beside the broken down cars were now two men. They were so dirty and scruffy it was hard to tell them apart. Both were holding shotguns. There was a look of desperation along with a hint of craziness in their eyes. *Shit. Not one of us has our weapon drawn. How could I be so careless after all this time.*

"Son," Randall spoke up, a hand gliding to his hip. "We didn't realize this was your place. We'll be on our way."

"Fuck you will!" one of them shouted out, spittle flying from his lips. "Nice and slow now. Drop everything, then we will see who goes where."

"Everyone, do as they say," Hannah said, sliding her backpack off.

The other one, who hadn't spoken yet, licked his lips as his eyes darted between them and the backpacks. "You're the prettiest thing I've seen in a while, we definitely might want you to stay with us, help keep us warm."

Hannah blew the men a kiss and both of them turned slightly towards her. During Hannah's distraction, Randall drew his gun and fired in one smooth motion, like he was in some old western show. His shot was on target and blew a hole right through one of the attacker's head. A boom enveloped the area and echoed off the building. Randall went down, his front now a shredded mess of blood and fabric.

Ignoring the protest of his knee JT charged the one who shot Randall. The man turned, fumbling with his shotgun. JT crashed the man into one of the junk cars so hard the whole thing rocked. The shotgun clattered to the concrete.

JT wailed on the man, who didn't even have a chance to fight back. JT's vision was red hot. The man slid down to the ground, his face a mess of pummeled meat and sticky blood, which ran from his nose and his mouth profusely. JT gave him kick after kick for added good measure until his right leg was burning. The man was completely motionless after JT's assult.

The return of his rage was as comforting as the return of a old lover. He forced himself to stop. He walked over and sat down with his back against the wall of the store. He looked at his hands, cover in blood, and started to rub them on his jeans furiously. He tried to keep his eyes down but they kept sliding up to Randall's still body. Linda had rolled him over to his back. Her hands hovered over his body. Her look was one of resignation. Randall was gasping for air. JT was reminded of his childhood pet goldfish that had jumped out if its bowl. It too laid on the ground, it sides laboring for breath, when he had found it. Randall's chest stopped moving and no sound escaped from his lips. Linda felt for a pulse. After what seemed like forever she looked up and shook her head no.

JT looked down and then back up again. Hannah was coming over towards him. She sat down in front of him and clutched his battered hands. "This wasn't your fault, we all let our guard down," she said, as if they didn't just kill two men and lost one of their own. "I'm going to go inside. See if there's anything we I can find to help Randall."

JT gave Hannah a death stare. "Nothing can help Randall now. Go check out the store. I don't care. I'll be waiting out here." He jerked his hands away. "Please, don't touch me right now."

JT thought Hannah was going to challenge him. His look dared her to. The rage of an argument with Hannah would be better than feeling this guilt. Randall was right. He loved his anger because the world was shit. Instead, she got up with a sigh. She walked over to Randall's corpse and stood over it. Linda rose to her feet and the two of them embraced, then went inside the gas station. Gus stood over Randall looking somber and in shock. JT didn't know how long he sat there, looking between his hands and the body of Sheriff Randall. *The man didn't get to enjoy his retirement for long.*

Hannah came out with a threadbare throw. On it was a picture of a wolf howling at the moon. She covered Randall's body with it. JT thought it was a poor excuse for a grave. The man was hard but he deserved better. The others all stood around his body and held hands. Hannah didn't even look over at him. At that point JT decided to he'd go inside, see if there was something to wash his hands off with.

Through the broken glass he could hear Hannah's voice drift into the store. She was saying a prayer. The words made a pulsing throb in his head. Its color was red. He found some hand sanitizer and poured it all over his hands, relishing the stings where his skin had broken open. He ripped open a pack of paper towels and dabbed at the blood until he was satisfied.

While he was inside he rummaged through the store for some alcohol. *Wouldn't want this stop to go to waste.* He found three bottles of whiskey and figured it was enough to get hammered on. He jammed them into his pack. He couldn't wait until the black abyss took him tonight.

On the way out JT caught himself looking at his reflection in the mirror on one of those spinning sunglass trees. Thoughts of what Randall had said to him ravaged through his mind as he looked at himself. *God damn JT,* he thought to himself, *you had to rush to the storefront to look for alcohol. You left your position and made everyone vulnerable. This is on you. Bad enough it was Randall. It could have been Hannah.* With that thought JT grabbed the display and violently shook it. Cheap sunglasses fell to the floor. He picked up the whole display and slammed it into the ground, sending plastic shards flying everywhere.

JT stopped to catch his breath before heading back outside. He took his hat off and poured some water on his hair before replacing his hat. That's when he noticed it. A rack on the checkout counter of cheap DVDs. Only $5.95 the bright neon sign advertised. One of the face out cases was the movie *Red Dawn*. JT felt like he could laugh and cry all at once. He stuffed all that bullshit down violently snatched up the case. He fuddled with the outer pocket of his bag and slammed the movie into his pack. It felt right.

WORRY WORRY WORRY

"You do see what's going on back there, don't ya?"

Gus had slid up next to Hannah as they walked on towards what felt like the edge of the Earth. Hannah snatched little glances back over her shoulder. She saw JT sway down the shoulder of the interstate. He wore sunglasses today, saying the sun was too bright, even though it was overcast. He frequently held his hand to his head, rubbing his temples.

"Yes, JT looks tired and is struggling to keep up." Gus gave her a look that said are you kidding me.

Of course she noticed his increasingly erratic behavior. How could she not notice, with the four of them being so close all the time. They were two days passed the death of Randall. She had grieved and moved on, confident in her faith. Randall was now in a more peaceful place. This was one death she knew wasn't her doing. It was this world's fault. It didn't seem JT could do that though. She didn't know if she could help him either. He had rejected her attempts at praying together or accepting any condolence at all.

"You want me to say something little lady? I know you two have been on the outs since that Albright business."

"You don't need my permission Gus. Do what you can." She tried to keep the urgent worry out of her voice.

With a pat on the shoulder Gus paused, waiting for Linda to catch up to him. The group marched on. It was another uneventful day. Which gave Hannah plenty of time to chew on her worry. She talked to God, asking him to take the burden from her and come back with an answer. She kept JT at the edge of her vision all day.

Hannah called camp at dusk. There was still nothing but flat, brown grassland all around them, as far as she could see. With nothing to build a fire with, it would be another cold night on the hard ground.

"It's getting so cold out here, my nipples are gonna poke an eye out," Gus said, as he ate a dinner of cold Spam with a chocolate chip cookie for dessert. "Don't you try to sneak a peak, Linda."

"What's there to peak at? You need to get some meat on your bones," Linda said, opening up her own Spam tin. "You're not doing a good job keeping me warm at night."

Gus shot a finger gun at JT. "That make you jealous over there handsome?"

JT simply shook his head no with pursed lips. He played with his tin can, flipping it end over end. He sat apart from the three of them and when he ate, it was in silence. He grabbed his backpack and stood up when he finished.

"I gotta go do my business," he announced.

"Hold up boss," Gus said, waving him back. "I've tried to be silent, but I gotta speak up now. You okay there JT? Anything you want to share?"

"No Gus, I don't think so. Unless you are wanting to come help me wipe," JT half smiled. Hannah could tell he also looked annoyed. She jumped in.

"JT before you go-"

"Hannah, don't you start in too," JT interrupted.

"JT, what do you think I'm going to start?" she said, in a more commanding voice. "I just had something I need to tell you. I've decided to take you off the lookout position. At least for a while."

JT shot Hannah a dirty look.

"Come on now son," Gus said. "It's for your own good. We should have never put so much stress on you without a break. Randall, Hannah, Linda, me, we all should have taken turns. Dial it down JT. You're not a superhero."

"You're not my father Gus, so don't try to act like it," JT said, sounding like a whiny teen.

"Then start acting like an adult, damn it!" Gus shouted. JT looked at Gus like he had been slapped. "Now look what I've gone and done. Sorry JT."

"JT, this is what we're going to do. Linda, Gus, and I are going to go on rotation," Hannah gave him a knowing look. "You act like you are guilty of something. What did you think I was going to bring up? You have something to share?"

JT stood there, clutching his backpack. She felt bad about ganging up on him like this. She didn't know if they would get through to him or just push him away more. He looked on the verge of saying something, then turned and walked away into the twilight.

"The kid is hurting," Gus said when JT was out of sight, lost in the darkness their little battery powered lanterns couldn't penetrate.

"I've seen lots of it in my time," Linda said. "He's has so much grief and anger he is clinging on to. Most of it he has to work out himself. I'm no psychologist but I could help some, if he would let me."

"Maybe, with more time," Hannah said, understanding some of the grief JT was carrying. More and more she was coming to feel some of her own rage. She made a disgusted laugh. Those were things she still shared with JT. "You're still a stranger to him Linda. No offense, but I highly doubt he'll talk to you."

He wouldn't open up to her but Hannah guessed JT blamed himself along with her for Tyrone's death. God knows she blamed herself enough without JT piling on her. Maybe he also blamed himself for Alan and Dusty and Ashley too. Then she felt the rage, one which was close to the surface, like an oil slick on a body of water. Was that how JT felt all the time? It had been with her since leaving the church behind. Tapping that anger made her want to strangle JT. Slap him in the face and tell him to get over it. Hadn't she been traumatized more than anyone else here?

Christ, she about had sex with a lying, murdering slime ball. Before that a psychopath tried to kill her. He wanted to stuff her and mount her like a hunter's trophy. Those things were on top of all the zombie attacks. The death of her dear friend. Not knowing but fearing her mother was out there right now, walking around as one of the undead.

It was crazy to think about all she had been through. Yet she wasn't numbing herself into oblivion with drugs or alcohol. Instead, she laid awake long after everyone else was snoring away, thoughts of all she had endured chasing each other like a dog chasing its tail. Most mornings she woke up, cheeks hot and wet. She turned to her faith at those times. God had been silent but she knew, deep down, he would answer her when the time was right.

She drew in a deep breath and let it out. She needed to calm down. This wasn't a grief competition. She had to admit there was the other part of her though. The part which still had feelings for JT. It wanted to comfort him, tell him they had both been through so much yet they were still here. Everything would be okay. They had to lean on each other was all. She hesitated to do it though, because she wasn't sure he still felt the same way about her. Where did they stand now after all they had went through. He barely looked at her now, let alone talked to her. How much of Tyrone's death did JT blame on her? What if he utterly rejected her? Could she take it right now?

They broke apart for the night. Gus said he would take first watch. She set up her tent, crawled inside, and read her Bible by flashlight, until the words started to blur together.

She gave up and settled down into her sleeping bag, hoping tonight at least the bad dreams wouldn't come.

The next morning frost covered everything. The road and the grass twinkled in the dawn's early light. The tents crunched as the crew packed them up. Hannah had taken last watch, so she was already up when the others rose. She sat on the concrete shoulder, knees up to her chest, looking off into the distance. The first to come over was Gus, stomping his feet and rubbing his gloved hands together.

"Morning darlin'," he said, standing close to her. The sun looked swollen as it topped the straight line of the distant vista. "I don't know what I miss more, central air or heat."

"Gus, morning" Hannah said, perkier than she felt. "It's too bad we ran out of coffee. My inside's could use some warming up."

"That's what she said."

It was a half hearted attempt. Gus only chuckled slightly and Hannah smiled a little. She had indeed had a bad dream last night. Randall had died. How she couldn't remember, but he didn't stay dead. He had come back as a zombie. He had eaten part of JT when she discovered him. Randall rose and came for her. Behind him was a zombie Harold and a zombie Albright. She woke up panting heavily. Knowing that sleeping was done that night, she took over guard duty from Linda.

The sun shone down weakly. Hannah stuffed her gloved hands into her coat pockets. It was the coldest day they had encountered yet. Linda stood beside Gus. Moments later JT stumbled up to join them, sunglass on. Hannah shook her head slightly and motioned that is was time to go.

Gus shivered dramatically, rubbing his arms. "Either we are about to Colorado or winter is almost here."

It wasn't long after a midday break for food when they found another car along the side of the road. It was a little Honda Accord. More out of habit than of any real hope, she checked it out. It looked in good shape and when Hannah looked inside, pistol drawn, the keys were dangling in the ignition.

She slid behind the wheel, closed her eyes tight, and tried it. Weakly the engine turned and then roared to life. She got out, jumping up and down and waving her arms.

"Jackpot!" she shouted. "Everyone pile in."

"Ford tough my ass!" Gus cackled. "Give this old fart a Herculean Honda any day!"

JT took shotgun. Gus and Linda went in the back seat. Hannah eased the car into drive and out of habit looked in the rear view mirror. There were a pair of pink fuzzy handcuffs dangling from it.

"Kinky," Gus said from the backseat. "You want to pass them back here? I might have a use for them later."

Hannah saw Linda smack Gus in the arm. Hannah smiled and pulled onto the Interstate. Soon they were blazing down the highway, heater cranked to the max. The car even had over half a tank of gas. Hannah felt the happiest she had in awhile. Funny how it took something so simple nowadays. She was humming a song to herself as the miles they would have struggled to walk flew by in a blur.

The state sign to Colorado came and went. As they passed it they all cheered. Even JT, who had been silent and spent most of the time looking out the window. The warmth and the break from walking seemed to put everyone into good spirits.

Signs for Denver began to appear over the Interstate. More and more broken down cars and big multi vehicle pile ups began to appear as well, like icebergs in a frozen sea. Hannah knew there was no way she wanted to go into a city that big. In fact, while pouring over the state maps, she decided she would skirt the mountains to the south and approach that way, going past Colorado Springs. It was still a big city but not the metropolis Denver was.

She guessed maybe the winter would be less severe and maybe start later as well if they went further south. In her previous life she had never been any farther west than Indiana for a cheerleading competition, but she had heard some roads could close as early as November up in the mountains. She didn't know what month it was now but she guessed it was late in the year. The trees they passed were all but bare. As they took I-70 deeper into the state and saw no snow on the ground, she felt hopeful they would make it ahead of any major winter storms.

Anytime they got to an on and off ramp for a town the snarl of cars got worse. Hannah had to be careful maneuvering around and through them. Besides those times, the going was relatively open, like most of Kansas. They had seen no sign of people or zombies.

In what seemed like a short amount of time they arrived in the city of Limon. Hannah gave a thankful prayer to God. Without the car they wouldn't even be to the state border yet.

Although it was only mid afternoon, Hannah thought this would be a good place to stop. She knew from the map in Limon they would be jumping off the I-70 interstate and taking a highway down to Colorado Springs. She didn't know what condition that highway was in and she was getting sleepy from the heat. She knew she didn't want to be entering a bigger city like Colorado Springs at night.

Driving slowly through the town, Hannah offered. "How about we stay someplace a little nicer tonight?" pointing at the Holiday Inn Express they were passing. There were no objections. Hannah turned into the mostly empty parking lot.

"How we going to do this?" JT asked as Hannah killed the engine.

"We'll go together, floor by floor and room by room. Once we know it is clear, we take the top room by the emergency stairs. That location should give us enough warning if something were to happen."

"Sounds like a plan darlin'," Gus said, opening his door and stepping out with a stretch. "Damn it was great to rest these old bones. And to have feeling in my fingers and toes."

Hannah popped the trunk. Each grabbed a gun from their packs, except for JT, who had had his shotgun on his lap for the entire drive. The only other thing everyone grabbed were their headlamps. The rest, Hannah thought, would wait until they were sure the place was safe to stop for the night.

Gus and JT pried open the sliding glass doors to the lobby. Inside looked relatively clean. A few suitcases laid half on, half off an overturned luggage cart. A body was slumped over the check in desk at the waist. Its arms look like they had been chewed on by an over sized toddler going through their teething phase.

"Not too heartwarming," Gus exclaimed. "You sure we should be going in here?"

Hannah waved her hand forward. They continued on.

The first floor was clear except for the laundry room. In the big canvas box on wheels that usually held dirty towels, they instead found a variety of body parts all hacked up. There was no blood, so Hannah assumed they were zombie parts. Back when this began she would have gagged and thought how strange it would be that someone would do such a thing. Now she shrugged at JT and moved on.

They did come across one zombie at the end of the hall. It was between the inner and outer doors of the side exit, trapped like a fly in a window. Hannah held open the door and JT pulled his knife. He stabbed it in the head. Down it went. Hannah closed the door, leaving it where it fell.

Up to the second floor they went. Every room was cleared. There were no incidents. The third floor also checked out clear.

"Well aren't we lucky today! Check in's at three and checkout is at ten," Gus said as they stood outside the door to the stairwell.

"Not a bad choice Hannah," Linda said. "It will be nice sleeping on a bed, out of the wind for at least a night."

Hannah smiled, pleased with herself. She went through the stairwell door and down to the car. The rest followed her. Single file down and single file up they went, carrying the rest of their supplies up to the third floor.

"I'll take this one," Gus said, pointing with his free hand three doors down from the exit to the stairs. "Ladies first."

Gus dropped his stuff to open the door for Linda. "What a gentleman," she said as she passed Gus to go inside. JT raised an eyebrow and Gus winked at him. Hannah rolled her eyes.

"Night night all." Gus closed the door.

JT took the room next to Gus and Hannah took the one next to it, right next to the stairs.

It wasn't exactly warm inside but at least they were going to be out of the wind for the night. She put her backpack on the dresser, her gun on the table next to the bed. She threw open the curtains to let the sunshine lighten up the room. Maybe the hotel wouldn't feel so much like a tomb.

Hannah picked the bed by the window and pulled the sheets off the other bed so she could double up on her blankets. A knock came from her door.

"Come in," she called. The door opened and JT came inside.

"Can I help you sir?" she asked, smoothing out the additional comforter.

"Well, I had a crazy thought," JT said, smiling sheepishly. "Maybe we should share a room tonight too. There are two beds. That way, neither one of us are alone and separated from the other. If something should happen."

"Uh huh," Hannah said, a little sarcastically to tease him.

Even with all that had happened there were still moments like this. Where it felt like they were back to when they first met and sparks had flown between them.

She watched his puffed out chest deflate and his shoulders sag. She gave in to him then. After all she didn't want to discourage his reaching out to her. Maybe if they were together tonight, he would even refrain from drinking. Him trying to hide it was the most worrisome part. Doing that showed how JT knew he shouldn't be doing drinking so much.

"Alright. You'll have to go get your own blankets though."

JT bounced out like a boy on Christmas day. He came back with an armload of blankets and made up the second bed. He made a second trip bringing over the rest of his stuff.

"I want to go down and see if the lobby has any snacks. Some water too. JT, want to come with me?"

"Yeah. Let's go. What else am I going to do? Watch *Big Bang Theory*?"

"Heat and running water would make this place perfect," Hannah said, taking the stairs at a trot. "I wish I could take a shower, get this stench off. I feel like I'm covered in inches of gunk."

"Me too. You smell like a garbage dump," JT said.

Hannah took a step backwards to bonk into JT with a smile. JT smiled back but she could also see him cover up a grimace.

"I didn't know I had gotten so much stronger," she said, slowing down now. She could see JT favoring one leg as he took the stairs.

"It's this knee still," JT said. "It has been bothering me a little more lately. It usually does when the weather changes. Plus I've been walking on it way more than I normally would have. I guess I should be taking better care of it."

"I'm sorry JT. I wish there was something I could do to help it. Did you bring it up with Linda?"

"Eh, I'll live with it," JT said, blowing it off.

"I'll be gentle with you then, since you're fragile," Hannah smirked.

"Watch it. I could still kick your ass. I'd do it too, even if you are hot," JT growled playfully.

They went to the breakfast lounge area and rummaged around. They each took two bottles of water and some bags of pretzel sticks they had found.

"I remember when people complained about how stupid bottled water was," JT said. "Those same people would be happy so much of it is lying around. Funny huh?"

"Everything else has been so hard, I don't even want to think about safe water being scarce too."

They were both quiet as they made their way back to the room. The sunlight pouring in was now much dimmer, as low grey clouds rolled in. It made Hannah drowsy. She yawned deeply.

"It's going to feel so good, not sleeping on the ground," Hannah said, closing the curtain shut. "Do you mind crashing early?"

"Not at all. Do us some good I bet. My knee will enjoy it."

Hannah crawled under the covers, putting the water and a bag of the pretzels beside her on the table between the two beds. The gun was moved to under the pillow next to her. She let out an audible sigh as she sunk in.

"You need some privacy over there for a few minutes?" JT joked.

"Ha ha. Ignore any buzzing sounds you hear. Good night, JT."

The silence was non hotel like. She wondered if Gus and Linda were already asleep. It made the hotel spooky, all that silence. Reminding her of too many horror movies her and

Ashley had watched between parted fingers, about haunted houses and hotels. It was also a reminder to her how dead the world was now. She rolled on her side, looking through the gloom at the wall next to her bed. The drowsiness was disappearing since her mind wouldn't shut up.

"Hannah," JT called softly.

"JT."

Sheets rustled. "Do you ever have these random ass thoughts race through your head? Like what if we had met before the Outbreak started? If you and I ran into each other at a party or bar, would we have hit it off? Would we even speak to each other? I am older than you. If we did, would this connection I feel still be so strong? I know you don't want to hear this but I still have feelings for you Hannah...I think. I don't even know what I'm trying to say. Am I rambling or does this even make sense?"

Hannah swallowed. She guessed he might but then again after the whole Albright thing, not to mention Tyrone, she couldn't be sure he'd even want to be friends with her.

"I won't lie, I have feelings for you as well. At times, I wish every night that we could go back to before Albright and Harold. Before all this zombie crap. We could have become the stereotypical cheerleader and ex football player, dating."

She laid where she was, continuing to stare at the wall. It made it easier to talk freely.

"We sure have been through some shit. Still, Hannah, here we are. The two of us are still together. I've already come to peace with the whole Albright thing. So you know...I'm willing to give it a go again."

Hannah swallowed. Did he really already forgive her for what happened to Tyrone? Could that be the alcohol talking? She wasn't sure if he had any earlier in the day or not.

"Well I haven't yet. I'm not sure you have either. JT, how much have you had to drink today?"

"What's that got to do with-Ohhhhh. You think I'm like drunk dialing you right now? Trying to get laid? Why can't you believe me? Is it because you are being too hard on yourself?" His voice rose in the dark.

"I've noticed, even if you think I haven't. It's not healthy." Hannah hated the self righteousness squirming into her voice as she spoke.

"Oh and following some book telling you what a sinner you are and beating yourself up all the time is?"

"JT, I helped kill Tyrone," Hannah was getting frustrated now. "Jesus has to forgive me for that before I can forgive myself."

"Fuck! Hannah, for the hundredth time! Albright killed him!"

She didn't reply right away. She could hear him breathing heavily on his side of the room. She sat up, her back up against the headboard and looked at him. She tried to drop the tones of judgment from her voice.

"Look, JT. I ask because I do still care. You say I'm beating myself up. What's the drinking about? You weren't doing that when we first met. Have you forgiven all? For real? Are either one of us in any shape to be having a relationship?"

"You're right, forget it. Good night, Hannah." JT huffed.

With a grunt Hannah jammed herself back down under the sheets, looking up at the ceiling. The squeaks of the bed and the rustling of sheets is all Hannah heard from JT until the sound of snoring came on loud from his side. Hannah continued lying on her back, looking up into the dark. Outside she could hear the sound of rain mixed with sleet hitting the hotel window.

What a mess.

DEAD OF WINTER

ICE CAPADES

JT tossed and turned most of the night. He didn't mean for it to happen again. Too many times their talks had fallen into arguments. Then she went and brought up the drinking. He wished he had drank before talking to her. It had been hard to bring up he still wanted to be with her stone cold sober.

A weak light crept through the edges of the curtain. He decided he might as well get up. He walked over to the window and peeked out. There were still steely grey clouds hanging low, like he could reach out and touch them. Everything was covered in a thin sheet of ice.

"How's it look?" Hannah asked from behind him.

"It looks clear. You pack your ice skates?"

Hannah stretched and reluctantly slithered out of her covers and came over. She groaned at the view.

"I guess we're in for the day. Let's go down to the lobby. See if we can find anything better to eat than pretzels."

They chewed on some stale danishes they had found, still in the wrapper, and sat by the lobby window. JT looked out the window at the glazed over world.

"Want to risk a fire to make some coffee or hot chocolate?" JT offered. "I found some packets."

"I wouldn't want to be responsible for burning the hotel down."

JT took another bite of his pastry and sipped his water. "If it did burn down it wouldn't hurt anybody. It's not like you could get in trouble for arson or something. It would probably be years before anyone else even knew."

Hannah smiled at him but the by the look in her eye he knew it was a closed case. He went back to looking out the window. He hoped Hannah wouldn't bring up last night. He wanted to just forget about it and carry on.

"JT, I'm sorry about last night." Hannah started. *Fuck.* "I've come a long way in a short time since leaving Albright and the church. Not that I have to justify anything to you but without God I would be a wreck right now. I don't need you to have faith in anything except me. Give it time."

She extended her hand across the table and he took it. She smiled at him. The first real genuine smile since Albright he felt. He sighed then reached across to squeeze her hand gently. The sparks still existed after all. He could almost feel the heat.

"Aww look at the lovebirds," Gus said as he walked in. He put his hands together and tucked them under his chin. JT threw one of the pastries at him. Gus ducked to the side.

"Like you have room to talk Gussy," JT said. He let go of Hannah's hand. "Where is your much better half?"

"Still sleeping. I had to take a crap and thought I better do it down here. So we ain't' stinking up where we live. Then I heard voices on the way to the throne. I also thought I'd grab a nine month old newspaper. Always goes easier with some reading materials."

"Gus, we can always count on you for TMI," Hannah chucked.

"You mean TMA? Too Much Awesomeness? I know, how can I help it? See you kiddies in a bit."

JT looked at Hannah and they both shook their heads. Gus grabbed his newspaper and left. As he disappeared down the hall Gus shouted, "Well I'll be darned! Powerball is up to three hundred and thirty million! Old Gussy is feeling lucky!"

Hannah and JT burst out in laughter as they slouched back in their seats.

Later in day JT paced up and down the hallways of the second floor. He was feeling restless and trapped. This was the first time it hit him that the zombies had taken something else from him. His freedom. Before the Outbreak, he was able to jump in his car to get out and clear his head. His mood turned fouler at the realization. He didn't even realize Gus had joined him until he bumped into him.

"You look like a bee whose honey was eaten by a bear. What's going on big guy?"

"Restless I guess, Gus. Being stuck in here."

"Let me walk a little with you JT. Should keep my strength up. Lord knows we will be doing more walking."

JT and Gus walked side by side at a slower pace.

"You know, being up in the mountains, or wherever we stop, will be a lot like this," Gus said.

JT sighed. "Yeah, I know. I was just having the depressing thought about how the Outbreak also stole our freedom. I can't go out, jump in my car, and go anywhere. I can't do anything. If zombies don't try to kill me, other people might."

"Huh, I never thought of that. JT, you sure are in a funk."

JT shook his head like the motion would clear it out. "Don't I know it buddy. What am I going to do about it?"

They reached the big window at the end of the hall. JT put a hand against it, feeling the cold seep into it.

Gus put a hand on his shoulder. "I like a beer or two as much as the next man but drinking so much you pass out every night isn't helping. Like my father would say. 'Gotta face things head on or they turn around and bite you in the butt.'"

JT thought he would get angry. He knew he would have before. Now when he felt that old rage, he thought of about the little girl. Or Tyrone. Or the last words Randall said to him. He sighed out a puff of hot air.

"I'm that poor at hiding it, huh?"

"Like you love to point out, I've been around the block a few times. I have seen my fair share of real alcoholics. I also have a good idea what the bee in your bonnet is. Listen, JT. I was around in the church and around Albright a lot more than you. Albright was a slick son of a bitch. My radar broke with Harold but I was picking up and putting down what the so called 'Reverend' was selling right away. Hannah, where she was at the time, she couldn't. She was vulnerable. He pried and pried and won her over. He wanted Tyrone dead. It would have happened without her if Albright wanted it to. He had you and Tyrone under his thumb."

JT took a moment to think over what Gus was saying. Letting it sink in.

"What you are saying is probably true-"

"No, it's true," Gus interrupted firmly.

JT didn't feel like arguing and changed tracks. "I made a promise to take care of Tyrone. I failed. Then I failed Randall. I might fail Hannah, Linda, you. With my track record I probably will."

"Man listen, I'm still here because of you. Don't wallow in only the bad. That's easy. I'm not denying things aren't shittier than a Chinese restaurant's bathroom . You want to know what can help, then take this advice to heart. It's being with Hannah."

JT took his hand away from the window. It was almost numb. He turned and they walked back down the hallway.

"Hannah? You think one fucked up person plus one fucked up person will cancel each other out?"

As soon as it was out of his mouth he wanted to take it back. It was too harsh. It sounded like the old him speaking. It didn't seem to bother Gus, he went right on talking.

"I'm saying, you should stick with Hannah. She is a woman you can get behind. Or in front of. Or she could get on top of you. It's all good."

JT laughed deep, from his belly. It was like a breath of fresh air, light through dark clouds."Gus you are a funny bastard."

"Good thing I am, too, or I'd just be a bastard."

"You're right about one thing, Gus. I am turning into a old sourpuss. I'm a grumpier old man than you are," He wasn't going to dismiss what Gus was saying outright but he did want to change the subject. "So you and Linda huh?"

"What's to say?" Gus shrugged. "I was looking for love in all the wrong places. Who knew the right place was a zombie apocalypse."

RUMMAGE

JT's cabin fever returned not long after Gus left him. He found himself scavenging through every nook and cranny the hotel had to offer. He found everything from a closet full of miniature toiletries to what appeared to be a lost and found junk yard. As he was venturing around he wound up in room 217. The room was left in a state of more disarray than most of the others. There were clothes strewn about, pillows on the floor, even a box of condoms with a couple missing on the bedside table.

He dumped out a black leather bag he found on the floor of the bathroom. The first thing he noticed was the package of mostly used birth control pills, then the small, almost full, bottle of perfume. The words on the glass bottle read "Still by Jennifer Lopez." JT shoved the bottle into the pocket of his hoodie and moved onto the fridge in the room.

"Well what do we have here?" JT commented to himself. Inside the lifeless fridge was one bottle of champagne and one bottle of red wine. He gathered the bottles and headed back to the third floor.

Upon arriving back at the room he and Hannah shared he found Hannah doing some yoga type stretches out of a fitness magazine. He couldn't stifle his laugh at how silly she looked there on the floor, on one knee with the other kicked leg up in the air behind her.

"I have something way better to loosen you up," JT exclaimed.

Hannah finished her stretch and came back to a standing position. She crossed the room to stand beside him. He had the bottles of alcohol hidden behind his back and brought them around to show her. He could feel her apprehension right away.

"Ok, wait before you say anything I have another gift for you! Now it's no hot shower but you may enjoy it a little." JT pulled the perfume from his pocket and handed it over to Hannah, bringing a smile to her face.

"I want to be mad at your insinuation that I really do stink but it's such a sweet gesture I guess I'll let it slide, thank you!" Hannah startled JT with a kiss on the cheek. JT wanted to grab her and kiss her again but he wouldn't let himself.

There was awkward tension building in the room when Gus came in.

"Well, well, well, looky here! Champagne and wine, you two gonna hit the hot tub later and play honeymoon?"

Hannah gave JT a cheeky look.

"Actually Gramps, I thought you and Linda might enjoy some nice old folk friendly adult beverages tonight. In fact I was just about to deliver them with some fresh picked strawberries and warm bathrobes."

"Hey oh, watch it, JT. Linda's not old. Don't let her hear you saying that."

Gus waltzed over to the bed with an invisible partner to where the bottles laid. JT was lying through his teeth. He wanted them for himself but felt like he had just been busted by dad . Gus took advantage of the opportunity to thwart him. He picked up the bottles and with a shimmy of his hips gleefully burst out "Amen, Amigo! I will tell Linda you will be by to give our couples massage shortly."

JT plopped down on the end of the bed and stared at the blank TV screen. Now he'd have to renew his search. Hannah walked by and ruffled his hair with a smile before leaving the room.

When Hannah declared the next day they were moving on, JT was so happy. With a feeling Hannah and Gus were watching him closely, he hadn't had anything to drink the whole time they were at the hotel and it made his nights miserable.

They loaded the car back up and continued on the highway to Colorado Springs. Hannah was driving and he sat in the passenger seat, trying to find a way to place his legs where his knee would feel the most comfortable, while also having the shotgun not poke into him the whole way. He was glad for the car but wished it could have been bigger.

The flat land began to give way to what JT guessed you would call foothills. The road gently rose and fell. A dark smudge in the distance at first made JT think another storm was coming in. It came into focus as they got closer. JT realized he was mistaken. Those were mountains.

The sun glared, making it look deceptively like a warm summer day. JT broke out his sunglasses and settled back, trying to relax. He wasn't up for talking, he had too much on his mind today. Missing alcohol, the chat he and Gus had at the hotel, Tyrone, Randall. He even found himself thinking about Jelly back in Gateway City. But mostly it was Hannah on his mind.

He must have dozed off because the next thing he knew Hannah was shaking his arm and saying, "We're at Colorado

Springs. We're going to skirt around the city if we can and start up into the mountains here. Stay sharp everyone."

JT yawned and looked out the window. The view raced along. It was mostly hotels, restaurants, and car dealerships for now. Behind the buildings, behind the city, rose the massive bulk of the mountain range. JT felt it was brodding over the city, the craggy peaks watching over the dead city. One of the towering peaks was already white. From the map JT wondered if that was Pike's Peak.

The highway began to have more cars stopped here and there. Hannah slowed her speed down as she swerved around them.

"Glad I don't get car sick. This would make me green in the gills," Gus said from the back.

"Are we going to stop here for the day and start up tomorrow or are we taking our chances tonight?" Linda asked. "I didn't hear any specifics about what we're doing next."

The car came to a screeching stop and the momentum carried JT forward into the resistance of their seat belts.

"Jesus Christ, now what?" Gus complained in a breathless voice.

JT saw what they had feared. Across the highway in a tight clump, mixed in among the wreckage and debris, was a pack of zombies. Between the pack and the Honda there were no exit ramps. The sound of tires squealing on concrete made the zombie pack turn in their direction.

JT couldn't believe now, of all the times, he didn't have his shotgun on his lap. It had slid down to the floor as he slept. He reached for it and thought better of it. If they weren't getting out, his pistol would be a better idea. It was in his holster. He reached for it as best he could against the seatbelt as Hannah decided at that moment to floor it.

The car jumped and slipped sideways a little. The engine revved and it became clear to JT that Hannah was just going to ram her way through. Zombies bounced and careened off the car as it plowed ahead. JT's side of the Honda shrieked as the metal rubbed against one of the wrecks.

Hannah shot through the pack. Somehow one of the zombie had gotten hold of the hood well enough that it was still there. JT rolled his window down and reached out. He shot at it and missed as Hannah juked the car left and right.

"JT you idiot," Hannah yelled at him. "Don't do that. If you miss you could shoot me through the windshield."

JT powered the window back up. He wanted to slap himself in the forehead as his face burned. *What a rookie mistake.* His eyes felt like they were coated in fuzz, along with his brain. Had he been so asleep?

"Get ready everyone," Hannah said, stepping hard on the brake again.

The zombie flew off, skidding hard on the pavement. Rotted flesh on its exposed chest tore off and bone was exposed in patches all over its torso. It laid there, twitching.

JT looked behind and saw the rest of the pack coming their way.

Again Hannah floored it, running over the prone zombie. The car rose and thudded back down. Hannah took the next exit that came up at a speed JT wasn't comfortable with. She turned left on a curving side street. Lucky for them it was empty. The car bounced as it hit some rough road. Hannah turned again and again and then got back on the highway. Looking behind him JT didn't see the pack anymore. Hannah's crazy maneuvers worked.

"Hannah, I think we're clear," he said, letting out a breath he hadn't known he was holding in. "Sorry about what I did back there. That was a dumbass move."

"Nobody was hurt, just don't try something like that again you knucklehead," Hannah said, trying to joke about it.

JT fake smiled and wanted to move on. It bothered him though. Why had he thought it was a good idea?

"Nice driving darlin," Gus said.

"Thanks, Gus."

"For a woman," he added, not missing a beat.

"Linda please smack him," Hannah grinned into the rear view mirror.

There was a small smacking sound and a 'ow' from Gus.

"I'm going to sue. I had no idea you were so abusive, Linda."

JT chuckled despite himself. Now that he was fully awake, he scanned the road ahead like a paranoid maniac.

Hannah drove on, letting off the speed again, taking it careful around the abandoned vehicles. Dusk began to fall as the sun lowered itself behind the mountains.

"To answer your question Linda, that little run in tells me we're not stopping in Colorado Springs. Let's try our luck up in the mountains."

JT had a grim feeling that up in the mountains they weren't going to find things to be any better.

CARSON

Three large brown stones rose up along the left side of the road, lit up by the car's headlights. A sign on the middle stone read U.S. Army Fort Carson. A black fence ran along the highway, with a gate closing off the entrance and exit road to the base.

"This could be a good place to stop," JT suggested to Hannah.

If he were in charge, they would be stopping here. They would be sure to find some small building or a house to hole up in. Driving through wintery mountains at night wasn't something he wanted to keep doing. This was one of those times it was hard to bite his lip and not just demand they all do something he wanted.

"Or, it could be infested with zombies or some other crazy survival group," Linda offered. "Should we go poking around in there, in the dark?"

JT knew Gus liked Linda, but there were times she just got on his nerves. Always questioning things. Sure she was smart when it came to being a nurse, but that didn't mean she knew everything. *I know there's beer in there somewhere.*

Hannah took his questioning in stride. Hannah's lack of annoyance or frustration just made his that much worse. "I think it'd be okay if we go in for a little bit, check things out. If it looks like it's in bad shape or we see signs that the place is inhabited, we go on. No more fighting."

Luck was with them, the gate stood wide open. Hannah drove in. She did a U turn at the first crossroad then stopped.

"Linda, the three of us will get out. You'll stay here. I want you in the driver's seat."

"Hot damn Linda, you get to be the wheelman!" Gus exclaimed.

Linda cleared her throat. "Don't you mean wheelwoman." She over exaggerated the woman part for dramatic effect. Gus gave her a kiss on the cheek as he slipped out the passenger door.

Hannah pushed the button to pop the trunk and got out. JT stepped out the passenger side. The air outside was bitter after the toastiness of the heater. Linda passed her and slid in behind the wheel. Gus and JT joined her at the trunk. Headlamps on and pistols in their gloved hands, the three of them walked along the road into the base.

"Man, if Dusty was with us, he would have his military boner going for sure," Gus said. "This would be like a homecoming. Or Heaven."

"Can it, Gus," JT hushed at him. "This is suppose to be a stealth operation."

"Why you're channeling ole Dusty britches himself," Gus said, not in a joking manner.

JT wanted to glare at him but in the near total darkness, it would be pointless.

"The both of you need to be quiet now," Hannah said.

They continued on deeper into the base. Their flashlights didn't penetrate the blackness much beyond the confines of the road. They came to an intersection. To the left in the distance JT could tell there were the shadows in the shape of houses.

Hannah stopped them. She held her pistol high up in the air and pulled the trigger. The shot rang out through the night, echoing all around them. JT waited tensely, trying to look in all directions at the same time. She could have warned them first. He wanted a drink, to take the edge off. Minutes seemed like hours. No zombies came swarming at them. No human attackers came charging out, guns blazing. Hannah nodded, more to herself than to him or Gus, and the three went on straight.

At the next intersection, Hannah motioned to her right. JT looked that way. He saw the shadowy bulk of some long, large building. It was hard to judge just how far away it was in the gloom. JT cursed the cloud cover.

When they got closer to what appeared to be the front of the building, JT looked up and could see the sign on it said 'Exchange', with a big X above it. They crossed an almost full parking lot. Each car they passed JT ducked down to shine his light inside. Each car was empty. He had learned his lesson. He wasn't going to have anyone spring out of a car and have what happened to Randall happen again.

The entrance to the building had the wide automatic doors which of course didn't work now. On either side of the electric doors were regular glass doors, with stainless steel handles. Hannah tried one of those doors. She pulled the handle. It opened.

They walked into a large expanse. It was something like a mini mall. To the left was what looked like a food court area. To the right were rows of windows and fencing, which were more than likely stores.

As far as their lights would puncture the dark they could see everything was in shambles. Bodies, most of them in army fatigues, laid in scattered heaps. Around them and on top of them were bits of broken furniture, large shards of plastic, and piles of all kinds of stuff. As JT swung his head around, his light showed bullet holes in just about anything he looked at. Even the glass door had a few, when he looked closer. Looking down he saw empty shells littered the floor. He guessed it must have been one hell of a firefight. Maybe even a last stand situation. Then the stench hit him. It wasn't the first time he had come across piles of bodies but he didn't think it was a smell he was ever going to get use to.

"I don't like the looks of this," Hannah whispered to them, her nose crinkling up. "Let's go back."

JT couldn't agree more. His gung ho, let's kill some zombies, take what we need attitude was pretty much gone. Sheriff Randall's words were something he thought on everyday since he died. His words seemed to be the last nail in that attitude's coffin.

JT walked backwards towards the doors. Headlights splashed through the windows and a low, powerful rumble of an engine vibrated from behind him. He didn't have a moment to wonder if it was Linda. JT turned to look out the glass doors, then flipped back around when he heard noise behind him, in the mall.

"What, now the zombies take naps?" Gus exclaimed. "This is the first time I'm jealous of these sons of bitches."

Looking around in a sweep, JT could see what Gus was surprised about. Some of what JT had assumed were dead bodies stirred among the wreckage. The zombies rose up as one all along the open gallery that ran the length of the building. JT's quick count was twenty five at least. This was new behavior, lying in wait. JT felt his panic rise and his confidence plummet.

"Out the door, now!" Hannah shouted.

JT was already turning back towards it. From outside he now heard the slamming of several doors. The parking lot was brightly lit up. JT had no idea who could be out there. Maybe Linda came looking for them?

"I knew following them would be a good idea. Look at this place," a man's voice spoke, muffled by the glass between them.

JT skidded to a stop. Hannah did as well right next to him. Gus bumped into her. He was still walking backwards.

"You know exit is the place where you leave," Gus said.

JT could see the figures outside now, silhouetted in the headlights of their trucks. They were armed and headed their way.

"Run," Hannah commanded, jigging off to the right.

JT popped off his pistol as a runner streaked across the littered tile floor, stumbling as it closed in. JT got it in the head when it was only a few feet away. Its momentum caused JT to hold up for a minute as the zombie flew between him and Gus. Then the two took off after Hannah towards the mall stores.

"Over there," JT heard a woman's voice now. He did a quick over the shoulder look.

Four figures stood in the dark. They were inside the mall now. They didn't have lights but they seemed to be able to see. The head shots they were popping on the zombies proved it. One of the newcomers turned in his direction and debris puffed up at JT's feet. JT took off with renewed effort, his knee already throbbing from the extra push. This was why he wasn't in charge anymore. Here was another decision he wanted which could result in them all getting killed. It was a bitter thought he didn't have time to contemplate at the moment.

"Gus, they aren't friendly," JT said in a pant as he caught up to him.

"They usually aren't," was about all Gus could breathlessly reply.

JT thought *fuck it, they shot first*. He stopped, dropped to his one good knee, and fired at the shadowy figures still standing by the entrance way. He pulled back his teeth in a smile that was more of a snarl when he heard one of them cry out in pain.

"Gerard, Lydia's been hit," he heard one cry out.

"Let's go then," a different, more gruff sounding man said. "We can let the skin jobs take care of them. Plenty of other buildings to hit."

A wall of zombies cut off JT's sight of the attackers. The man may be right. The zombies might take care of them. There was a shitload coming towards them.

"JT, wake up!" Hannah shouted. "This way."

She was kneeling behind a big trash container bolted to the floor, taking shots at the zombies. JT ran towards her, not looking back. Ahead Gus was crawling under a half lowered metal gate into one of the stores.

JT blew past Hannah, slid under the gate trying to look like a hot shot. He regretted it right after as his knee popped. He jerked to a stop on the carpet on the other side of the gate. He tried to scoot out of the way to make room for Hannah, holding his knee which screamed in agony. Gus came over and gave him a hand up. He stood one legged like a stork. Hannah tossed her rifle under the opening and then rolled under. Zombies began to smash into the gate, making it screech as it jostled on its track.

Dead hands tried to reach through the opening of the gate. Grey and rotten flesh peeled back on the metal as they reached for the living. Some didn't even have fingers left. Bony stubs of fingers flapped without muscle and arms ending at the wrist tried to grab them as well. They strained for them without expression, without a sound. JT felt a pit open up in his stomach. This was Tyrone's state the last time he saw him.

Hannah shot two in the head at point blank, turning away as the gore splattered in every direction. She got her fingers in the gate and tried to push down it quickly to latch it shut, but had to jump back as more zombies rushed the gate.

JT got himself back into action and looked around for something useful to help. If they didn't get the gate closed, the zombies might figure out a way to get through it. He laughed out loud when he realized they were in a Gamestop.

"Game on," JT said, still chuckling.

How he would have liked to ransack a place like this back in the day. He had the feeling of someone who had won one of those five minute shopping sprees, where you got to keep whatever you could get in a cart. He greedily looked around.

"When you're done laughing like a loon, a little help would be nice," Hannah grunted, kicking down at the gate to get it to close. A hand grabbed her ankle at just that moment and Hannah went down on her ass with a squeal.

JT came back to reality. He picked up a metal pole that use to be the side of a display rack and began stabbing and smashing the zombies through the gate. Gus rushed up and helped Hannah off the ground. Together the three of them struggled getting the gate closed and locked.

JT shoved the metal pole as hard as he could into a zombie's head. It sank in deep and JT let it go. The pole caught on the gate and the zombie hung from it. It waved its arms and legs uselessly. It didn't have any leverage to get off the metal that impaled it. The remaining zombies mindlessly pushed on the gate, which shook and rattled under there collective weight.

"Great Hannah," said Gus as the three made it to the back of the store. "We're safe for now. What's the next move kemosabe? What about Linda, you think she's okay?"

"I bet she saw them coming and hid," JT said, patting Gus on the shoulder.

"Let's check out the stockroom. There could be a back way out of here," Hannah said.

JT looked longingly at the video games around him. Even though he didn't have a way to play them anymore, he was tempted to stick a couple video games in his backpack. With a sigh he turned and followed Hannah. In the back room they did find a door that opened out into a hallway of yellow cinder blocks. Hannah took point, with Gus behind her. JT brought up the rear. They came across a body a few feet down the hallway and another at the door that opened out into the mall. Thankfully they were of the actually dead variety.

Back out in the open mall, Hannah ducked down and took off in a sprint for a door marked emergency exit. JT did his best to follow her, but he more limped than sprinted. *I really did a number to my knee. Fuck, like it wasn't bad enough already.* At least now the pain had dropped down to low and dull. It didn't feel like Freddy Kruger was sticking his fucking blade glove into it. Outside, huddled up against the side of the building, he couldn't see any of their human attackers.

"Lights off," Hannah said, reaching up and switching hers.

JT did the same and his eyes began to adjust to the darkness.

"How we going to find Linda?" Gus asked.

Just then headlights flashed across the street as a car turned on the road in front of them. The three of them hid back around the corner, until a figure got out and stood in front of the headlights and looked around. It was Linda. They scooted across the parking lot, attempting to stay low. JT thought they probably looked like the world's goofiest ninjas.

"There you guys are," Linda hissed to them, waving them over. "I was at the gate when what looked like a convoy turned in, so I turned off my lights and rolled back into the shadows. Later I thought I heard noises in this direction."

"It was just the always pleasant welcoming committee of the undead," Gus said.

"Along with some armed fuckwads," JT added. "I heard them say they were following us."

They all climbed into the car. Hannah took the passenger seat next to Linda. Gus and JT got in the back. JT winced and tried to keep from yelling as he bent his knee. He ended up falling in more than anything.

"It was dark but there was no mistaking one of the vehicles was a dump truck." Linda said.

"Those guys? No way." Hannah was incredulous.

"What now?" JT asked, massaging his injury.

"We keep looking for supplies," Hannah said, gritting her teeth. "I'm not going to let them chase us away. For all we know they may be gone. If not then we will just deal with them."

"Let's not bring a knife to a gunfight," Gus said. "I recall they had a whole bunch of explosives."

"Which won't do them shit in close combat, unless they want to blow themselves up too," Hannah retorted. "Linda drive on."

As they rode on JT was afraid he was going to have to swallow his pride if they did stop again. He didn't think he could get out and run around. Having to fight, would be even worse. He might have to ask to stay with the car.

"There, that building looks promising," Hannah said, pointing out her window. "Maybe we'll find a something useful."

Linda pulled over in front of it. It was a long, low brick building. A short set of stairs led up, past the pole where the American Flag fluttered in the breeze, to the front doors.

"I don't see any sign of the others." Hannah reached for the door then stopped.

"Linda drive around, see if there is a way to get to the back. I want us all to go in."

There they found a loading dock. Linda backed up the car and popped the trunk. There were two dock doors and a set of stairs going up to a grey metal door.

"Linda, always thinking," Gus said, giving her a wink as he opened the trunk.

"A compliment from Gus? You'll have to go on without me, I might faint right here," Linda said in a dramatic southern belle accent.

Hannah went first and tried the door. It opened. They all went inside, JT bringing up the rear, swallowing down his pain.

"You okay there buddy?" Gus asked when he noticed JT's limp.

"Popped my knee is all. I'll be fine."

"Try not to put too much pressure on it," Linda advised. "I'll look at it when we stop someplace safer."

"Yes doc."

"JT, you want to wait here?" Hannah asked.

"No way. In movies it's always a bad idea to split up. I don't want to be picked off. I can make it fine. Not like my knee hasn't bothered me before." *Later some whiskey will numb the pain right out anyway*.

Their headlamps were on, illuminating their way. They were in a plain hallway. Their shoes squeaked on the linoleum floor. They came across a sign pointing the way to the Armory.

"Bingo!" Gus said. "Hannah my sweet, you may have just won the damn lottery!"

The building was as silent and empty as a tomb. JT figured whatever fight happened at the base, all of it must have taken place down at the mall. There was no sign of anything being disturbed here.

Hannah stopped them at a door with a plaque on the wall that said Armory. A machine which looked like a credit card swiper was below the plaque.

"You think the door will open with the power off?" JT asked, more to himself.

Hannah tried the door. She just about fell over when she yanked on it, she was so surprised it opened. JT made a move to catch her but she corrected herself.

"Ladies first," JT said, grabbing the door and holding it open.

Along one wall was a row of small lockers. To JT they almost looked like Post Office boxes. Some of them stood open. Along the wall across from them were six rows of gun racks, three on top and three below them. Each rack looked like it held eight weapons. Each rack seemed to be a different style. Some of the racks had empty slots in them.

"Either things were taken during the Outbreak, or we're not the first ones here," JT said.

"Still, there is plenty for us," Hannah said, heading over to the boxes. "Let's load up everything we can."

JT went over and with a firm pull he got a shotgun and what looked like a semi-automatic rifle from the rack. Slinging one over each shoulder he went over to Hannah. The boxes were filled with ammunition. None of them were experts on firearms, even now. They had been able to pick up and use what they had found along the way. She wasn't sure what magazines went with what guns. Hannah was just dumping what she could into her empty pack. When they had taken what they could, Hannah declared it was time to go.

"Now that we are armed to the teeth, are we going to run around the mountains calling ourselves the Wolverines?" Gus joked.

"Why would we do that?" Hannah said, looking puzzled.

"Kids these days," Gus sighed.

"Fucking Randall..." JT smiled as he said the words to himself.

CHATEAU

The little car sputtered and wheezed as JT coaxed it up the mountain road. The road twisted back and forth, this way and that. A mountain stream tumbled among the rocks on the left side of the road. It was pretty in the dawning morning light. He would have rather been in the passenger seat to admire it.

After leaving the army base with a trunk full of new toys, Hannah had said she was too tired to drive. Gus volunteered but JT didn't want to be stuck sitting in the back. Driving was painful but being stuck in the small space of a backseat for hours would have been worse.

So JT had driven all night from the fort. The sun lit the now clear blue skies, which JT could only catch glimpse of between the towering walls on both sides. He followed the climbing road deeper into mountain territory. He felt the pull of sleep on his eyelids.

"Look out," Hannah called out beside him.

JT, startled, jerked the wheel. He didn't even know she was awake. He compensated with a sharp turn in the other direction to find himself heading straight for a truck lying on its side across the entire road. JT turned the wheel hard right. The little car went off onto the small, narrow shoulder and the passenger side screeched across the rocky face of the mountain. The back seat window shattered. The car then careened in a circle when it hit a patch of slick ground.

JT was able to get the car to stop before he completely lost control. They were backwards on the road, facing the other side of the truck they had just barely missed crashing into.

The Honda sputtered again, then the engine died. JT tried to get it started again, cranking the key, but the engine refused to catch. Hannah pushed against her door, grunting as she applied more force. It wouldn't budge.

"Damn it!" JT shouted, slamming his hands on the steering wheel.

He got out of the car and walked around to the passenger side. It was dented in places and had huge scrape marks running from front to back.

"You're not going to be getting out that way Hannah. You either Gus. You're going to have to slide out," JT said.

"You're license is revoked," Gus called out through the broken window. "We walkin' now bossman?"

"It would do you some good anyway Gus," Linda said as she got out, then extended a hand to Gus. "Get some fresh mountain air in those lungs."

"Yeah, and a heart attack from the steep mountain roads," grunted Gus. "I'm not some damn billy goat. After our luck of finding that car, I thought it was going to take us to the promised land."

"You should know by now our good luck never lasts for long old timer," JT said, going around to the back of the car.

"I don't know if that's true," Linda said. "If you had swerved harder left instead of right, we would have fallen right off the mountainside."

JT looked to his left at the open space and shuddered. She did have a point. He walked to the back of the car and popped open the trunk. Inside were everyone's winter coats, hats, gloves, and three backpacks. Along with all their new weapons and a bag full of ammo. JT distributed them around. Everyone got a backpack except Gus, who was still too weak to carry much more than himself. However, Gus did take the ammo bag, along with a automatic rifle.

JT shrugged on his backpack, settling it into a comfortable spot. Hannah stepped up next to him and put her gloved hand into his. Though it was still early winter, they were high enough up now that the cold was getting bitter, and snow was starting to stick to the ground. Every time they spoke, little puffs of steam trailed their words.

"A romantic winter getaway in the mountains. You know how to touch a woman's heart," Hannah said, smiling.

JT chuckled. "Sure, we can pretend." He squeezed Hannah's hand. The sudden show of affection was surprising and welcomed.

"It better have a fireplace, Captain Morgan, and some snow bunnies," Gus said.

This got him a light punch in the arm from Linda. Hannah and Linda both laughed at Gus's over the top outrage as he rubbed his arm.

"Seriously though, I just hope we find someplace safe," Hannah said, pulling away from JT. "There has to be someplace isolated enough up here. One that not many people were around when the Outbreak started. I'd think any zombies or people left around would be hampered by the rough terrain. Like we are now. I'd love to find some food and supplies in a place that hasn't been raided yet. The mountains still seem like our best chance."

"Yeah," JT agreed. "Maybe we can have a chance at something like a normal life after all."

"This is all fine and dandy, but I'm freezing my man titties off here. Can we get to moving before my blood freezes too?" Gus said.

"You always become a grumpy old man when it gets a little cold outside?" JT asked.

The finger was Gus's reply.

"You do know that before you were born I walked over mountains like this barefoot to go to school both ways? Let me show you kids how it's done," Gus said, walking off up the incline.

"Don't blow a gasket Gus," JT called. "You might have your own personal nurse now, but that doesn't mean you need to show off and over do it."

"I just want to find someplace to get inside before it gets dark," Gus said, his breathing already getting heavier. "It's going to be real cold out here tonight. I can feel it in my bones."

They walked on for most of the day as the shadows lengthened behind them. Clouds began to gather among the peaks. A light snow began to fall as the sky darkened towards evening. Hannah led them off the highway heading up into the mountain and down a dirt road that led to a rather large house at the end. The group took a long staircase up to the red stained front deck, which wrapped around the side of the building. Hannah tried the front door. It was unlocked.

"Hello...Hello..." Hannah called out as they entered. JT was right behind her.

"This is quite a swanky place. Back before, this house was easily a million bucks," Gus said.

The four gathered in the large living room, which did indeed have a ornate brick fireplace. Pictures of a happy family lined the mantle along the top of the fireplace. It also had huge windows running along one side of the room. The four of them stood at them and looked out at the land below them. The nearest city was just dots in the far off distance.

"Isn't it strange?" Hannah asked. Her voice sounded as if she was far off, lost in thought.

"What's that?" said JT.

"From up here, the world doesn't look any different."

Hannah turned away with what seemed like a struggle. JT looked at her and looked out the window. The city far below almost didn't look real. More like a model someone had put together.

"Nobody has answered us. Guess the place is empty," Hannah said.

"Let's go check it out Hannah," JT offered, pulling himself from the window. "We'll want to make sure there are no surprises."

They left Gus and Linda downstairs to check things out while they went up. The wood floors creaked with every step. JT gave up trying to move quietly. Hannah was right, if something or someone was here, they would have known it by now.

The first room they investigated had to have belonged to a kid. It had Mario decals on the walls, a desk with Lego pieces scattered all over it. The floor was a mess of clothes and bed sheets. Hannah looked at JT as if to say what the hell. JT went inside, poked around the piles on the floor, checked out the closet.

"It's clear," he said, coming back out.

They moved on. The next door down the hallway was closed. Hannah turned the handle slowly while JT covered her. It was locked. Hannah switched places and with a mighty shoulder rush JT banged the door open. A huge bed with a solid oak headboard and footboard dominated the middle of the room. They could make out shapes under the heavy red comforter. Next to the bed the window was open. The curtains flapped and there was a puddle on the hardwood floor under it.

"Hello," Hannah called out.

Nothing stirred. JT was not liking this. He felt like he had just entered a slasher flick. They stepped inside, got closer to the bed. The sheets were pulled all the way over the bodies, only a little hair was sticking out the top. There were red stains on the white pillowcases. Hannah reached for the comforter.

"Hannah, what the hell are you doing?"

She pulled it back without hesitation. JT raised his weapon. Two people, surely husband and wife, lay dead on the bed. A gun lay between them. They were surrounded by a red bed sheet which at one time had been white. Both figures had traumatic head injuries.

"Gruesome," JT said, turning away. "That makes me not want to sleep here tonight."

"We don't have much of a choice," Hannah said, covering them back up. "That's sad, to be so desperate and out of hope..." She trailed off.

"Let's not tell the others what we found Hannah. No reason all of us have to be disturbed by this."

Hannah nodded her head and the two went back downstairs after checking the last room, which was an empty bathroom.

Gus called over from the fireplace when he saw them. "If you wouldn't mind JT, can we see about getting this started before it gets fully dark out there?"

JT stood looking out the window, disturbed by what they had found upstairs. Some thought was on the tip of his tongue but he couldn't wrangle it. With an effort he tore himself away.

"Sure Gus, let me get on that."

"You want any help?" Linda called out. JT was just leaving the room and twirled around, wincing as he did. "Your knee could use a rest."

"No, I got it Linda," he gave a weak smile. "Thanks."

He could go out, get some firewood, and also some sips of a nice whiskey he had stashed at the bottom of his pack. He had found it at the army base in Carson. He thought no one had seen him swipe it and stash it away. He was rationing it, there wasn't enough there to get blackout drunk, but he could get a good buzz going. After everyone else was asleep, he could search around the house. A nice place like this they surely had some quality liquor around.

He went down some stairs and out a door to the garage. He waved his flashlight around. Inside sat a nice Audi in one spot, the other was empty. On the wall across from him, tools were arranged neatly on a pegboard. One of them was an axe. Just what he was wanting to find.

JT stood in the doorway, digging out his whiskey, and took two shots. The warmth ran down his throat and into his belly. Taking the pack off, he stuck the whiskey bottle in his coat pocket, went over, and grabbed the axe.

JT pulled the cord to the garage door and pushed it up by hand. It rattled and squeaked on its track. JT took another look around with his flashlight, hoping to find something like a sled, to pull the wood back. The mountain wind whipped around his legs and he shivered.

I need to warm up. He took another two shots from his bottle, feeling a slight buzz coming on. He enjoy the feeling. It had become a comforting friend. In front of him, at the back of the garage, was a long wooden bench. Under it he was rewarded with what he wanted to find, a kids plastic sled, round and red. He grabbed it and pulled it out, swaying a little as he squatted and then raised himself back up. That's when he had a thought come back to the tip of his tongue. He took a few steps back and bumped into something.

"Damn it, Hannah, don't sneak up on me like that." He whirled clumsily. It wasn't Hannah his flashlight lit up.

It was a zombie. A boy who looked to once be ten or eleven. The right half of his face was scarred like it had been charred in a fire. The eye socket on the ruined side was empty. The boy stumbled back a few steps. Its mouth opened like it was hissing at him, but no sound came out. It lunged forward.

Its mouth clamped onto JT's coat and ripped. White fluff, so much like the snow outside, drifted through the air as the zombie pulled back. JT tried to fight through his foggy brain. It was like sirens were going off in the distance, fighting to make it through air made out of cotton.

It lunged again, shreds of fabric still between its teeth. JT dropped the flashlight and used both hands to bring up the axe. Light skipped around, like what was going on was some kind of rave or dance party.

JT blocked the zombie. Its face smashed into the wood handle. Teeth, cracked and shattered, fell onto the floor. The boy's jaw jutted out the side at a weird angle. It still worked though, it gnashed its jaw as best it could as it made another run at JT.

JT swung at it with the axe and missed wildly. It banged off the concrete, making small sparks in the dark.

The zombie was behind him. He twirled, almost losing his balance. It was already coming again. JT lifted up his left arm, blocking without thinking about it. The boy dug into his coat again. JT held his arm up and swung low with the axe, cutting through one leg. The boy was wearing shorts, so there wasn't much resistance.

The zombie dropped, pulling JT's arm down with it. JT yanked, ripping the coat open again as he backed up, panting. The boy attempted to pull himself along the concrete. Without much to grab onto and with a half a leg missing, it more wiggled back and forth making JT think of a snake.

JT raised the axe up with trembling arms and brought it down, splitting the zombies skull in two. It stopped moving. Huffing and puffing JT stumbled over and leaned against the car. He cursed himself for being sloppy. For getting soft. He cursed the zombie. Cursed the world.

Once his tirade was done, he scooped up the flashlight. He scanned the whole garage again, even under the car, axe in hand. He took a few steps outside of the house, casting his light around. He saw nothing.

Going back inside, he grabbed up the sled, rolled the zombie onto it and pulled it out into the snow. It still tried to reach out to him. He thunked his axe into its skull and pulled on into the woods, where he planned to dump the body.

Maybe I should cut back on the drinking. That was pretty close.

By the time JT got back with the load of wood he had chopped, the whiskey bottle was empty.

SMALL COMFORT

JT decided it best to stash his war tattered gear in the garage before lugging the wood inside. The snow had picked up since their arrival but he was sure he could find a replacement in the house. When JT returned to the living room area he found the other three had arranged two couches and a love seat around the fireplace. Gus shuffled over to help JT as the two of them got the fire going pretty easily with the matches they had found.

"Well ladies and gentlemen we are in for quite the treat tonight, not only did we get lucky with the matches but in the pantry off the kitchen I found one box of unopened graham crackers, some hot cocoa, and the main event..." Linda modeled each item like she was on The Price is Right. Gus cheered outlandishly as Linda showcased a five pound can of baked beans with bacon and a mostly full jar of extra crunchy peanut butter.

"Sweet mother of the legume world we thank you for your gift." Gus mocked a cheesy prayer making the room fill with laughter. JT was feeling good enough now that his laughter was genuine.

Gus and Linda went to the kitchen to find a big pot to use to prepare their meal in the fireplace. JT put his leg up, relishing the heat and the relief. He ravished the peanut butter and crackers in record time. While they sat around the fire each enjoying their bowl of beans they discussed their plans to move further up the mountain after everyone had a chance to rest. They all liked this oasis they had come upon but were all in agreement the house was too close to the main road to stay for long.

Later that night, as Hannah laid snuggled up on the love seat and Gus sawed logs from the couch nearest the fire, JT got up to relieve Linda of watch duty. Linda offered up JT the last of the cocoa but he declined saying to save it for one of the others. Besides he had plans to do some deeper searching into the cabinets over the sink, where he had spotted some promising looking bottles earlier.

JT sat in the chair Linda had positioned to look out the large window towards the road. If he wasn't mistaken he even heard the distant call of an owl over the crackles of the fire. He waited awhile, watching the snow continue to fall and build on the trees and the ground, before going on his adult beverage recon.

Satisfied he had waited long enough JT lurked his way over to the kitchen area. On his way there was when he noticed a wine cabinet tucked neatly between two oversized fake potted plants. He slowly slid the wooden door open and saw what he desired The good stuff, the smooth stuff. He quickly decided on the bottle of Amaretto and went back to his perch for watch.

He twisted the cap off and took one swig. He was about to take another when a hand fell on his shoulder. He jumped, spilling some of the Amaretto on his lap. He turned in his chair.

"Hannah! What the fuck?!" He fumed.

She didn't say anything. Hannah just pressed a finger to his lips to quiet him. She moved the bottle to a nearby shelf and adjusted her blanket as she crawled into JT's lap.

"Not tonight, please," Hannah somberly requested as she snuggled her head into his shoulder, while intertwining her fingers with his.

"Ok." That was all JT could muster up to reply.

A different warmth spread through his body when Hannah kissed him on the cheek and thanked him. Feeling overwhelmed JT adjusted his seat and leaned in to kiss Hannah. She met him with no hesitation. There was such a rush between them JT wished he could pick her up and carry her to a bed. Perhaps even the floor right here. JT was sure Hannah could feel his arousal. He wondered what she exactly had in mind.

Just then a coughing fit from Gus froze them like teens caught by their parents. Gus, still asleep, called aloud, "Linda honey bear, come back to bed and keep papa bear warm."

Hannah and JT covered their mouths to stifle their laughter. As they regained their composure JT tried to get back to where they left off, placing his hand on her inner thigh. Hannah seized the moment, taking his face in her hands, "not here, not like this, okay?" JT complied giving her one more long kiss before she snuggled back into his lap.

Not long after sitting there, holding her in his arms as she breathed the softness of sleep, JT found himself looking at the bottle just out of reach through bleary eyes. He longed for the taste and comfort of alcohol, but he even more so craved what lay in his lap right now. JT wondered if he would ever let his desire to drink get to the point where that changed?

THE MORNING AFTER

JT didn't recall nodding off at all. He woke now only because Hannah was climbing out of his lap. The morning light was bright through the large windows. JT stood and stretched, looking out into the forest. The sun glistened off of the snow which made a white blanket over everything. Hannah stood beside him looking too, then walked off to the kitchen.

Gus and Linda were already up and around. Linda was sorting through what appeared to be a folder full of brochures. JT got up and looked over her shoulder. They pitched things from around the area, anything from restaurants in the town below to avalanche survival training.

"Well good morning to the two of ya'!" Gus said cheerfully. "I was going to relieve whoever this morning but the dawn was already rising and you two just looked more snug than two kittens in a mitten."

JT just smiled as they shook the sleep off. He wondered just what all of that was about. Was Hannah trying to come on to him? Keep him from drinking? Both?

After breakfast, at Hannah's request, they spent the rest of the morning turning the house upside down looking for anything useful. Nothing much came up they didn't already have. JT did find a new winter parka. It was a bit snug but it would do.

Linda came up with the idea to put snow in the pot over the fire, melt it, bring it to a boil and then use towels for warm sponge baths. There were no complaints from anyone about that. JT even gave Linda a giant hug when she told him to wrap his knee with one of the hot towels. He sat looking out the window again, enjoying the relief.

"Hey there partner," Gus said, taking a seat next to him. "Good to see something other than a scowl on yer face. The woman are off upstairs in the bathroom. You want to have a chat with me?"

JT looked at Gus out of the corner of his eyes. "Depends, honestly?"

"Look. I get it. I do. What happened to Tyrone, well it sucks donkey balls is an understatement. I've lost lots of people and it ain't any easier from the first to the last. I've learned to deal with it though. You've got to as well."

"Oh yeah? How so?" JT couldn't believe Gus.

"For one thing, you can't go around being angry all the time. The situation we're in is grim but you going to carry this boulder around on your back until a zombie gets you? You gotta deal with it bud, not drown in it." Gus put a hand on his knee. When JT turned to look at him, Gus raised an eyebrow.

"I hear you, Gus. Alright? Geez." JT turned away before scowling.

It felt like Gus was going to say more but Hannah came bounding over, looking almost radiant.

"That was wonderful. I feel like I've removed a pound of grime and zombie goo. What are you two up to? Manly talk?"

"Ah, you know," Gus said, getting up. "Just chewing the fat."

"Before you go, Gus, I've already told Linda I think we're going to stay here one more night and then continue on tomorrow morning. What do you think?"

"That's fine with me, little lady. It's warm in here."

JT grunted, indifferent to either option. Gus had gotten under his skin and he wasn't in the mood to talk to anyone.

"Okay. I'll take that as a yes. It's to bad we can't stay here longer but there's no way we could survive the whole winter here. If we do try to go up further and the weather doesn't cooperate, this at least is a good place to fall back on."

The two then left. JT continued to sulk and stare out into the whiteness. He looked around and couldn't find the bottle he was going to start on last night. Hannah had probably hidden it. Maybe even threw it off the deck for all he knew.

In what seemed like minutes the light had faded. JT turned, muscles stiff. Gus sat stoking the fire as darkness imprisoned the outside world. Linda was already nodding off on one of the couches. JT walked over, wanting to warm up.

"Well Hannah, should we play rock, paper, scissors for first watch tonight?" Gus asked as he continued poking the logs.

"Nope, no need. I'll stay up first. I want to read some." Hannah answered as she held up her Bible.

"How about you read a little of that book out loud tonight for us beautiful?" JT asked. Without any alcohol around he thought the sound of her voice might help distract his thoughts and send him off to sleep.

"Atta boy!" Gus clapped JT on the shoulder as he made his way to the other end of the couch where Linda snoozed. "Alrighty darlin', the floor is yours." Gus kicked his feet up on the coffee table in the middle of their little couch fort.

Hannah's teeth chattered as she made her miserable way across the open, snow covered field. It was up past her ankles, making her legs burn as she powered and plowed through it.

Light flakes drifted lazily across her vision. Ahead the mountain face rose dramatically on either side of a opening. Hannah thought of the possibility there may be a road there under all that snow. The opening was her destination.

It was times like this, she wished they hadn't left the nice, warm house. After two days though, any food not spoiled was gone, so there wasn't much choice but to go on. Not long after they had left that day, the sky opened up with what had to be at least eight inches of snow.

Hannah paused for a moment, looking back over her shoulder for a glance at the others. JT looked like a furry bear, covered in brown winter gear. It fit snugly on him. Only his mouth and eyes were visible. She couldn't see his eyes just now, his head was down as he trudged along. He had gotten it from the house, his other one he said got snagged and torn on a tree.

Not far out of the tree line they had just emerged from came Gus and Linda, straggling behind JT. Gus still leaned on Linda for support as the two of them struggled through the of uneven terrain and waves of snow drifts.

Even though it hurt her chapped lips, Hannah smiled at the sight of the two of them. Now if they could only go faster. She waved her hand over her head at them.

"We're comin' little missy!" Gus shouted back, mocking her with a wave of his own variety.

He stopped, bent over a little, hands on his knees. Hannah felt her impatience melt away. It was hard for her to make it through all this snow and she was in her twenties.

The crunch of disturbed snow snapped Hannah's focus away from Gus and to the right of where she was standing. A hand, grey and covered with open wounds that didn't bleed, burst out of the snow like it was rising out of the grave. The rest of its body followed, creating a miniature snow shower. It was maybe twenty feet away from her position. Hannah's heart sped up.

Another, a man wearing cargo shorts, hiking boots, and nothing else rose up. It was even closer to Hannah. Snow clung to its dead but preserved body in clumps here and there. Fresh enough to almost look alive. They started moving towards the sound of Gus's voice.

Across the snowy plain more and more zombies ascended from the snow, like they were waking up from hibernation. Hannah hadn't accounted for this. She thought none of them did. It made sense now that she saw it. Of course being already dead, the cold didn't affect them. They moved closer to Gus and Linda, oblivious to the weather, cutting the two off from Hannah.

Ten, twenty, thirty. The number kept climbing. Frozen in shock, Hannah watched them shamble to their feet. Their presence disturbed the once pristine snow field.

Like a bull JT charged through the snow, stopping when he reached Hannah. Almost slipping and falling down, he recovered by grabbing her arm. That roused her from her waking nightmare. JT pulled out a pistol. He took shots at the nearest ones, missing more often than not in the treacherous footing. If he wasn't slipping and falling, the zombies were as they plowed brutishly through the deep snow.

The grey hazy sky, which had looked threatening all morning, opened up, like a switch had been flipped. Snow began to fall down, in small floating flakes at first, but then became faster and more intense.

"No, no, no," Hannah mumbled to herself, swinging her rifle from her back into firing position.

The wind began to pick up as well. The snow whirled and twirled and Hannah began to feel like she was inside a snow globe. She barreled through the snow as fast as she could, leaving JT behind, trusting he would catch up. She was trying not to lose sight of Gus and Linda as the storm threaten to obscure her vision.

"JT, don't worry about me," Hannah yelled over the gunfire. "We have to get back to Gus!"

It was a white out as the storm kept building. She lost sight of everyone, even the zombies. Panic nibbled at the corners of Hannah's mind. She could still hear JT firing, it sounded as though he wasn't far behind her. She wasn't worried about him, he could take care of herself.

From the white gloom, two hands grabbed at her without sound. She twisted away, the snow helping to root her in place. She swung with the butt of her rifle, knocking the zombie over back into the snow. A shot to the head stopped its struggling.

In addition to the sound of JT's pistol, Hannah began to hear the pop of gunfire ahead and to the left of her. She honed in on it, knocking a few more zombies out of the way as they suddenly loomed into sight. The wind began to howl, making it harder to pinpoint Gus. Her hands began to throb and stiffen inside her gloves. Her face ached. She took a gamble and called out to Gus.

"Here darlin'!" was his breathless reply.

More to the right now, she adjusted her course. A tug on her shoulder and suddenly she was yanked backwards off her feet. She went down into the snow in a thud. Above her towered two zombies, a man and a woman, in summer clothes.

She shoved the rifle barrel up and into the male zombies mouth and pulled the trigger. The weight of his falling body ripped the rifle right out of her hands. The female zombie fell on her, clawing at the parka Hannah wore. Shreds of fabric drifted up into the air, joining the snowflakes before being violently blown away.

Hannah tried to roll but it was impossible in the deepening snow. Next she tried to scramble backwards. Her hands and feet kept slipping out from under her. Meanwhile the zombie kept tearing away. Real panic hit her then. Her flailing hands hit something hard under the snow. She pulled with all her strength and instinctively swung it with all her might.

It was a large, thick stick, which cracked in two as it knocked the zombie slightly off to her left side. She used the moment to try to get some leverage, get up on her feet. Then the zombie was on her again. She slipped back down, flat on her back. She held the stick's remains in both hands and jammed it sideways into the chomping mouth. Splinters rained down on her face. Her eyes squeezed shut to near slits.

This might be it. Dear God don't let it be.

A blurry shape whooshed over her body. The zombie stopped, its head dropped from its body onto Hannah's stomach. The rest of the body fell to the side in the snow.

"Don't lose your head to now honey," Gus said, materializing out of the storm and offering Hannah a gloved hand.

Hannah took it, along with Linda's who appeared alongside Gus. In Gus's other hand he held a gore covered axe.

"Another groaner from Gus," Linda said. "Keep coming up with stuff like that and I might die and turn into a zombie."

The wind shifted and for a moment the field of vision around them cleared. Hannah could see three zombies approaching from her left. Linda raised her gun and fired, taking them out. JT reached them, steam continuously rising from his mouth. His face was almost as white as the snow.

"We need to get out of this field. We are like sitting ducks," he puffed.

"Follow our footprints back the way we came," Hannah said. "Then keep straight and we will reach a narrow outcrop of rock. I think a road is there, under the snow. Maybe it will lead us to shelter. At the very least we will have a wall at our backs."

"Sounds like a plan," JT said, taking another shot at a zombie that rose up a few feet away. "I'll take the rear guard."

The four followed their back trail through the snow. There footprints in the snow were rapidly filling in from the falling snow. A few minutes later the blowing winds began to calm. The snow started falling more softly, more slowly. Visibility increased. Hannah didn't like what she saw.

Tens of zombies still stood on either side of them. The snow was slowing them down but wasn't stopping the baseless determination they had to bite living flesh. Some that fell just started to crawl through the snow, leaving lines that looked like sled tracks behind them. Hannah counted her blessings at least no zombies were in their path. Even a runner wouldn't have been able to close in rapidly. The snow was both a curse and a blessing.

On they plowed, yet the outcropped rock didn't seem to be getting much closer. Hannah began to worry about Gus. If his body would be able to take the strenuous effort they were exerting. She could feel her heart pounding, her lungs working hard to keep up the pace. She could hear the occasional fire from JT's pistol behind her.

Another pair rose out of a drift not twenty feet to the right. Hannah got one before it could even move. The other was a runner. It was almost comical how it pumped its arms and legs so hard but was getting almost nowhere. Hannah took it out before it could reach them. She prayed no more popped out in front of them now. She needed to reload and she didn't want to stop here in the field to do it.

Hannah reached their destination. She slammed her back against the rock wall so hard she almost knocked the wind out of herself. She could see Linda pulling Gus through Hannah's tracks, like a cowboy guiding a horse. JT was covering them. For now, any zombies pursuing them were back at the far end of the field, almost out of her sight. When all four were together, they stretched out side by side. Hannah could see JT was almost within reach of the other side of the rocky outcrop.

"JT, Linda, cover me," Hannah said, dropping to her knees with a crunch, sliding off her backpack. "Gus you going to be okay."

Gus nodded his head up and down furiously. There was a continuous steam cloud puffing from his mouth. His complexion matched the snow around him.

She fumbled with the straps, trying to get her pack open with her gloved hands. Realizing if she couldn't do that simple task there was no way she was going to be able to reload with gloves on, she gritted her teeth and took them off. Out into the snow plopped the empty magazine. Click went the new one. On went the backpack, on went the gloves.

"How's it looking out there?" Hannah brought her rifle back up.

"It looks clear." Gus retorted.

"I'm going to take a look at where we're going next. Keep me covered."

They were in no position to stay and fight. Hannah turned and squeezed between Gus and the wall. The snow fall over on the other side of the rocky walls didn't look nearly as intense. She could see a sharp descent, which ended at what looked like some kind of log cabin. Next to it a half frozen lake stood. Beyond that she couldn't see anything but whiteness. Between them and the cabin stood an army of evergreens, marching off on either side of a line cut through them. It had to be a road.

On the other side of the cut was something that looked like a transformer station. It was between her and the cabin. Lines rose from it and ran from poles into the whiteness, that looked like metal giants on a winter train set. She turned back around, cursing why it had to be a cabin.

"They're getting a little too close for my comfort," JT said, trying to keep the edge out of his voice and only half succeeding. "Where to next?"

"There's a cabin, by a lake and a transformer station, down on the other side. By down I mean a pretty steep ascent. If we're not careful, we could end up on our asses."

"Better than ending up as zombie chow," Gus said, all but panting still.

The scattered pockets of zombies had joined together to form a wall of walking dead. They trundled and scrambled closer.

"I wish I had a sled. Or a snowmobile. Or a airplane," Gus said. "No, an airplane. With an airplane I would fly away from all this shit. Ah, like my mom said if wishes were cows I'd be knee deep in manure."

JT laughed. Hannah gave them all a serious look.

"We have got to be standing on a road. We follow it down, watching our step, get to the cabin. If it's empty, we ride out the storm there. I see no zombie now. Lets hope there's no more surprises."

"You heard the Major, boots on the ground now," Gus joked, trying to lighten Hannah up.

Hannah let out a guffaw and gingerly started down the sharp incline. They continued on in formation. The footing was treacherous and there were some close calls but they arrived at the station without incident. Hannah turned around when she reached the station's outskirts. It was hard to make out through all the trees but she didn't think the zombies were following them any longer.

Hannah led the group across the winter wonderland to the cabin. She took the cabin steps fast, looking forward to getting out of the snow and the wind.There didn't seem to be any trace of activity in the cabin from the outside. She hoped no people or zombies were inside. She had lost all of her fight. Rest is what she craved.

Linda had to half drag Gus inside out of the cold. He was trying to move his legs, but the stubborn things weren't responding. He had a feeling when they warmed up they would be complaining up a storm. Gus was sick of the damn cold and snow.

Not that it was much warmer than a freezer in the cabin. His first thought was to call it a cabin but now that he was inside it was more like a two story log home. At least there was no wind inside. Gus was thankful. It had been cutting through him like he had no coat on at all.

The best thing about being inside, no zombies had attacked them. Not yet. Hannah had knocked on the door and called out but had gotten no response

Linda got him propped up against the wall just inside the door. She took out one of those packs you break and shake and it gets warm. She followed the steps and placed the pack inside Gus's coat. She smiled warmly at him as she did this.

Gus still couldn't believe how lucky he was as he smiled back. He hadn't been looking for it. If he had been, he didn't think he would find it in this world. A zombie filled world of death. Fucking crazy, even after all these months, to call it that. You had to call a spade a spade if that's what it was.

He didn't know how long this Linda thing was going to last. All kidding aside about his ex wives, which he had only had one, he liked her quite a bit. That also made him scared, as they had lost so many people along the way. He missed them all, even ole Dusty, pain in the ass that he was. Linda slid down beside him and the two huddled close together. He stopped reminiscing and enjoyed her warmth. Outside the wind howled like it was protesting in fury that it couldn't reach them anymore.

"Hannah I don't want to criticize, but maybe we should have made our way to a Caribbean beach instead," Gus said through chattering teeth.

Hannah finished scanning the living room they had taken shelter in and sat down across from Gus, rifle across her knees.

"How would we get there, Gus? Are you a seaman?" Hannah winked.

Gus laughed. "Touche' my dear. Touche'."

"Been hanging around you too long."

JT was pacing the floor. His eyes kept darting towards the staircase on the other side of the room.

"You trying to carve a racetrack slick?" Gus asked up at him.

JT stopped. He shot Gus a look. Gus was sorry he said anything.

"We have something to block this door with?" JT asked, resuming his frantic walking.

"JT, buddy. Sit down here next to me. Cool your jets. We have been in worse scrapes than this. Come cuddle with Gussypoo."

That got a smile out of JT. It was a glimpse of the old JT, from when they first met. Gus was happy to see something besides anger or hurt inside of him, if only for a moment. He thought the talk back in the hotel and on the road here would have helped. It did for a little bit but Gus had seen JT fall back into using the bottle when he could find one. Even though JT thought he was being a sneaky SOB.

JT sat down next to him. He started to rummage through his backpack but then stopped. He looked at Gus a bit sheepishly. He reminded him so much of a kid caught in the cookie jar.

Gus tried to reassure JT. "If the zombies are still coming, it could be hours before they find us. If at all. It's like stirring up a beehive. Now we're out of range, they should just calm the fuck back down."

"If you say so Gus," JT said. He closed his backpack and pushed it aside. "Now hold me." JT made a big gesture of putting his head on Gus's shoulder. He tried to wrap his arm around Gus' shoulder.

"Get off me you big lug," Gus said, pushing JT's head away and laughing.

"Do you think this is already someone's hiding place?" Linda whispered.

Hannah scanned around again.

"If it is, they keep it spotless. Doesn't look like a soul has been here." The words had no more left her mouth when someone called out.

"What are you all doing in my house?"

Hannah spun around and Gus caught a glimpse of an old man. A real old man, not joking around like with everyone did with him. He looked to be about eighty. He was holding a shotgun in his hands, which shook up and down, pointing between the floor and them. He wore a white t-shirt, red and black checkered pj pants, and brown slippers. His voice attempted to be commanding but it sounded more like a rasp of a long time smoker.

"We don't mean you any harm," Gus said, slowly rising to his feet, using the wall to push himself up. "We just needed a place to duck away from the zombies."

"Zombies? What kind of drugs are you people on? No such thing as zombies."

The shotgun wobbled around some more. The old man looked like he was running out of strength to hold it. A voice came from upstairs, a woman's voice.

"Grandpa, are you talking to yourself again or do you need my help?"

Gus noticed the confused look on the man's face and took a guess as to what was going on here.

"Hello up there. We are just traveling along. We don't mean you any harm. Your grandpa has a gun on us. I'll be upfront with you, we have zombies chasing us. We thought this was a deserted place to hide."

"You must be on drugs, there is no one here but me." He took a step closer to the group, who were all lined up on the far wall now. "Are you here to rob me for your drug money? Last warning, get out or Betsy here will blow holes clean through you."

Rapid footsteps announced her presence. A young lady raced down the stairs. She looked to be about Hannah's age and her blond hair, fashioned into a braid, bobbed with each step. She was dressed as if she as if she had been swallowed by Smokey the bear. She was short and had to stand on her tiptoes when, with a deft touch, she grabbed the barrel and pulled the shotgun up and out of the old man's hands.

"Just who do you think you are miss?" the old man protested, reaching for the gun.

"Grandpa it's me, Amber."

The old man paused for a moment then grumbled. "Right, Amber. Is lunch ready yet?"

"Go back into the kitchen, Grandpa. I 'll be there shortly." Amber shooed him along. She watched him go back through the swinging door before she whirled back around to face them. She pointed the shotgun up to the ceiling.

"You need to go now before those things know you're here. It's just me and Grandpa. We'll never be able to fight off a pack of them. Who am I kidding, it would just be me doing the fighting."

"Please," Hannah stepped out, hands up, palms facing Amber. "We are not sure they are even still following us. We encountered them up over the top of the mountain pass. Where the road cuts through."

"We can fight," JT came forward beside Hannah. "We've had to more than once. If it comes to that, you and your Grandpa won't be harmed. We can protect you."

"No, leave. We have survived this long by not drawing attention to ourselves." Amber looked hesitant but she did drop down the shotgun and train it on them.

"Whoa, whoa miss," Gus said. "No need for violence. We could help, clear these things out once and for all if they come but we will leave if-."

There was a crash against the door. It shook but held. Then there was another crash against the wall. Then two more. Linda was closest to the window and peaked out.

"Looks like a pack of six Runners, by the way they move," she informed everyone, moving away from the wall.

"Damn you people," Amber said, looking as if she was about to burst into tears.

"Hon, don't worry," Gus said, pulling a pistol from its holster. "We got this." He hoped his cocky attitude was convincing in calming her. Because he had learned when tackling these things, it was never a sure deal.

"A pack made up of Runners, that's new." Gus said, sliding up next to JT.

"Yep." JT was taking off the safety.

"As they say, the faster they are, the faster their dicks drop in the dirt."

"Gus, I've never heard that saying."

"Amber, I'll go back in the kitchen with you," Hannah offered. "We will protect you and your Grandpa with our lives."

Amber looked hesitantly between them all, shotgun still pointed at them. With a sigh of resignation she lowered her gun. "Guess its to late. The zombies are already here. You can follow me into the kitchen."

Amber looked scared to death. Hannah put her arm around the young woman's shoulder and led her off, following her grandpa's route.

Gus turned to Linda, keeping up his swagger. "Linda, are you locked, cocked, and ready to rock?!"

"Gus you're such a stud. You're making me wet," Linda smiled broadly.

"I knew there was a reason I liked you," Gus chortled.

"Gross." JT made fake heaving sounds through a big grin. "It's like listening to my parents make out."

The zombies kept thudding against the door and now the walls as well. It was time to get serious. Gus was about to say so when one broke through a window. While it struggled, its torso was caught on some jagged glass, JT took two steps forward and blew its brains out.

"You two stop with the bedroom talk. Let's get this done."

Wind and sparkling snow flurried through the busted window. JT stalked to the window, kicked the zombie back out, and started taking shots out the opening. Gus was glad a sober JT with them today. He would not like to be shot, stabbed, or bitten.

"One down, five to go," Gus said.

"Look, Gus can count," JT said. He fired again. "Make that four."

There was another door rattling thump then a quieter thud.

"Three. Get the other window open and start crackalackin', Gus."

Gus unlocked it, lifted up the window, and then jumped back, just about tripping over his feet. A Runner lunged at that moment, startling him. It was half in, half out the window. It twisted around like it was possessed by a demon. Linda came up beside him and finished it off with her shotgun. The sound still rang in his ears as Gus hesitantly grabbed the thing by its rotting shirt and pulled it all the way in, clearing the line of fire.

Gus could see two more out there, both scrambling at JT's side. Gus hung out the window, fired, and missed. The zombies both turned as one, drawn by the sound. Cursing himself, Gus fired again, hitting one in the side of the head. It jerked back then kept coming. Gus went flying backwards again as within a second they were on top of him. He had forgotten how fast the son of a bitching Runners could move. JT leaned out the broken window and took a shot.

"One."

"Save the last for me. I don't want to look bad in front of my lady friend."

"Go ahead, I have to reload."

JT backed away from his window and did just that. *If those things could think,* Gus wagered, *the last one would be confused by the loss of its friends. Its compadres all gone, attacked from two directions.* Gus was ready to put it out of its misery. The door banged for a third time and the wood on the door frame splintered. The last zombie used to be a big man's man. Gus chuckled to himself, imaging the zombie man as a sterotypical lumberjack.

"Lumberjack Mac," Gus cawed out the window. It turned towards him.

Boom. Right in the middle of the forehead. Gus cheered after he took it down. Its forward momentum kept it coming. It slammed into Gus and he fell back, hitting the wall hard. Gus felt like his bones in his back had been crushed. JT pulled it back outside. Gus slid to the floor gulping in extra air.

"Gus, you show off," Linda said, dropping down to one knee. She looked concerned which made him smile.

"How's that for this old timer!"Gus crowed when he got his air back. "Hey ladies, it's clear."

In a few moments Hannah came back out with Amber.

"My God," Amber said, covering her mouth with her hand. "You people. Look at our house! Look what you've done!" Her face was turning red and she topped talking. Instead she hissed and spit like an alley cat.

"Shit, she's going to pop her boiler. She's going to blow," Gus said. He regretted the outburst when she came at him, hands clenched into fists at her side. She stared up at him like a Medusa willing Gus to turn into stone. He would have took a few steps backwards but he was already against the wall. Instead he put his hands up.

"Guys, I have even more bad news," JT said, getting between Amber and Gus. "With all that noise, there's a slim chance the other zombies could come this way. Sound carries and echoes up here I've noticed."

After hearing JT's statement, all of Amber's anger seemed to evaporate and instead she started crying into her hands. She plopped down on the stairs.

"As winter came we were bothered less and less by anyone dead or alive," Amber said between sobs. "Not that there were many people here in the high country to start. There were in Colorado Springs though. It was rough getting here but this was the first place I thought of when this all began." Amber took a deep breath. "With my Grandpa, the way he is, I thought we didn't have a chance anywhere else. This was his vacation house when he was younger. We fled, we made it. I lost my mom on the way but we've managed to hang on all this time. I had begun to think, the last few weeks, that after a while...I thought maybe the zombies were gone for good. What a silly thought. What am I going to do?"

Linda went over to her, put an arm around her. She went into full caring nurse mode. Gus felt his heart swell at her compassion. "We're sorry. We never meant to be a burden. We'll do whatever we can to help you."

"Really?" Hannah said, hand on her hip. "Linda don't you think we should talk about it first?"

"What, you think these two are a threat?" JT said.

Gus wished JT could have said it a little nicer. These two grumbling at each other was getting on his nerves. Hannah walked as far away from JT as she could and stood there. Her arms were crossed and a pout was on her face. Gus didn't have time to fiddle with them and their sensitive feelings right now. Linda was in the right and they needed to take action before the were overwhelmed with zombie assholes.

"You go on up stairs, hon," Gus said, softening his voice. He stepped up next to Linda. "Gather up what you need in case we have to skedaddle. I'll go in the kitchen while you're up there. Us geezers need to stick together."

Amber looked up at the two of them, her eyes wet. Linda held out both of her hands. Amber took them and the two went upstairs. JT and Hannah were having a staring contest. Gus thought it looked like a competition to see who could look the most pissy. He left them to it. Gus pushed through the swinging wood door into the kitchen. The old man was sitting at a table, staring off into space. He turned to Gus as he entered.

"Do I know you?" the man asked.

"I'm Gus. Acquaintance of your granddaughter, Amber. I didn't catch your name."

The man continued sitting there, looking slack jawed. Then a little spark came into his face.

"Byron," he said, excited. "My name is Byron." He spoke with a slight English accent.

Gus joined him at the little wooden table. He was trying to decide what track to take with this guy. "It's nice to meet you, Byron. You know what is going on with the world right? What happened?"

Byron scratched his nose. Gus was afraid the man was going to start picking it too but Byron put his hand down in his lap.

"Yes. People went crazy. We came up in the mountains to hide. Me and my Amber. My daughter in law Lindsay, too. I wonder where she's gotten off to."

"Right!" Gus was happy to see Byron still had some gears grinding away. "Well I got some bad news, pal. Some of those crazies are headed this way. I have a group of people here with me. We are going to help. Either drive the crazies away or get you and Amber out of here safely."

Byron just sat there, fiddling with his hands. Gus was afraid the lights had went dim upstairs again. Then Byron surprised him by standing up.

"I need to get my things then. Just in case. Don't you fret though, I can fight too. I was in the British Army." Byron puffed out his scrawny chest.

Great, we traded in Dusty for a older model. Gus chuckled to himself. He humored Byron. "Well what are we waiting for. Let's go out with the others."

Back through the swinging doors they went. The others were huddled together as far from the open window as possible. Except for Hannah, who was looking out the broken window. Snow and wetness gathered around her feet, puddling on the hardwood floor.

Amber came back down the stairs. She was carrying the shotgun in one hand and a large duffel bag in the other. She put them down to take Byron by the hand. She led him over to a closet by the front door.

"Grandpa, let's get you into your winter coat," Amber said, like she was talking to a child.

"You better hurry," Hannah said from her perch. "I see movement out there."

"I need to hit the bathroom now then, so I don't piss myself later." Gus bellowed at the others.

"Ugh," Linda and Hannah said in unison.

"No, really."

Amber pointed back towards the kitchen. "Right before you go in, turn right."

Gus gave a thumbs up. That was the hard part about being so funny, people didn't know when to take you seriously. After relieving himself, Gus came back out to the sound of gunfire.

"Gus! The undead wall is back!" Hannah shouted over the weapons.

"The hills are alive, with the sound of gun play," Gus said, picking up his weapon, which he had left leaning against the wall.

"Quiet!" Hannah shushed. "Stop shooting."

Everyone stopped firing. Gus settled down and strained his ears. He had never been in the mountains or around snow much but he had of course watched lots of movies, like *The Shining* or *Hot Tub Time Machine*. He could swear what he was hearing now was the sound of snowmobiles.

Whatever the sound was, it was getting louder. Then he heard the rapid eruption of gunfire. With all they had been through, there was no mistaking that sound.

Gus squeezed in beside JT, trying to see what was going on. Between the mass of zombies and the thickness of the snowfall, it was tough.

"I haven't seen this much white powder since the eighties." Gus's commentary fell on deaf ears this time.

Gus could see the dead turning towards the sound. About every third zombie fell face first into said powder. They couldn't walk in the snow worth shit either. It was comical and horrifying at the same time.

Everyone got their weapons ready again just in case it was another threat. Gus was beginning to worry about ammo if this was another attack. Two snowmobiles crashed through the undead line. Both had a person in a ski mask and a long coat driving them, semi automatics in hand. One rode right up to the porch.

"You people," he said in a hard tone, muffled through the mask. "What are you doing?"

Hannah stepped out the door and up to the man. "All we want is to be left alone."

The man answered back sarcastically. "You do know there is a pack of dead heads coming this way, over the ridge? Besides the ones already here. Behind them we've spotted some kind of crazy people plowing through the snow with a dump truck behind them. We have someplace safe nearby. You should come. The sound of your gun fire attracted us. You can be damn sure it attracted everything else around too."

"I've heard that before," Hannah said, indignant. "Both times the people in those supposed 'safe places' killed my friends and tried to kill me."

The other snowmobile pulled up alongside the man talking.

"I'm not going to stand here and have a debate with you. That's my offer, you can come right now or not." Two more snowmobiles pulled up and stopped next to the man speaking. "Last chance."

Amber strode out between them, Grandpa in tow. "We're going with you. These people have left us no choice." They both straddled one of the snowmobiles, Byron between the driver and Amber, and took off. Three remained.

Hannah looked at the others. Gus could see the lost look of panic on her face. She was afraid of making the wrong decision here. Fearful memories of Albright and Harold had to be paralyzing her. He had tried to stay out of her way and not put his two cents in most of the time. Now might be a time she would appreciate his opinion.

"Look, Hannah. I know the last thing you want is gettin' mixed up with some group. Hell, I want nothing to do with the lot of them. Our choices aren't looking so good right now though. Didn't expect to find packs of undead up here. Didn't expect to be followed by lunatics in a dump truck. Let's go with them, with all of our antennas up, so we can at least get our bearings."

He could almost imagine seeing the wheels spinning in her head as he watched her struggle with it. She looked down at the porch for the longest time.

The man turned to leave. "Sorry, we gotta go. We aren't getting tangled up in this. I wouldn't even be out here if my Dad didn't force it on me."

"Alright, alright," Hannah said, expelling it out in a rush. "Lead on and don't try anything. We're armed and we know how to kill."

"We could say the same thing to you."

THIN ICE

JT was extremely wary of this idea as he climbed on the back of one of the snow mobiles.

"Hold on tight." The driver yelled back as he accelerated so abruptly he almost bucked JT off the rear. JT considered cuffing this guy across the back of his head until the vehicle Hannah was on glided by and he saw her smiling at his near misfortune.

Their little convoy navigated the terrain at a brisk pace, weaving in and out of the trees and the outstretched arms of the undead horde on the hunt. As they cleared a break in the trees they saw the snow mobile carrying Amber and Byron stopped near the iced over lake they had passed in route to the cabin during their retreat. The driver was frantically giving hand signals bringing the other three mobiles to a halt.

Hannah looked ahead to see what the commotion was all about. A platoon of zombies were headed their way. She guessed the dead were directly in their path and gathering.

"What's our move here?!" One of the drivers yelled to another.

"Fuck! I knew this was a terrible idea!" Was his only reply as he lifted his goggles.

The driver of JT's vehicle began to fiddle with the holster housing his revolver. Nerves clearly had the best of him, his hands shook as he checked the cylinder of the weapon, nearly spilling the ammunition out of the chambers. JT had an idea but it would be dangerous. *Fuck it. At least I would die doing something.*

"Get back on JT!" Gus shouted at him. He threw a gloved thumbs up over his head.

JT walked towards the frozen lake with a purpose. He barely broke stride as he hit the slick surface and shuffled in long glides a few feet from the shore.

"What in the hell are you doing?" Hannah called to him, concern rising in her voice.

JT was about twenty feet onto the frozen lake when he started to fire his pistol into the air. The sudden noise drew the zombies attention as they veered in his direction. He remained poised as he hit the safety and secured his pistol inside a coat pocket. He drew the rifle from his shoulder, bringing it into position.

The flock of zombies began to shamble onto the ice with the grace of a toddler just learning to walk. Some fell, others just slipped around in place like a stuck penguin. Hannah leapt from her seat, training her own rifle on the clamoring group.

"No!" JT called to her, then started loudly singing The Wheels On The Bus.

"Hell of a time to audition for Star Search." Gus mumbled to Linda.

The zombies kept slipping and sliding their way across the icy surface towards JT who was now firing shots at their feet creating little spurts of icy water as they burrowed through the ice.

"Any of you guys ever played Don't Break The Ice?" JT asked over the sounds of his gunfire.

He gave himself a moment to turn around, seeing the group look at one another with shrugged shoulders and upturned palms. The sounds of the trucks engines were getting closer.

"Don't break the ice!" Gus suddenly shouted, nearly knocking Linda off the snowmobile as he scampered to his feet. "In this case break the damn ice!" He yelled again, taking aim at the front of the herd and firing at the ice.

Hannah and Linda caught on and joined Gus at firing at the ice, water spouts popping up rapidly. There was a big splash of water as the middle of the herd collapsed through the ice into the water, pulling some of their dead friends with them, others falling at the change in pace and terrain. A few of the remaining zombies stood still looking conflicted about the noise of their fellow brethren sloshing in the frosty water and the living people who put them there.

JT was done pressing his luck. He had to imagine the whole lake's icy surface was unstable at this point. JT slid his way back to the shore, a huge smile across the face of his mobile's chauffeur. The rest of the group hurried back to their vehicles as well.

"JT you slick son of a bitch! Here I thought you were just gonna cash in and head home!" Gus said to him as the vehicles started to move.

"Gus, I'm just glad they played that game back in your old folks home." JT retorted.

With a ornery grin Gus gave him a long thumbs up as the vehicles zoomed along their way, destination unknown.

THE GRAND TOUR

The big neon sign laid dormant, its gaudiness dead. Even though there were signs the settlement had some form of electrical power, it wasn't wasted on such extravagance it seemed. Waste like that was for the old world. JT and Hannah passed under it, entering the casino with their two escorts.

The town was quite a sight. It had a wall of junk around it, like a barrier, set in it was a gate. Hannah felt a sense of crushing foreboding as she once again entered a settlement full of people. There weapons were taken and the snowmobile men escored Gus and Linda off, along with Amber and Byron, stating they were taking them to a clinic.

It only set her a little at ease when everyone and everything they passed after meeting their new escorts seemed more like a regular small town. Everything seemed normal, like from before the Outbreak. People seemed to be happily going about their business, children played out in the streets and front lawns. Of course Albright's church also had an appearance like this at first.

Hannah's apprehension grew as they entered the old casino. The two escorts, weapons in hand, didn't say a word to them. They passed the silent slot machines and game tables to the staircase in the back. It was a small casino, only three floors. Hannah and JT took the stairs to the first.

At the top they took the long hallway down to the room at the end. One of the escorts knocked on the big door. A man wearing small frame glasses opened the door. He was only a little taller than Hannah. His black hair was shot with grey and was mostly gone. Only little wisps remained on both sides of his head. He wore nice business casual clothes and had the air of a more refined civility to him than most of the survivors they had met.

"Come in," he said, in a voice that instantly made Hannah think of the Sopranos.

The room was expansive. Hannah guessed before the Outbreak this was the top suite in the casino's hotel. A large window dominated the living area, with a view of snow capped mountains that was breathtaking. Everything from the couches and counter tops to the carpeted floor was spotless.

"Bobby, Joe. You guys can wait outside," the man said with a wave of his hand.

The two men left, closing the door behind them. Casino man took a seat casually over by the window and waved his hand again at the couch. Hannah looked at it like it was going to bite her, then reluctantly sat down. JT stood over her, his hands crossed over his chest, a sour look on his face. Hannah began to wonder if this guy was maybe the casino's supervisor or owner before the Outbreak. If so he has been riding it out in style.

"Suit yourself pal," the man said, crossing his legs. "I heard one of my guys found you and your group on the run from some of the cadavers. Oh sorry, pardon me. Where are my manners? My name's is Dr. Childs. And you two are?"

"Hannah," she said, speaking just above a whisper.

"JT," he spit out from his clenched jaw.

"You two don't look too happy to be here. Don't worry, we aren't going to hurt you."

"I've heard that before," JT said sarcastically.

Hannah spoke up. "Let me just get to the point Dr. Childs. We have no interest in being here. We want nothing to do with your settlement. We didn't ask for any help. We want our weapons back and to be shown the way out." The volume of her voice rose as she spoke. She reined it back under control before she started yelling at the man.

"I see," Dr. Childs said, shifting his eyes between Hannah and JT. "Can I at least give you the grand tour? We don't need anyone right now but hey, it would be inhumane to at least not offer you a safe haven."

Hannah's stomach clenched and a chill ran down her spine at Dr. Child's words. She sprang up. "We want out now!"

"Woah, woah. I don't know what happened to you but it looks like it wasn't a good time. What about you, JT? You two were brought here because my men were told you were the leaders of your group. You agree with your lady friend?"

Hannah saw JT look over into Dr. Child's kitchen. There was a line of bottles, ranging from gin to scotch to tequila along one counter. Hannah felt her stomach clinch.

"I don't see any harm in staying one night first. Making a plan," JT licked his lips. "I agree with Hannah. We're not looking to join another group of survivors."

Hannah scowled at JT, flabbergasted. She wanted to do no such thing. She would have an earful for him later. She pierced Dr. Childs with a scathing look.

Dr. Child's went on, ignoring her silent protest. "I will give you an abbreviated tour on the way to shelter. Then you can be on your merry way. I'm not sure I'd want such...negative emotions brought into the town anyway. Alright?"

Hannah unclenched fists she didn't even realize she had made. She took a deep breath, attempting to blow away the horror and the guilt threatening to overwhelm her. She nodded.

"Nothing funny out of you," JT said, still standing like a statue, arms crossed.

"Same to you, pal. These people, they take my safety seriously. Being the only doctor around since the Outbreak, I'm an important person around here. The most important a lot of them would say."

Dr. Childs stood up, crossing the room to the door. He grabbed a stylish parka from the hooks by the door and shrugged it on. He opened the door and waved them through.

"Our friends Gus and Linda. They are coming with us," Hannah demanded as she walked past Childs.

"Of course. No need for hostility. We will swing by our clinic, by no means can we call it a hospital, and pick them up. I had heard the older man you were with was hurt. I'll give him a once over before you leave, if he doesn't mind."

JT took Hannah's hand. Hannah squeezed it as hard as she could then let go. *JT you can go screw yourself and the bottle your dreaming about.* Yeah, so far it seemed like this Dr. Childs was okay and they were going to be let go unharmed. She had been through too much to fully trust him. There could still be a trap somewhere along the way.

Dr. Childs led the way, followed by JT and Hannah, walking side by side and in the back trailed the two body guards, Bobby and Joe. Their pistols were now in the belts around their waists, but their hands never strayed too far from them. Hannah wondered if at one time one or both of them were policemen or security of some sort.

Hannah blinked as they exited the casino. The sun's glare was harsh off of the snowpack. It temporarily blinded her after the gloom of being inside.

"I'd guess we're the most self sufficient town you will find in this area," Childs continued on. "Possibly even the United States. I don't know where you came from, but it sounds to me like you have done some hard traveling. Yet here you are. You haven't been killed yet. You're survivors."

"I don't believe anywhere is safe," Hannah said sullenly.

"I think you will beg to differ, once you see our joint."

"How did you get here?" JT asked. "You don't sound like you're from Colorado."

"Ha, you got that right. I'm New Jersey, born and raised." Dr. Childs said, as they continued down the snow covered street, following in the footsteps of the others who had came this way. "I was vacationing with my wife, Glenda, when the Outbreak happened. We were down in Colorado Springs, doing the tourist bit. My wife likes skiing and shopping. I like sipping umbrella drinks by the pool. That you can do anywhere. I liked to keep my wife happy and this is where she wanted to be. Then bam, the world goes to fuck. I'm just a family physician, not a pathologist or infectious disease specialist. Still, I can't wrap my head around what appears to be a virus with a one hundred percent infection rate and a incubation period of minutes."

"Is your wife here?" Hannah asked, curious in spite of wanting nothing to do with these people.

"She umm, she didn't make it. I was in my hotel room. She was out looking at antiques or some such shit. I had the radio on. The emergency broadcast broke in. I couldn't believe what I was hearing. So I turned on the TV. Saw the photos and videos of the devastation in New York, Washington D.C., Los Angeles. I called Glenda's cell, couldn't get through. I was about to go out the door when I happened to look out the window. Down from my suite on the sixth floor, I could see I was already too late."

Dr. Childs stopped for a moment. Hannah thought he was taking a moment to help keep his composure. She softened just a little then. Not much, she still kept her eye on the two bodyguards as they walked. There was still no way she was trusted any of them.

Childs continued on. "Colorado Spring had turned into a massacre. It was a bloodbath in the Hilton parking lot, it looked like a war zone. From high up I couldn't tell who were the people and who were the zombies. All I could see was they were tearing each other apart. I barricaded the door and stayed inside until hunger drove me out. This was, I don't know how many days later. I scrounged up some food and hid back in my hole. It was summer until I ran into any other living people. They had come down from the mountains. When they found out I was a doctor, they went nuts. You would think they had just won the powerball or something. I came up here with them and I've been here ever since."

"So you didn't start this place?" Hannah asked.

"No, but I've been in charge ever since I got here. Before me it was Henry Evans. He's an engineer. He helped erect the walls, blasted a cave in the mountain side where we have food stored. Got some electricity going even. We get along okay but I can tell he wasn't happy about being replaced as the top dog. Wasn't my idea though. Just about everyone here said having a doctor around was the more important thing."

They stopped outside a building proclaiming itself as the number one stop for ski supplies.

"This is the clinic. We'll check on your friends, I'll give you all the abbreviated tour and then if you still want, you can be on your way."

They went inside. A surprising blast of warmth hit them as the door opened. A roaring fireplace stood in the middle of the store. Shoved against both walls were racks of winter gear. The walls were mostly stripped bare, but here and there skis, poles or boots were still hung up or sitting on shelves. Their footsteps tapped along the hardwood floor as they made their way to the back.

"The fireplace feels great right?" Dr. Childs said with a smile. "It was the top reason I picked this place to set up. Even in the summer, at this altitude, it can be chilly. Couldn't have been vacationing in the Bahamas when shit when down huh?"

Behind what use to be check out counters, huge red curtains ran from ceiling to floor. Childs parted them, revealing a big open concrete space. Whatever store inventory there had been was emptied out to make room for beds and medical equipment.

There were six beds. Two of them were occupied. One of them was by Gus. Linda was seated next to him, reading through a magazine. She stood and smiled when she saw them.

"Just like a real doctor's office, I found a year old magazine to thumb through," Linda said, chuckling.

"Gus, here you are lying around in bed again. Too much of this and I'm going to start thinking you like being pampered," JT said, chiding his friend.

"Well don't you have a bedside manner like catching my pecker in my zipper. Why are we even friends again?" Gus gave back.

"He popped a stitch in all the excitement," Linda said. "It was an easy fix with all the supplies they have here. Gus cried like a baby."

Gus gave Linda an over the top stare. "Well no more Mr. Nice Gus for you either!"

"Hi, I'm Dr. Childs." He extended his hand out to Linda, then Gus.

"Linda."

"Gus."

After handshakes he asked. "Linda, are you a doctor, too?"

"No, I'm a nurse," she said, sounding like a professional. "It's nice to meet you, doctor."

"Excellent," Dr. Childs said, rubbing his hands together. "I could use a good assistant, if you decided to stay. Sometimes my hours here are longer than I had back at my practice."

Linda looked to Hannah and JT and then gave a noncommittal. "Um, sure."

Dr. Childs fully turned to Gus. "Gus, I have been practicing medicine for twenty years. Would you mind if I gave you an examine, before you go?"

"Sure doc, as long as you don't ask me to turn my head and cough."

Dr. Childs frowned, then went to gather up a stethoscope, blood pressure cuff, and a pen light. He snapped on some gloves and came back over. He did the standard checks on Gus's hearts, lungs and then looked at the gash in Gus's side. He felt around it, asking Gus for feedback on how the pain was.

"You are in reasonably good health. Lungs could be a little clearer. I gather you use to be a smoker, right?"

Gus nodded. "That was a tough bitch to bust, but I gave it up many, many moons ago."

"The stab wound must have been nasty. It is healing nicely, all things considered. I don't see any sign of secondary infection. Try not to do anything strenuous the next few days."

"Good to know," Gus said, pulling his shirt back down. "Now are you going to bill my insurance? I don't know where I've put my card, but it was BlueCross BlueShield."

"I don't give away many freebies, but that one was on the house," Dr. Childs said, putting his equipment away.

"I'm free to go doc?"

"Yes."

"First Gus, the doctor here is going to give us the timeshare pitch on why we should buy a lovely condo here," JT said.

"He was?" Linda scratched her head. "Then he can start by telling me about the zombie out back in the cage."

"What?!" Hannah fumbled for her weapon, forgetting they were still unarmed. Just when she started to think maybe this place was on the up and up.

"I stepped out for a quick breath of fresh air after finishing with Gus and there it was on the dock," Linda said.

"Now, now, calm down," Dr. Childs said soothingly, raising his hands up in the air. "It's no secret I keep the specimen back behind the building. You can see it, if you like."

"Count me out, I've seen enough of those for five lifetimes," Gus said.

"I've seen it already." Linda sat back down.

Hannah didn't know why she agreed. She should have cared less than zero about seeing it. They were leaving no matter what anyway. She guessed it was just some morbid curiosity that made her nod her head yes. Maybe she wanted to hear what excuse the doctor could come up with.

Dr. Childs walked them out the back door. In a corner where the building jutted out a little, there was a large dog crate. It looked large enough for something like a German Shepard. There was no dog inside; it was a zombie. It use to be a toddler. It looked no bigger than a four year old to Hannah. Its right arm was gone all the way up to the shoulder. The bone of the shoulder socket stuck out around ragged grey and black flesh. It had silvery duct tape wound around its mouth. It looked towards them with empty white eyes as they approached. Hannah felt the urge to puke. In all the times she had seen the zombies, this was the first time abominations came to her mind to describe what she was looking at.

"Dude, disgusting," JT said, going pale.

Hannah could guess why. It had to be the same reason she turned her head quickly away. Seeing a zombie in a cage reminded her too much of what happened to Tyrone. She tried to keep the thought away but it rushed to the top. Not for the first time she wondered if the undead walked around with there souls trapped, unable to ascend to Heaven. She shivered and it wasn't because she was cold.

"We have a small patrol group. They go out once a week, gather supplies and have a look around. They captured it on one of their rounds. They thought maybe I could study it. I guess they thought maybe I could find a cure or vaccine." Dr. Childs' smile was condescending. Like he thought those people were simpletons. Hannah disliked him for that.

"Like I said diseases aren't my specialty, but I have been doing observational studies. One interesting theory I am charting now is even though the dead bodies are animated by the virus, the bodies are still decaying. I theorize eventually the body will rot away to such a state that the victims will actually die. There will be no brain tissue left. Then the virus too will die. It does seem the virus somehow retards the decaying process by some unknown degree. I am excited to see where testing leads, as limited as I am here."

"I'm done," Hannah said, holding her looping stomach. "Let's go, JT."

"Fine." Dr. Childs turned away. "Walk with me and we'll stop by the guard house. You'll get your weapons and supplies back and you will be free to stay or go."

"Sounds good," Hannah said, peeking at the zombie one more time. It was like looking at a horrific accident. She couldn't turn completely away until the metal door shut, blocking her view.

Back inside, Linda and Gus were sitting close to one another, chatting. Hannah turned her mind from the disturbing thing she just saw and the feelings it brought up. It was like walking through thick syrup but she needed to distract herself. She focused on how happy she was to hear Gus was healing well. On how happy Gus and Linda were together.

Gus got up from the bed. Linda helped Gus bundled up for the cold. Hannah realized with a pang that Linda had supplanted her in caring for Gus. *What a weird thing to be jealous of.*

She turned away to Dr. Childs. "We're ready. Can we go?"

"Follow me." Childs led the way.

She was beginning to think Childs was telling the truth and they would get to leave. It would be a first in this screwed up new world.

Gus spoke up just as they were about to leave the makeshift clinic. "What about Amber and her grandpa, Doc Brown?"

"I had them installed in an apartment building as soon as they got here. I was told over walkie talkie that the grandpa, I can't remember his name, started acting out on the way in. I'm going to talk to them both and get a medical history. I'll need to schedule an examination for him. Sounds unfortunate though. I believe he is suffering from early stages of Alzheimer's."

Gus looked at Linda and gave her a nod. Again Hannah surprised herself by not caring what had happened to the two people from the cabin. Even though she knew she should. After all wasn't that the Christian thing to do? It was their fault after all that Amber's house was damaged. If something happened to them here, if Childs wasn't safe, wouldn't something happening to the two of them be partially her fault too? She didn't think she would feel any guilt. Maybe that bucket was already full. Or she was kidding herself.

Childs held the door open for them. Little swirls of snowflakes swirled inside."If you weren't in such a big hurry, I could show you more reasons you should stay. It would be better than me just telling you," Dr. Childs said, walking deliberately in the slush. The sun was doing a number on the snow. Hannah gave Childs a harsh glare and shook her head no.

"Gus, Linda," Dr. Childs said, leading them on. "Like I was mentioning to Hannah and JT earlier, we have a storehouse inside a cave blasted into the mountain. We have so much food stored in there, frozen meat, fruits, vegetables, we could feed a population ten times our size. Obviously we have the clinic, a one room schoolhouse, a church. We have rigged up limited electrical power thanks to our engineer. Most houses have fireplaces and we have no shortage of wood. Close to all the comforts of before. We have easily defendable walls on the two ways in and out of town, manned twenty four hours. Best of all, no zombies or human attackers have ever made it inside. Not even close."

Gus whistled. Hannah had to admit it all sounded great and impressive. She did end up having another question for him after all. "And what? For this protection everyone just has to do what you say?"

Dr. Childs stopped and looked at her for a moment, tilting his head to the side and gave her a flat stare. "I wouldn't put it that way exactly," he said, adjusting his glasses. "I'm an important person here. I enjoy the privileges my status provides. Everyone must do their part to get any of the benefits."

Hannah made a sour face. Those comments solidified her decision. "We're leaving now."

"Suit yourself. Foolish as I think that is." Childs said. "I don't know what it's like out there now but I'm sure it's not fucking Disneyland."

"Hannah, really?" JT spoke up. "I thought we could at least sleep tonight in a warm house. Where the fuck are we going to go?"

"JT-" Gus warned.

"No, Gus. Fuck it. I'm going to say my peace." JT was getting worked up. "I think there is no harm in staying one day. Look, Childs is leading us out. He's been honest with us so far. Isn't this what you came to the mountains to find, Hannah?"

Hannah twirled on him. "You can stay. I'm not. End of discussion. Go have a drink on me."

JT reacted as if she slapped him in the face. His recoil turned into a petulant frown. His body drooped. "Now that's not fair."

"If you people are done bickering, we're here," Childs said.

In front of them was the guard shack. It stood next to the large chain link gate that let them into the town. It was build right into the wall. The shack was too small for all of them to go in at the same time.

"Wait here." Childs knocked on the door. Hannah and the rest stood behind him. A woman answered and Hannah heard JT gasp.

IN THE AIR

What struck JT first was her hair. It was pink. It made him think of cotton candy. It was done up in two ponytails that dropped behind the hood of her coat. She looked to be about his age. Her nose was pierced with what appeared to be a diamond, it sparkled as the sunlight hit it through the open door.

She scowled at Dr. Childs and the rest of them as she panned over them one at a time. When she got to JT she smiled and lightly bit her bottom lip. Her lipstick was purple. He couldn't help but smile back at her. His anger at Hannah evaporated, along with the thoughts that maybe he was tired of dealing with her.

"What Childs?" she grumped at him. "I was intensely watching a squirrel climbing a tree."

"Always such a pleasure to talk to you Lindsay," Dr. Childs said dryly. "These four people are leaving. I need you to give them back their personal property and the like. I understand they were stored here."

With exaggerated exasperation Lindsay got up and went over to a set of lockers, like the ones they had in school. She dialed four lockers open and returned to the doorway. JT could see one of the four had his weapons inside.

"You're leaving so soon, handsome?" Lindsay said, patting JT on the chest. "That's too bad. Most of the men around here are in a relationship or old like Childs here. We could use some new studs."

Hannah cleared her throat, clearly irritated. JT was flattered and he had to admit a little amused as well. He decided to mess with Hannah a little. He thought she deserved it after what she had said.

"If I knew they were hiding away a cutie like you around here, I might have changed my mind."

Hannah cleared her throat again, even louder.

"If you want you can leave, Miss Frumpy. Take the oldsters with you. I think the big man would like to stay, at least for tonight" Lindsay flirted with a wink.

"Can we get on with this please, before daylight is gone," Hannah said, throwing JT dirty looks.

JT laughed and gave a wink of his own at Hannah. "Two can be fun, but three's a party."

That got Gus laughing along with JT, but Hannah just fumed. Lindsay gave JT a smirk.

"Lindsay, can you get out of the way. I don't want any damn trouble stirred up. These people want to go and I'm starting to feel that's fine with me," Dr. Childs said.

"Sure," Lindsay said with a huff. "Wouldn't want to do something extreme like have fun." She backed out of the way and took her place in a chair in front of a window slit that looked out beyond the wall. "One at a time. As you can see it's a little small in here."

They went in single file, each getting there gear out of one of the lockers. JT went last. Lindsay sat in her chair, chewing some gum and watching him. "What's your name, hon?"

"JT."

"Well, JT, you need any help getting your stuff out?" Lindsay got up and brushed past him, making sure to rub up against him as much as possible. The thought of staying here and forgetting Hannah rose in his mind even stronger. She handed him his pack. It took considerable willpower to put it on and leave the shack.

At the doorway he turned around. "Gotta say, it was nice to meet you Lindsay. There's a good chance I'll be coming back this way." He figured Hannah was probably burning a hole into the back of his head but he didn't care.

"I'll be here. It's going to be cold out there. I've got a nice warm place here." She saved and smiled before shutting the door. JT was going to remember her.

"You happen to have anything you can spare for the road?" Gus asked Childs. "Some food maybe?"

"No I can't. I'm sorry," Dr. Childs said, not sounding sorry. "Like I said, I don't give freebies often. We work around here for our supplies. Our supplies are for our people"

JT thought that was a pretty shitty move. From the way the guy had been bragging it's wasn't like they couldn't share a little bit. Dr. Childs seemed like even more of a tight ass than he first thought. As much as it would be nice to rest for a bit, maybe Hannah was right, they should just go. He couldn't deny he had just met another tempting reasons to stay though.

"If you don't mind me asking, where is it you plan on going?" Dr. Childs asked with a detached curiosity.

"Someplace like this, only it will be just the four of us," Hannah answered. "I'm sure we could find another place like this."

Childs cocked his head and furrowed his brow. Yet he didn't comment on what she said. He went on with his sales pitch. JT had to give him credit, he didn't give up easily.

"Now is one of the worst times to be just wandering around out there. You don't seem to have lots of experience up here in the mountains. You have to be careful, the cold, the altitude. It can quickly overwhelm your body. Your lungs can freeze. That's a nasty way to die. If you need to come back, the offer stands. You'll have to work but you'll have all you need. Do you need to talk to the other two who came in with you? They are part of your group, right?"

Linda looked as if she wanted to say something so Hannah jumped in quick. "No. We just met up with them right before we were found by your people."

"I see, very well then." Childs gestured through the guard shack window. Lindsay came out. She unlocked and opened the gate for them.

The four of them went through the smaller door set into the larger gate. JT shouldered his pack, adjusting the weight distribution, and followed Hannah. He had to give Childs a point, they didn't know what they were doing up here. So far no one seemed to be bothered by the cold or altitude sickness. In fact, his knee seemed to be throbbing a little less. But JT had to guess this was only the beginning of winter. If it was already this bad, which was worse than it ever got back in his hometown, what would they be facing if they didn't find some place to hole up?

JT turned to give the place a last look. It was a fairly imposing wall they had cobbled together between the rocky outcroppings. It would probably look strange in the springtime when the snow melted, to see the road stretching on and suddenly stopping at this ten foot structure of wood, metal, and who knew what else. It made him think of Mad Max.

With the fantasy of sitting by a warm fireplace, maybe snuggled up with Lindsay, JT reluctantly turned away. They trekked on and on through the snow. The day grew later, their shadows began to grow llike black giants on the mountain face.

"Hannah? What are we doing?" Gus asked as the sun hung lower in the sky.

JT had been wondering the same thing. He didn't want to join those people but thought staying one night, trying to persuade them for more help, even some directions to someplace promising, would have been a good idea.

Hannah stopped and burst into tears, hands covering her face. "I don't know Gus. I... I just couldn't stay there. I'm sorry. Please don't you all hate me."

"Darlin', darlin'," Gus said, soothing her. "Never."

"Hannah, we're all in this together," Linda joined in.

His retort about how they should have stayed with Childs died in his throat. JT felt sorry for her then. He knew how it felt to have the others in the group look to you and then to totally blow it.

"Let's try to find somewhere to set up before dark," JT tried to encourage Hannah as gently as he could.

She sniffled, her nose turning red. "Yes. It's just so much harder than I thought it would be. I wasn't expecting this much snow. You can't even find the roads. All the maps I tried to memorize...turned out to be useless. Then there are still zombies..."

JT swallowed down any harsh comments he felt bubbling up inside. Instead he spoke as nicely as he could. "Just pick a direction."

They didn't make it far or to any place that offered much protection for the night. The next day was a repeat. It was mountains, trees, and snow as far as JT could see. On the third day Gus began to complain of dizziness and a feeling like he was going to heave that never went away. Linda said it was altitude sickness getting to him. The cold didn't help. Rest and water is what Gus needed.

They were exposed and miserable. They made camp as best they could next to a rock wall. They lined up their tents in a row. You could hear a tiny mountain stream splash on some rocks nearby. JT didn't know it could get so cold as he tried to get a fire going. The wind would cycle down then whip through in a frenzy. At the times when the wind did that, it didn't even feel like JT had layers and a coat on. He wanted to start yelling at the weather and at Hannah. He wanted a drink to at least warm up his insides. He wanted to rage at the world. Instead he kept trying to light the fire. During one of the wind lulls, it finally caught.

He helped Linda bring Gus over to it. Gus made a sound like he was sucking on air through a straw. He was also an alarming shade of blue. Ice and snow were clumped in his scraggly beard. He was shaking like he was having a seizure.

"D-d-do you guys get t-t-tired of taking care of m-me?" Gus stuttered.

"Yeah, sure as hell do." JT sat beside him, the heat feeling delicious.

"Fuck you too buddy."

"Nothing can freeze your sunny disposition."

As the two of them sat there JT watched Linda go off out of earshot with Hannah. Whatever the discussion was, it looked like there was some disagreement. Hannah broke away, stomped over, and went into her tent. Linda then came over.

"She is determined, I give her that," Linda said in a huff.

"If she wasn't, would she still be here?" Gus asked, teeth chattering.

"Gus, if we don't go back to Dr. Childs' settlement, I'm worried about what might happen to you." Linda looked more afraid than when the zombies were attacking them.

"She doesn't want to go back. Can you blame her?" Gus said.

"No but being a good leader isn't just about doing what you want to do. You think about the welfare of all you lead." Linda looked like she was going to say more then stopped.

"I know we had shitty luck in the pas but-"

That's an understatement big enough to push your ego through," Hannah interrupted.

JT blew his breath out, watching the steam whip away in the wind. He didn't raise his voice or call Hannah out. He just continued on with his point. "Staying and checking things out would have been the better choice. We could have been more careful and thorough. We know what to look out for now, with all of our experience. I think that would have been the better call than tramping around out here until we freeze to death." JT's teeth chattered as he spit out the last sentence.

None of them said anything for a few moments. The fire crackled and popped. A huge gust came and almost blew it out.

"Gus, let's get inside," Linda said. "The more you can rest the better. You have pushed yourself too much as it is. I'll melt some snow. You need to drink."

JT pushed his way into his tent. The heat from the fire didn't penetrate inside. He laid in the sleeping bag with his coat on, shivering. At that moment, as he laid there, he despised Hannah. He thought any chance with her was now over. Just as he felt, with his head clearer the last few days, maybe he could forgive her for Tyrone, here she was pushing Gus to his death. She had nothing but snide remarks for him all the time. Nagging and nagging about his drink. About how he should just get over the deaths he caused by his failures. What about her? They weren't inside a house, with a fireplace going, because she couldn't deal. JT had these dark, ugly thoughts and many more all the way down into a fitful sleep.

In the morning they awoke to several more inches of snow. Linda grumbled under her breath as she shook it off her tent as they packed up to go on. JT woke up thinking he should say something to Hannah. This was ludicrous. Would standing up to her even help? She loved Gus, he knew she didn't want anything to happen to him. What would it take to get her to turn around. *With all this stress, I could use a drink or five right now. What if we go back and Childs is some kind of psycho like Harold or Albright?* In the end he decided to keep his mouth shut.

Their pace was glacial. Gus had a hard time keeping upright, one foot in front of the other. It began to snow again. JT began to feel like he wasn't even on Earth anymore. Maybe he was on Hoth. He felt like he could cut open an animal and crawl inside if it would make him warm. If he never saw snow again it would be too soon. The more he cursed it, the harder it seemed to come down.

It reminded him of the Lord of the Rings movie, which he had watched the first one and hated. This was like that part though, where the group was trying to get over the mountain and snow, while the mountain itself was coming down on them. He looked around nervously, now expecting something like an avalanche. He had the bad thought, it was bound to happen now.

In the distance was a strange shape. By late afternoon JT could make it out. It was jutting out of the snow like an ancient artifact. The tail section of an airplane. JT thought it must have been a big one. He wondered if the whole thing was there, the front half buried in the snow or if this was just the back part of the jet. Snapped off in the crash, like some child's toy.

Hannah made a line straight for the crash. JT didn't know why. Maybe because it was the first landmark out here that wasn't a rock or a fucking snow pile. It ended up being another bad choice.

They came across bits of debris, like a breadcrumb trail, to the bulk of the crash, made up of sheet metal, airplane pieces, and body parts. Here and there the snow turned from white to black, red, or some disguisting mix of the two colors.

"Hannah, where the hell are we going?" JT called out to her. "What do you think will be in there for us?"

She didn't answer, she just trudged along, head down. If she had horns she would have made a perfect mountain goat. She was certainly stubborn enough.

JT kept his eyes up, scanning the wreckage. He licked his lips, wishing for a drink. Not for the first time that day he wished he had stayed in town long enough to get some liquor.

They were close enough now that JT could make out some of the interior through the ripped open side of the plane. Seats, some dead bodies, luggage strewn everywhere. Then he saw movement. He blinked rapidly. Several figures were moving among the wreckage, he was sure of it.

"Hannah," he called out, trying to keep his voice level. He paused to watch her. They were in no shape for a fight. Gus was barely able to walk.

"Hannah!" he called out again, a little louder.

Hannah turned to face him. Her expression was blank. He could also see the figures turn their bodies towards the sound of his voice.

"We need to get out of here now!"

Hannah turned and looked towards the plane, then turned back to JT. She started working back towards him through the snow, following the path her legs had just plowed. When she reached him, he could see ice crystals around her eyes and on the scarf pulled over her nose and mouth. He took her hand and pulled back to Gus and Linda.

JT kept glancing back at the wreckage as it fell further behind them. The zombies, he was sure that's what they were, he didn't need his scope to confirm it, tried to follow. Luckily the snow seemed to slow the undead down even more than it did the four of them. Hannah picked another direction and on they went.

Later in the afternoon, still in the middle of nothingness, Gus fell down in the snow not once but three times. On the third time Linda had finally had enough and broke down.

"Are you trying to kill him!" she screamed at Hannah. "We need to go back."

Hannah froze. She turned around and ripped off her scarf. She looked rocked to her core. Her cheeks were red and cracked, like she had been crying all day.

"I know, don't you think I know!" She shouted back. She dropped to her knees, her scarf brushing the snowpile. "What do you want me to do?"

"Come on, Hannah," JT said, keeping his distance, like she was a deer he was going to spook. "I know you're not dumb."

Hannah looked ready to shatter. JT thought he was going to have to step up after all. Back into a position he didn't want to be in.

"I-I don't think I can, JT. After Tyrone-Ashley-"

JT took a step closer. "I know, Hannah. For fuck sakes I know. This isn't the place for a therapy session but if you can't live with the guilt now, then how are you going to go on if Gus dies out here."

Hannah looked down at her knees. She gathered back up the scarf and wrapped it around her mouth and nose again. That done, she began to pound at the snow with both of her fists, as hard as she could. JT watched her get swallowed up in a blizzard of her own making. When the flying snow cleared, Hannah was standing back up again.

"JT, help him up. We'll turn around."

"I just hope it's not too late. Who knows how many days it may take to get back," Linda spoke softer. She went to Hannah to try and embrace her but Hannah held her hand out, gloved hand palm up.

JT was shocked at the impulse that was still inside of him. He wanted to go to her, tell her he would protect her. He had thought those feelings had died. The thought of Tyrone then jumped up in his mind. Instead of going to Hannah, JT helped Gus struggle to his feet. JT was a little scared, it felt like he was lifting a child. How could Gus deteriorate so fast in three days?

It ended up being four more days before they got back to Dr. Childs' settlement. For most of those days JT thought they were lost and were never going to find it. The heavy snows had erased all traces of their previous path. He never thought he would hate a color but he found himself hating white. He breathed a sigh of relief at the site of the cobbled wall of Child's makeshift colony.

Hannah pounded on the gate while JT and Linda held Gus between them. It was a long wait while the person at the gate went and got the doctor but they were eventually let in.

"Nice to see you back," Childs said, a little too smug for JT's taste. "How was the weather out there?"

"We need to get Gus to your clinic and get some IV fluids into him right away," Linda said. "One more day and I'm not sure he would have made it."

Childs seemed unfazed by this. "Sure, go ahead. I'll be there in a moment. The rest of you, pick out an empty place, we have got plenty of vacant dwellings. Get a good night's sleep. Tomorrow we can talk about what we'll do with you. After you do some work, I'll check the rest of you over. It would be fucking lucky if one of you didn't get frostbite."

Dr. Child's got Gus situated on the same table he had been on a little over a week ago. Gus was unresponsive. He must have passed out.

"It's a good thing you brought him back. I'm not sure he would have made it if you stayed out there any longer. What were you thinking, listening to the girl?"

Linda, who had been worried about hypothermia the last two days, now added frostbite to her list considering Childs had brought it up. Why hadn't she thought to check his extremities?

"I'm the only person within a hundred miles who could help him. You want to strip off his coat, hat, and gloves?"

Linda ignored the doctors arrogant manner and focused all of her attention on Gus. It wasn't the first time she had to work with and ego driven doctor. She was relieved when she didn't see any signs of frostbite herself. However she wouldn't be done worrying until Childs finished his examination.

"Linda, I assume you'll want to stay her with your friend?"

"You assumed correct."

"I expected no less from a professional. Can you get and IV drip started the?. You will find supplies over there," Childs pointed to a wall with cabinets, "along with hand sanitizer."

Linda rushed over and scrubbed up as best she could. She rummaged through the supplies as fast as she could. She rubbed sanitizer up to her elbows once again before practically running back over. Finding a vein she got the drip started.

Childs finished looking at Gus' hands and toes. Next he looked at Linda's work. She rolled her eyes.

"It's nice to have an assistant again." That was as much praise as she got. "No one else in this town was bright enough to train as one." Childs continued examining Gus. "Lucky for, Gerry wasn't it?"

"Gus."

"Right yeah, Gus. He doesn't have any frostbite damage. You take his temperature, blood pressure, and pulse. I'll be back."

Child's stopped and spoke to a women standing at the counter on the other side of the drawn curtain. The woman scurried out of sight then returned with pillows, blankets, and a small green cloth lunch bag piled in her arms. She transfered everything to Childs, who returned to Linda and Gus.

"What are the results?" he asked, standing there with his hands full.

"All are low but not dangerously so." Linda let herself feel relieved. Pressure, like two enormous hands which had been holding her down, gave way in her chest.

"Right. Again good. I've got your friend now Linda. Take these." Childs held out his arms. Linda scooped them up without thinking. "I don't think there is more you could do here right now. If you need anything I'm sure one of the town people could help you. Go find an empty place and get settled in. Know that Gerry is in good hands."

Linda found herself somewhat taken aback by his generosity so she didn't correct him. "I don't know Childs. I don't want to leave him. What if he needs me."

Childs gave her a stern look. "Lidia. You might not be as in bad a shape as your friend but your body needs rest, hydration. As a nurse you should know that you can help your patient if you can't help yourself. I'll be here all night. you go."

Reluctantly she had to admit Dr. Childs had a point. She gave Gus a kiss on the cheek and looked down at him. Taking him in. Trying to stop that thought that she would never see him awake again. She stopped at the door that led outside the clinic. She undid the Velcro on the bag to find a bottle of water, box of raisins, a granola bar, and small can of Vienna sausages. There was even a plastic spork.

Linda chuckled to herself. *Boy Gus, just wait until you wake up to this. I can only imagine how many small weenie jokes must be in that dirty old brain of yours.*

LIQUID ANGER

JT barely spoke to Hannah as they settled into the little place they had chosen for their nights stay. JT wasn't even sure why he agreed to share a space. Habit he guessed. JT watched Hannah unpack. He could tell she was clearly swallowing anger. Wasn't he the master at that according to Randall. He watched her as she changed out of her grubby clothes and into the fresh fleece hoodie that lay on the bed. He felt nothing.

He threw his stuff down and went over to the fireplace. It already had wood in it. He searched around and found some matches.

"Thanks for getting the fire going, you're getting really good at it..."She trailed off, probably realizing a comment like that wasn't going to help the current situation.

"Yep, yay me." JT angrily threw the words out as he rummaged through a trunk for blankets and tossed them onto the sofa along the wall.

"I can sleep on the couch if you want," Hannah offered. "Or we can share the bed. I'm ok with that idea too."

"Nah, I'm good." It wasn't that long ago they had done that very thing. It had been thrilling. Now, he just wanted to be left alone. *Christ my head hurts.* "I need some time to unwind. Enjoy having the bed all to yourself, fearless leader." *Shit*, JT thought to himself as the words rolled off his tongue, he hadn't meant to be a dick to her like that. Hannah quickly turned away and crawled into the bed without another word.

Later in the night, as JT lay on the couch staring into the fire, all the grudges he carried flipping through his mind, he could hear the distinct sounds of muffled sobs from Hannah. He could go over there, try to comfort her. Every time either of them tried, it always seemed to end in disaster. She would be better off without him. He hated himself right now. First thing tomorrow he was going to look for something to soothe his feelings; something of the liquid variety.

The next morning JT and Hannah were awoken by someone drumming on their door. It was a persistent lite knock. JT rushed to the door and yanked it open in complete annoyance. He was ready to rip someone's ass for the undue wake up call until he saw the teenage girl standing there looking timid and nervous.

"Um, hello sir, Dr. Childs, he um, he asked me to bring you these, you're uh, you're JT and Hannah right?"

"Yeah, that's us, kid." JT was trying to dial it back.

The girl handed JT two envelopes, one for each of them with their names written on the outside. As soon as she handed them over to JT she simply wished him a good day and hurried away.

"Awkward." JT let the word hang and drag out, high toned and extra sarcastic. He watched the girl turn a corner and closed the door.

"Mail call!" He exclaimed and tossed Hannah the envelope addressed to her. "He misspelled my name. Says JD. How good of a doctor is he if he can't remember two letters?"

JT plopped down on the edge of the bed where he and Hannah opened their envelopes in unison. Both of them looked at each other and rolled their eyes at the penmanship of Dr. Childs. Emblazoned on the paper were orders from Childs on what job JT would be doing and where he should report to. Peeking over at Hannah's, he saw she had been given a different job.

"Great. Now we've gone from running from zombies to being potential slaves for doctor know it all." JT scoffed as he said the words.

"What exactly is it you expect from me JT? Do you think I have the answers you need to hear or something?"

JT was surprised at her ridicule of him. He stood up quickly and spun to face Hannah.

"You know Hannah, I don't think anyone knows what they should expect from you anymore! Have any of us asked you for answers? Not by my count. Stop blaming yourself for Ash and stop playing the victim with the church bullshit! That song and dance has been on repeat for weeks and it's gotten old. "

JT took notice of the tears welling up in Hannah's eyes from his sudden outburst. I'm an ass.

"Hannah, look, I'm sorry, I didn't mean to-. You know how I feel about you and it drives me crazy to see you blame yourself for everything that happened to us. You know what I mean?" Shit. Why did I say that?

Hannah's eyes became plates. She got out of the bed and brushed past him. She grabbed her shoes, put them on, grabbed her pack and headed for the door. She made a mad show of it all.

"Come on Hannah, don't do this, I'm sorry." JT pleaded with her.

Hannah stopped in the doorway as she left. "Which part didn't you mean JT? The part about me pretending to be a victim? The part about me being scarred for life by the fact my best friend was murdered by a crazy motherfucker in the woods? Or the other part where we found ourselves in a place which turned out to be a real prison? Sorry, I don't feel totally comfortable here? I'll spare you my feelings and just go. Meanwhile, you just go find another bottle to be your friend. At least then you can only hate yourself." Hannah stormed out bursting into tears as she did.

"FUCK!" JT screamed as he grabbed a vase of fake flowers and threw it against the wall shattering it into colorful confetti.

"You really screwed up this time asshole." JT said to himself as he leaned head first against the wall, slapping it for good measure.

ALMOST BATTY

Hannah had an instant disliking for Roy from their first interaction. It wasn't like he was off putting, like Harold. She sure wasn't going to be taken in by him like Albright. Roy simply made no effort to hide what a dick he was.

She had been asked in her letter from Dr. Childs to see if she could help Roy, whoever that was. Childs had wrote Roy's crew of workers were short handed and they were trying to finish some repairs on the town's makeshift schoolhouse as soon as possible.

She was surprised by what Childs wanted her to do but what the hell, she was eager to be doing something. She couldn't stop thinking about the fight with JT.

On the way to meet Roy, she had stopped in at the clinic to see Gus. Angry at JT was replaced by worry about Gus, even though he was stable and Linda was by his side. Gus was still sleeping so after giving him a gentle kiss on the forehead, she had went on, following the crude map she had been given.

At the schoolhouse she found Roy leaning against the side of the building, smoking a cigarette, while the other three men were ripping off siding riddled with bullet holes.

Roy wore a black cap, backwards. His curly brown hair came out the back down to about his shoulders. He wore a flannel button up top with jeans. A chain came from his belt around front to his wallet, which was poking out of his front pocket. He gave her a sneer as she approached, and blew smoke out the side of his mouth.

"You one of the new people Childs sent over?" He asked, in a tone that said he could care less one way or another.

"Yes, I'm Hannah," she said, sticking out her hand.

Roy looked at it, took another hit off his cigarette and then pointed with it to the workers. She noticed had black gloves on, with the fingertips cut off.

"You have any experience, doing work in construction?" Roy sneered down at her.

"No. I learn pretty fast though."

"I thought not," Roy said with a laugh. It was not a humorous one. "That's not a mistake my Dad would have made. Childs may be a doctor, but my Dad was way more qualified to be in charge. Why didn't he send you over to the kitchens?"

Hannah stood there, thinking she could care less if there was any drama between Childs, Henry, and Roy, who she guessed was Henry's son. She didn't say anything, she just stood waiting for more direction. Roy's raised eyebrows and straightened stance seemed to be daring her to argue with him about it. She didn't rise to it.

"Fine," he said, throwing the cigarette butt to the ground and stomping on it with his boot. "At least tell me you can use a hammer."

"I've helped my Dad hang some paneling before. Pictures too."

Roy sneered again, adjusting his hat."Grab a hammer and some nails from the tools over there. You can go right at it, you old pro you." Roy stomped off.

Hannah was left to look at the piles of tools and supplies spread out on a tarmac. The hammer was easy to find, but she didn't know which size nails she was suppose to use.

"Need some help?" she heard over her shoulder.

A man walked up beside her. "This stuff isn't my thing either. Computers and IT were. Not much use for that now, huh?" He laughed nervously. "Still, I picked up some things working in the town. Name's Josh."

Josh wore a ball cap that looked like a stormtrooper's helmet from Star Wars. It was the first thing she noticed about him. His hair was long, black waves of it escaped from under it. His voice was soft and kind, as were his eyes, which were behind glasses that had seen better days.

"Finally, someone who isn't a jerk around here," Hannah said.

Josh laughed nervously again, looking around her but not making much eye contact. Hannah checked her annoyance. This guy didn't deserve it.

"No problem," Josh said, pointing to the nails Hannah needed then grabbed the side of his glasses to adjust them up. "You haven't met most of the people around here then. Roy is the exception."

"Does he always come off like that?"

"The nerve right?" Josh was hard to hear over the hammering. "He complains about everything. We have all heard it multiple times. Guy's sure butthurt. You would think it had happened to him and not his dad. Follow me, I'll show you what we're working on."

Josh let her over to a pile of lumber, sitting on the concrete that was the school's playground. Hannah tried not to think about where the kids who went to this school were now. They worked away the rest of the day without even a sighting of Roy. The two other men working on the building were more welcoming as well. Hannah soon learned their names were Emilio and Kevin.

They quit as it began to get dark. Hannah was tired, her hands were frozen and numb. Her arms felt as if they had been hammered. She was putting her hammer down when Roy showed back up. He looked over the wall then walked away. Hannah was no expert but she thought it looked good.

"First day here, you know where dinner is served?" Josh asked.

"No, I didn't even know they served dinner. So far I've just been eating what I brought in with me."

"Oh yeah, they have a buffet every night, up in the old casino. Since every house can't have power to cook, Henry set it up so that at least one place could make everyone some hot meals."

Hannah rubbed her hands together. "Makes sense. I can't even remember the last time I ate something resembling a meal. Never thought I would be living off of Spam, even back when I was in college and couldn't afford much."

Josh laughed. It was as soft as his voice. "I've eaten more bags of chips in the last few months than probably my whole life. That's saying something. Jerky sticks for sure. I never even thought about eating those until after the Outbreak."

They walked along the sidewalks cleared off while they were working on the schoolhouse. Hannah didn't like feeling she was impressed by what the people had here or that she was enjoying it.

People filed into the casino doors and past the dormant games. This was Hannah's first realization of just how many people were in the town. The line stretched outside the doorway to the restaurant that use to be the casinos actual buffet.

As Hannah got closer to the food the smells made her mouth water. Smells of cooking vegetables and meats she didn't think she would ever have again filled the air.

"How is it possible what I'm smelling?" she asked Josh.

"From what I have heard when Henry started here, food preservation was his first goal. They took all the frozen meat, vegetable, fruit, you name it and stored it in the mountain, where it would be cold enough to keep it from going bad right away."

"Crazy," Hannah said. Maybe Roy was a little right to be mad about what happened to Henry. Sounds like most of what the people here had a better life because of him.

"So you haven't been here since the beginning?" Hannah asked as they inched closer to the food.

"No," said Josh. He took a plate from the stack. They were almost to the front. "I'm from Boulder. I got out of there alive, barely, and arrived here, I don't know, sometime in the summer. Henry, Roy and a few others were already here. Right after me Dr. Childs arrived with his own little group."

Hannah felt like her eyes grew as big as her plate when she saw there were strawberries, spinach, grilled chicken breasts, mashed potatoes and red jello. She greedily filled up her plate until food began to threaten spilling off the side.

"Guess you're a little hungry?" Josh teased.

Hannah was too happy to be embarrassed. They exited the buffet and she looked around the room. She was shocked and happy to see Gus and Linda at a table. JT was there, which dampened her spirits a little. Gus saw her and waved, giving her a big warm smile.

"Can't keep this old man down for long darlin'!" Gus called to her.

"There are my friends! You want to come over and join us?"

Josh shrugged. "Sure."

"Josh, this is JT, Gus, and Linda. Everyone this is Josh. We worked together today, repairing a school." Greetings were exchanged all around.

"That sounds better than what I had to do," JT complained. "I spent the day clearing the sidewalks. My back's never been so sore. I think the blisters on my hands have blisters."

"How about your knee?" Linda asked. "That's a lot of strenuous activity for it. Why didn't you ask to do something else?"

"It was fine." JT dug back into his plate, shooting glances over at Josh. Hannah wondered if JT was going to act all jealous already or if he was still mad about their last conversation.

"If you say so JT," Linda sounded exasperated. "You can probably guess where I've been all day."

"At least all I needed was some fluids," Gus said between shoveling in mouthfuls of food. "Now it's chow time."

Hannah put her hands together and whispered a prayer, thankful for the food.

"Praying?" Josh asked when she was done.

"Yeah, why?"

Josh sounded defensive and put his hands up. "No big deal. Just, most people I've run into have lost faith, you know, after what happened." He was practically whispering by the end.

"Buddy you're lucky you didn't run into anyone who was the exact opposite!" Gus said.

Josh looked puzzled but Hannah wasn't going to get into that now. Especially with a stranger.

"Let's just say he was someone you wouldn't want to...cross," Gus stressed the last word and waggled his eyebrows up and down.

"Oh Gus," Linda moaned.

JT nearly spit his bite of potatoes out. Hannah rolled her eyes.

"Ba dum ching, I'm back!" Gus snorted.

CREATURE COMFORTS

After dinner the four went back to the house JT had picked out for himself. Hannah reluctantly came along. It was a nice two level, painted red, with a small porch on the front. The houses on either side looked empty.

"What a first day," JT said, putting his hands on the small of his back and stretching. "Hate to admit this but it felt....good."

"I got a nap, can't beat that," Gus said.

JT plopped down on the couch next to the easy chair Gus was in."Speaking of which, it's going to feel weird, sleeping by myself tonight, separated from you guys. We've been in close quarters so long. How am I gonna sleep without the soothing sounds of your snoring Gus?"

JT kind of trailed off then. Hannah hadn't thought about that but JT was right. She was going to have a big place all to herself tonight, even if it was only a few blocks away from the others. She didn't know if she felt happy or scared.

"So that's it? We're already deciding to stay here?" Hannah paced around, looking at the artifacts left behind by the previous owner. Knick knacks, pictures on the wall. One was of a man and a woman on their wedding day. Those people were either dead or zombies now. Here they were living in their place. It was sort of creepy to think about.

"Hannah, talk about goin' from zero to one hundred. Darlin' nobody's saying that yet." Gus assured her.

"I sure as hell ain't saying that," JT exclaimed. "Man, can't I make a statement without you jumping down my throat?"

He exploded up off the couch. He went into the other room and came back with a beer. Gus gave her a sad look. Now that JT had broke the booze out, she was ready to go.

Hannah excused herself and left. Even with all the work she'd done that day, she felt more exhausted than ever. Emotionally as well. She had no desire to get into another argument with JT right now. Or anyone else. Maybe it would be good to have some privacy tonight. I could have some privacy and put down the burden of worrying about everyone else so much.

She walked passed the stores in the middle of town to her place on the other side. Daydreams of bed filled her mind when she heard some commotion to the right. She turned and squinted, the day was losing its light but she had the setting sun on her shoulder.

She saw two figures go down a narrow alley between two brick buildings. The way they were dressed and the way one looked around nervously caused an alarm to go off in her head. She patted the gun in the shoulder holster she carried whenever she didn't want to lug her rifle around. Having a weapon made her feel safer, she had learned that lesson. With light footfalls, she crept towards the sound.

She could make out the figures arguing as she got closer. She thought she heard the words payment, time, and doctor. Then the talking stopped. She stopped moving. After a minute she took another step forward. Roy burst out of the walkway, turned, and nearly ran her down.

"What in the fuck do you think you're doing!" Roy barked.

Hannah staggered back, one hand reaching for her gun. Roy looked almost sweaty, he ran his hands over the front of his coat. Now that she thought about it, she hadn't seen Roy at dinner tonight.

"I'm just going home. I thought I heard a commotion. Was that you?"

"None of your damn business. Get out of my way." Roy stalked off, looking over his shoulder several times.

"Who were you talking to?" Hannah whisper to herself, watching Roy until he was out of sight.

With her sense that something funny was going on dinging louder than ever, Hannah turned from going back home to having a stop at Dr. Childs first. Then she hesitated. She just got here. She didn't want to stay. This would be getting involved in a big way. Did she want to do that?

What swayed her was a feeling from outside of her. If something were to happen she could have prevented, she would feel the guilt. It would be as much her fault as Roy's if he was up to something, this presence was telling her.

"Roy? He's a loser. A miserable little shit, too," Dr. Childs said. He'd been in the middle of reading a book when she walked in. It was sitting beside him now, face down on the table. She could see the title was The Shining by Stephen

King. Ironic, considering where they were now. "He's a pretty good builder but that's it. He is nothing like his old man. I bet if I didn't keep most of the medicine locked up, he'd be hitting it like a meth head."

"Could be, you know him better" Hannah said. "But doesn't resentment make it even more possible? I know what I heard. He's up to something."

"If you want to spend your free time following around that schlub, go right ahead. If he tried something, he would have to go through the rest of the people in town. I would have heard something by now from some of the others here. He's too much of a loser to pull off anything significant."

Dr. Childs got up and made himself a drink at the rooms wet bar while they talked. *I bet JT would like to have a bar like that,* she thought to herself. Hannah knew it was childish and petty and mean. JT, and what he meant to her, was another problem for another time. Possibly. Right now her concentration needed to be with Childs.

He made a deal of looking surprised to see her still standing there when he finished making his cocktail. "I have heard you. I will mention it to Henry."

Dr. Childs took his drink, sat in his chair by the window and crossed his legs. He gave her a look that was pretty much a dismissal.

"Fine," she bit out, turned and left.

She went home and spent her time worrying about the problem. If something fishy was going on what else could she do about it? She went to bed, thinking maybe she could go to Henry. Except, she realized, she doesn't even know what Henry looked like. She hadn't even met him yet. She could just imagine how good that conversation would go. A complete stranger talking trash about his son. She tossed and turned until she realized she had done something. Now it was out of her responsibility and in Childs' lap. With that she fell asleep.

Still the nagging feeling, which seemed to come from somewhere outside of her, wouldn't go away completely. It would epp in the morning when she saw Roy, who would spit out some commands and then disappear all day. Then the more the day went on the more it flowed to the back of her mind. A couple days later though, she awoke determined to do something about her feeling.

Since JT was spending a lot of time with his new drinking buddy, Lindsay, it was Gus she knew she would need to go to. Anyway, talking to JT right now would just lead to arguments and headaches.

"I don't know, sweetie," Gus said, after she filled him in.

She sat in the little house Gus and Linda took over near the center of town, not far from the clinic. All the shades were open and the little house was bright and cheerful. It made the worries Hannah had seem like wistful dreams. Maybe Roy was all talk and bluster. She didn't know him.

"Do we want to get involved with the people and what's going on around here? We've already left once. We came back out of necessity, but so far the place seems legit. Are you wanting to stay long term? Does JT? Or am I wrong, like I was about Harold?"

"No, you're not," Hannah conceded. She'd been cautious and kept her eyes open this time. Most people in the town just wanted to build up the community here to stay alive.

Even with her investigation so far telling her the town was okay, she wasn't sure if she wanted to stay here. She had no idea anymore what JT wanted. Right now she saw no reason why the two of them would stay together. JT might leave tomorrow for all she knew. Gus was right though, pursuing this would mean she was putting down some roots here. Did she want to? If this got back to Roy, would she want to live with what would surely become an even more antagonistic attitude?

"If you did want me to tail him, I could help. I'm not up to much most days, which bugs the hell out of me. I'm not ninety, I'm fifty five. Linda is gone at the clinic just about every day. I thought the guy said we had to work around here for our supper."

Gus put on a bad detective voice. "You want me to tail him sweetheart?"

Hannah rolled her eyes. "Nah, but if you happened to run across him doing something suspicious, just let me know."

"Maybe we should leave, before anything starts up. I believe you've been through enough, dollface." Gus continued with the accent.

"I might very well decide to do that."

Hannah left after some more pleasant conversation with Gus. For the next few days, she read her Bible, she went to the outskirts of town to practice her shooting, and she put up with Roy's verbal diarrhea, when he was around. In those days she didn't see JT anywhere outside of dinner. There he usually sat off by himself or with Lindsay.

The day came when the repairs on the schoolhouse were finished. She got to see the twenty or so children of different ages file inside on opening day. It gave her a melancholy feeling, seeing so many kids had survived but how this was now their world.

Hannah went home, wondering what she would do next. A filling of accomplishment filled her. That's when she realized most of her guilt and worry had vanished. Was this place God's sign?

It couldn't be. Now that she was done, well fed, and of more sound mind, she felt she could make a decision. Thoughts of packing up and moving on by herself were on her mind when a knock came at the door. She was surprised to see it was JT.

"Hi Hannah. What are you up to?" he said, his hands stuffed into his coat pockets.

"Not much as of right now. You?"

"About the same." He stood there, looking at her and looking away. "So, mind if I come in? I was wanting to talk and ..." JT hesitated a moment. "I was missing you."

"Before you even start, just no, JT. No."

"What?" he said, a little slurred.

"I can smell it from here. You can't just come over here because you are drunk and feeling lonely and expect to work things out between us. Just stop."

JT looked mad then. She didn't fear his anger anymore. She knew a little of what carrying rage was like. She realized then there had changed within JT since the church. She had to work to remember the last time he flew into a true rage.

His mouth dropped, making him look stupid. Did he think this was easy for her? It hurt her. He promised back when they met that nothing would ever hurt her. How naive they both had been.

"Fine," he spit out. He took two steps down, stumbled then caught himself on the railing. "I'll go see what Lindsay's doing."

She didn't know if that was suppose to make her jealous or to cut her. She felt she didn't care one way or another. It already hurt, what had happened between them. They couldn't pull it together, no matter what they had tried. They weren't a couple. She sure wasn't his mother.

"Well have fun then," she said with mocking cheerfulness, closing the door.

PORT IN A STORM

JT was laughing so hard his stomach was hurting. Lindsay was holding herself as well. At least a dozen beer bottles lay strewn about the floor between them.

"Whew," JT said when he could finally get ahold of himself. "That's crazy."

A fire roared in the fireplace. JT couldn't even remember starting it. It was nice though, being so warm. He felt like taking his shirt off, so he did.

He popped the top of another bottle and knocked it back. He was sitting half slouched over on the couch in his house. It was funny to think of it this way, his house. Before he could barely afford the shit apartment he had. He giggled again and checked out Lindsay, who sat across from him curled up in a chair.

He had already stripped down to his baggy grey basketball shorts. Appropriate winter attire. He snickered again. Lindsay was wearing a long sleeve dress, red, that went down to her knees with black leggings. JT thought she wore it well as he enjoyed the view during their chat. It had been a pleasant surprise when she knocked on his door earlier carrying a six pack.

"That's like when all this shit went down. I jumped into the first car I could, turned on the radio and the song that came on was Zombie by the Cranberries."

"Get the fuck out of here," she said, reaching for another beer herself." That did not happen."

JT thought it was only her second, or was it her third? Either way the rest of the bottles on the floor belonged to him. Fuck it, what did it matter.

"True story. Swear it on whatever you want me to."

Lindsay laughed. "Okay, I believe you." She took a deep breath. "Those first days, they were well...they were something."

Lindsay's voice took on a far away quality.

"I use to live up in Portland, before. Don't laugh but I was taking a shower when the zombie apocalypse happened. I had a roommate. Her name was Heather. We weren't close friends but we got along okay. I was in the shower, cranking up Imagine Dragons on my shower speaker, lathering up my hair, singing along.

I heard some banging around outside but figured it was just Heather being loud or looking for something. Then something shook the whole damn apartment. I heard more noises I thought were strange. I poked my head out of the shower curtain and called out for Heather. There was nothing and then she started pounding on the bathroom door so hard it made me jump. Then she started screaming. It was muffled so I couldn't make out everything she was saying. I turned the water off and reached for my towel.

I stood there frozen for what felt like hours. I reached for the door to unlock it but then I thought better of it. What if someone had broken in? I was only thinking of myself then. Don't know what that says about me.

The pounding stopped but I heard her out there. Sounded like she was running around crazy. Our apartment was all hardwood floors and the sound carried.

Right about then my phone went off. I jumped about five feet off the floor. Let out a little scream. I snatched it up off the counter. It was blowing up with text messages. I scrolled through them all, not believing what I read. You can guess what they were saying.

Heather came back to my door. This time she wasn't screaming. She was knocking and sobbing then. Someone was out there. I need to let her in. Let her in. That's what I kept thinking but my body wouldn't move.

Something hit the wall, hard. The door moved on its hinges but didn't open. Fingers poked under the small opening between the bathroom door and the floor. She began to scream then. Her fingers were suddenly jerked away. I sat there, huddled in the corner by the toilet, listening to my roommate be eaten alive by zombies.

I don't know how long I was there. Days I guess. In nothing but a towel. I had my phone. I kept checking it, checking messages and Twitter and YouTube. I tried calling my parents but couldn't get through. I watched helpless as the battery ran down, flashed red and the phone died.

I would climb into the shower, stretch out and drift off, only to hear the sounds of movement outside and jerk awake. I drank from the sink until it stopped working. Hunger is what finally drove me out.

I've seen plenty of slasher flicks. I knew what I was going to do. Go straight for the kitchen, grab the biggest knife I had. If it was clear I was also going to grab some food and run right to my room.

I threw open the door, one hand holding onto my towel, and flew to the kitchen. Good thing that was my plan too, as there was one zombie still in my apartment. I tried not to look straight at the remains of my roommate. I just concentrated on getting the knife, keeping the zombie in my peripheral vision. I made it, pulling the blade from the knife block. The undead thing shuffled its way across the room, its steps sounding like someone was scraping the floor with a wet mop. I didn't want to fight it. I just wanted to get past it and get the hell out of there.

It came at me, faster than I thought it would. I got in a lucky blow, stabbing it in the side of the head. Just like in the movies, it went down. I couldn't catch my breath and thought I was going to hyperventilate. Thinking of passing out on top of the zombie forced me to calm myself. I went to the fridge, grabbing things without really looking and ran to my room. Locked the door. Dressed and ate at the same time.

I felt a little better after doing that, a little more normal. I went over and took a few glances out my window, we were up on the second floor, then stopped. What I was seeing made my stomach turn."

Lindsay gave a empty sigh when she was done. Her normally cheerful expression had soured.

"How did you end up going from Portland to up here in the Colorado mountains?" JT asked.

"Probably as many crazy coincidences as brought you up here. Nothing worth going into. Unless you want to share more. I don't like thinking about it."

No he did not. The less she knew about the people he killed, the things he was responsible for, the better. He liked Lindsay. He was still deciding how much.

"Nah. I don't feel like doom and gloom right now. I got a good buzz going."

"What about your friend Hannah? Is she more than just your friend? Because I have to tell you, I don't see you two hooking up. She seems like no fun at all."

What was Hannah to him now? Most days she looked at him with disgust or disappointment. The wall that went up after Albright, any time he thought they were making cracks in it she would retreat and fill them back in. He should stop kidding himself and move on. That was proving more difficult than he had planned. The chance they had was gone. He found himself even thinking about her less. Now with some physical distance between them, maybe it could help.

"She didn't always use to be so, I don't know..."

"Stuck up?" Lindsay sneered.

JT jumped her harshly. "Hey, she is still my friend."

"Sorry," Lindsay replied in a timid voice. "Fucking hell man."

"I was going to say gung ho. Like 'I'm warrior bitch now, don't fuck with me.'"

"I can't call her stuck up but you can call her a bitch?"

"I meant it in a complementary way."

They looked at each other then they both started laughing. When they were done, JT finished off the drink in his hand.

"You know, I'm not going to lie. I thought the zombie apocalypse would be kind of fun. I use to get into fights all the time, in High School, in College. I was a football player. I guess I was a cocky one too. I wasn't going to take shit from anyone and I never backed down. One guy, six guys, ten guys, it didn't matter. Even if they beat my ass I would get right back up. When I couldn't be a football player anymore, I was a bouncer. Putting the hurt on people. Guess that's all I'm good at."

"This isn't going to be a pity party is it?" Lindsay shifted in her chair. "Because I'm not looking to fix anybody. Way I look at it, I'm lucky to be alive, so I'm just going to have a good time while I can. If that makes me shallow, so what. Who the fuck is left to impress?"

JT vehemently shook his head no. "I'm not going to lie, I don't know why I brought it up," JT opened up the last beer he had. "I don't feel that way anymore. Too much bad shit has happened. How long has it even been? Has Christmas come and gone? Is this a new year? Whatever, I'm not that guy with the killer instinct anymore. I'm not going to lie, I miss him sometimes."

"Dude, I'm glad that's the last beer because you don't need anymore. You're heading into wastedville. It's a new world, you be who you want to be. We have all done things we wouldn't have done before to survive."

"You are too cool, you know that?" JT pointed in Lindsay's general direction. He was feeling real good now. He didn't know what she was saying about stopping. He didn't want to stop now. He was just starting to feel it.

"I met this crazy guy once. Called himself Jelly. Had a crazy idea. He told it to a friend of mine who passed it on to me. Maybe people infected and turned into zombies weren't really dead. They were still in there," JT knocked on his head. "They were just being controlled, like puppets. By the virus. Trapped watching themselves fucking eating people alive. Wouldn't that make them cannibals? Fucking crazy. I can't get it out of my head now, when I see any of those zombie fuckers. I hesitate to kill them because of it. It can't be true but still..."

JT lost where he was going with this, so he just took another drink.

"That's a fucking chilling thought. I wish you hadn't shared with me. If you're concerned about zombies though, you can't be a bad guy. At least not all bad."

Lindsay got up from her chair and sat down next to JT on the couch, close to him. Her leggings felt nice as they rubbed against his leg.

"How about we change the subject? That's enough zombie talk for me." She had one arm around him now and leaned in. Her breath tickled his ear. "Enough talk all together."

When he turned to face her, their mouths were only inches apart. It didn't take much of a move for him to start kissing her. He got into it wholeheartedly. Her lips felt good. He devoured her like a man who had been without food for months. Then he pulled himself away.

"Wow, that was good," Lindsay said, breathless. "Don't stop now."

He couldn't help it. A picture of Hannah flashed through his mind. The memory of her heat against his body. How much he wanted to go all the way with her but she had always stopped him.

"It's not her is it?" Lindsay asked as JT just sat there. "I'm not looking for any drama JT, I'm just looking for some fun."

He didn't want to admit it to her but that's exactly what it was. He had to accept Hannah was a closed book anyway. Hannah was gone. Lindsay, she was right here.

"Ok, let me help you make a decision," she said as she stood up and pulled the red dress over her head. She was naked now except for the leggings. A colorful tattoo covered her arm from shoulder to wrist. It weaved in and out in patterns, floral like in design. Blues, green and reds filled in spaces. JT was surprised with himself. She wasn't usually the type JT was interested in but Lindsay looked beautiful there in the warm glow of the fire.

She stood there, a look of longing in her eyes. "Like what you see?"

He pulled her back down on the couch.

"Where did we leave off?" He asked as he began to kiss her again, this time even more intensely. JT wriggled, pushing off his shorts. The feeling of their now naked bodies intertwined was almost enough to push JT over the edge as he scooped Lindsay up and they moved to the floor in front of the fire where after two rounds of intense love making they passed out in each others arms.

COMING DOWN A MOUNTAIN

Hannah looked at herself in the mirror. Her hair had never been so long, well past her shoulders. She had to sweep it all back into a ponytail when when she wasn't wearing a hat to keep the front part out of her eyes. It was tangled and kind of dirty looking. She hadn't bathed in a couple of days. It was just too much hassle to get water out of the stream that ran through the town, carry it back, heat it up over a fire and so on. Besides she wasn't trying to impress anyone, so what did it matter.

That led her back to thoughts about JT. He rattled her more than she wanted to admit last night. She had spent most of the morning reflecting back on all the good times they had. Joking around in the car during the countless hours on the road. Cuddling up during the long nights, feeling safe in his arms. How he had tried his best to protect her, to let her in.

Maybe she could go over to his house and get him to sober up. For her. Then they could see if they could start over or if it was indeed time to move on. She was done playing games. She was done feeling sorry for him or for herself for that matter. She felt so much older now. It hadn't been but maybe eight months since the Outbreak, but she felt like she had grown about ten years older.

"Closure." she told her mirrored self.

She put her coat on and walked out, stocked full of determination. She walked the few blocks over to where JT was staying. She was about to knock on the door when it opened.

"Oh, hey Hannah," Lindsay giggled. She bounced down the stairs, turned and waved goodbye at the bottom, then glided down the street over enthusiastically.

Hannah immediately started scowling. JT now stood in the open doorway, leaning against the frame. He wore the biggest smile she had seen him have since before the whole church thing.

"You look to be in a good mood this morning," she commented, trying to sound much calmer than she felt.

"Hannah," JT said, in a standoffish way. He was wearing a robe. Hannah didn't think she'd ever seen him in a robe before.

"Is this a bad time, JT? Maybe I should come back."

"Nah, I'm feeling great. Come on in?"

She hesitated for a moment then walked in.

"So you had Lindsay stay the night here with you?"

As soon as she asked, she wished she hadn't. It came out sounding jealous. It must have sounded that way to JT too because he went off.

"I've protected you to the best of my ability. Kept you safe. I even bled for you. You just kicked me in the dirt and gave me the cold shoulder routine when Albright showed up. Flashing that smile of his, preaching some shiny golden God bullshit in your ear. That seemed to get you to jump into bed with him real quick. You sure as hell seem to have caught his holier than thou attitude."

Hannah inhaled sharply. She felt like someone had just punched her in the gut. For him to go there, just like that. The nerve. She was so mad and upset she could feel her tears start to fall despite attempting to hold them back.

"Sorry. God dammit. I didn't mean that Hannah."

"Fuck you JT, you aren't allowed to be a complete dick to me and then apologize like it makes it fucking okay!" Hannah said with her voice trembling. She willed herself to stop crying. She would not give him anymore satisfaction than she already had. When heading over here, a hesitant voice whispered to her it was a bad idea. She wished she'd listened to that voice. When she had second thoughts about something, when was she going to start listening? If she would, it would save her lots of grief.

"You obviously look much happier with Lindsay. Not that you need my permission but go ahead and fuck her brains out. I'm sure most the guys here already have. I must have been mistaken that you actually cared about me. Not just getting in my pants, like some typical guy. I'm so tired of being used."

She turned to leave. He grabbed her shoulder.

"Hannah. I didn't mean it, honest. I just, I just got mad..."

"I...I guess you can't change can you, JT? By the way, good job saving Ashley."

She ripped JT's hand from her shoulder. JT stood there, like he had just died standing up, pale and silent. She felt like punching him in the gut but instead she walked off.

She was able to keep her tears in on the way home. Her anger had taken over keeping her face blank, expressionless, until she got to her house. She ran to her bed and threw herself on it. Her sobbing was like that of a child. Her whole body convulsed. Then she screamed. It sounded so loud to her, she was surprised later that no one came running to check on her.

A thought, sounding like her Dad's voice, told her to calm down. She pushed herself off the bed slowly. She walked out to the living room. Her stomach hurt, her chest still hitched, her eyes stung. Even still, she followed the voice's advice.

She stood in the open area between the couch and the television, taking deep breaths. That voice inside her urged her on. Be calm. Before he died her Dad insisted she take some martial arts or self defense classes. Before and after practice they always spent a few minutes in a meditative stance. She called on those skills now.

The tears stopped. Her breathing slowed and her mind emptied. When she felt normal again, she went back to the bedroom, stripped and went to bed. She slept away the rest of the day and night. She awoke the next morning, feeling refreshed.

Hannah spent the next few days feeling like she was floating. When the work on the school was done, she was assigned to the kitchen next. They were short handed she was told. She worked and talked to people. Yet, when she would arrive home at night, she couldn't remember a single thing that was said.

As she drifted off each night, she thought about packing her things and leaving. Yet every morning she got dressed and went out to work. Hannah forgot about her suspicions about Roy. She didn't care what JT was up to. She had seen him by himself more often than not, mainly at dinner time. Sometimes he would be sitting with Gus then get up to sit by himself when he saw her looking for Gus and Linda to sit with. She lived in her own head for at least a week. She showed up one afternoon in the kitchens and was surprised to see Gus there.

"Well hello darlin'," he said, taking in his surroundings. "They've finally given me something to do. Watch out everyone, Chef Gus is here. I can make a scrumdiliumcious bowl of mac and cheese, don't you worry."

Hannah smiled and nodded, then headed over to what she now considered her station.

"Shit, I need to work on my routine," Gus said, more to himself.

A long pause stretched out. "Hannah, you haven't visited Ms. Linda and I for awhile. Is everything okay?"

"Mmhmm"

"Let's just say your reply didn't stir confidence in my heart. What's going on? Is it the fact that we said we would never join another group, yet here we are?" Gus gestured wide with his hands.

Hannah looked around. The lights were on as the electricity was allowed to the casino at all times. That thought made her think how she still hadn't seen this mysterious Henry.

The two of them were the only ones in the kitchen for now. Still Hannah came over to Gus and whispered to him. It was like a cork popped off a geyser and she spouted out everything that was bothering her: JT, Roy, Dr. Childs, Lindsay.

To Gus's credit he listened without interruption, not even with a bad dad joke. When she was done he pretended to wipe sweat off his brow. "Girl, you've given yourself a plate full of trouble."

"Implying I've asked for it?" Hannah snapped back.

Gus cocked an eyebrow.

She didn't expect to feel even more frustrated after talking to him. "And?"

"Isn't it wonderful that this place seems normal? No one has tried to kill us. Or control us. None of that Harold shit. For sure none of that Albright fuckery. It's a thing to be thankful for. As for JT, we told him how we feel, it's up to him to turn it around. I would bet money on it he will and quite frankly if he won't well then screw him."

She took in what Gus was saying. She mulled it over while working open some cans. Getting out the pots and pans. Mixing and stirring. Son of a bitch. He was probably right. She had spent so long wallowing in the darkness, she couldn't see the light right in front of her.

"Gus, you might act like a clown but you sure know how to cut through my bullshit."

"Age, wisdom, blah blah blah." Gus gave her a wink.

Lance came in to join them and the three worked through the rest of the prep as the crowd of hungry people lined up out in the former restaurant. She saw JT and gave him a tentative smile as he passed through the line. He scowled back. She thought that was his choice, it didn't bother her. She also gave a smile to Lindsay as she went though. Lindsay smiled back and gave her a little wave. Roy wouldn't even look her in the eye. She had done what she could, if there was anything going on, it wasn't her problem. She was feeling better, cleaner. She hadn't felt like this in a long time. She thanked God for it and for putting Gus in her path.

After everyone left she ate with Gus and Lance. After clean up, she was exhausted. Leaving, she was feeling lighter than a cloud. She was prepared for bed, feeling she would sleep good tonight.

It was a shock when she passed through the casino's doors to find Josh pacing back and forth on the street in front of it. He was holding a large flashlight, its beam bouncing and bobbing.

"Josh," she said, pleasant enough. "This is a surprise. You been waiting out here for me this entire time?"

"No," he said, shining the beam up at her. She squinted and raised her hand. He smiled, obviously embarrassed by his mistake. He adjusted his glasses along side of the lens with his free hand. "Yes. I just thought, after working together on the school, that it would be nice to see you again. It's been awhile. Maybe I could walk you home?"

Hannah was struck by the altogether sweet gesture. She guessed he was crushing on her. She wasn't interested in him or anyone. It was time for her to be on her own. She wanted to make it crystal clear, so he wouldn't think she was leading him on.

"Alright. Just as friends though okay? I'm not looking for anything beyond that with anyone. I'm sure your are the nicest guy in this town. I'm just not looking for any romance or relationships. Clear?"

In the dim light given off by his flashlight, she could see his body deflate, his face fall. It might hurt now but it was better this way.

She came down the steps near him. "You know, I don't need an escort but I appreciate the offer."

"I know," his smile brightening again. "You might be the bravest person I've ever met."

"I don't know about that," Hannah said, on the verge of blushing.

"Modest. I've heard some of the tales of the zombies you have faced from your friend Gus. I don't think I could have made it in your place."

"Well, tip for the future, Gus has a tendency to embellish, besides you're still here," Hannah said. "That means you survived situations just as bad I'm sure."

She heard Josh's breath inhale deeply then come out in a slow shutter.

"There was one time. I thought I was going to melt into the floor. My legs felt like Jello. I kept thinking this is the end."

They started walking towards Hannah's house.

"There was a group of five of us. We had gone into this military base, down in Texas. We walked down this long hallway. The floor was vinyl colored government gray. Our steps were the only sounds in the place. It had a drop ceiling with several tiles missing. Like a loony smile of a madman missing some teeth. That's what it made me think of.

I was in front. Why I don't know. Behind me were two women and behind them two other men. Down this hallway we walked. First it was brick also grey. Then these skinny windows appeared on both sides. They had the wires inside that made patterns of x after x. I made the mistake of shining my light into one.

Inside were row upon row of them. All facing the same way, standing still in formation. Like they were still soldiers, out on the parade field. They turned their heads as one in the direction of my light.

Quickly I flipped the light to the other window, to find the same unholy sight. The woman behind me, it broke her nerve. She screamed. The woman behind her clamped a hand over her mouth so hard, the slap reverberated through the now silent passageway.

I had never experienced the saying 'my heart is in my throat' until that moment. I scanned the light around back and forth to either window. It looked like a lighthouse, warning of dangerous seas ahead.

We were all surprised to see the zombies just continue to stand there. I've never seen anything more bizarre before or after this encounter. The man at the end of our party, Robert spoke two words. Holy God.

That's when we heard pattering feet in front of us. Heading our way fast. We turned as one, just like the zombies had. Now I was at the rear. It took all the humanity I had not to push the women in front of me out of the way and sprint past them.

We had descended the stairs down from the main hallway into this corridor of hell. We were rapidly approaching them. Not rapidly enough for me. I felt fingers brush up against my back. Now it was my turn to scream. I didn't have a weapon. Physical violence makes me ill. The first time I had to kill a zombie I puked until my stomach was empty. Funny, I know, when that is the only way to survive this new world.

Robert peeled off to the side, pressing himself against the wall. We flew by him. He raised his bat with thick, long nails driven through it. He jokingly called it the ventilator. Robert, he was a real man. I heard him yell 'bring it', then the thunk and suck of him unloading on a zombie. That was the last time I ever saw him."

Josh burrowed his chin down into his chest, like the bad memory had overwhelmed him. "Sorry." He finally muttered out as they neared Hannah's place.

"Hey, it's okay Josh." Hannah was trying to be comforting by lightly rubbing his back and patting it in the most friendly way she could think of.

"We've all been through hell. If you ever need someone to talk to or just to keep you company, you can come here anytime." Hannah said as she decided a hug was in order.

"But just as friends right?" Josh teasingly joked as Hannah made her way to her door stuck her tongue out mockingly at him.

A STAB IN THE DARK

Gus chuckled to himself, breath escaping in short puffs in the cold mountain air. Seeing a younger couple walking the other way, it made him think about Hannah and JT. How they were acting like they belonged on one of those teen drama reality shows. Sure it wasn't the first time he had seen people who loved each other try to deny it and act the way they do. It still cracked him up every time. Life was too short for that shit.

Gus was out strolling around the town waiting for Linda to be off duty at the clinic. He needed to stretch his legs but also he was looking out for Roy. He was only half kidding with Hannah about following him. Kitchen duty ended up being only a temporary thing for him. This morning he woke up and thought what the hell? He had nothing to fill the long hours of the day, so he put his coat on and went out.

His hands were deep in his pockets and his shoulders felt like they were up around his ears. This deep of a cold still surprised him. He was already sick of it. What happened to retiring to the beach? He should have put on more layers, Linda would've been tanning his hide he thought.

Gus knew Roy had finished overseeing the school house from Hannah. What she didn't know was what he had moved onto doing next. She hadn't seen him after their last run in.

Gus found himself up at the front gate. It was an imposing structure. It looked like something from a Mad Max movie. We don't need another hero. He laughed at himself. Of course he was sure it was slapped together in a hurry. Some of the trees they used for support still had studs of branches sticking out here and there. Between the trees were pieces of drywall, wood pallets, siding, metal sheets and whatever else they could get their hands on.

He couldn't believe his luck when he saw Roy walking along the wall, over by where the gate was. Looked like he was inspecting it or something.

"Hey, you're Roy aren't you?" Gus asked, approaching him.

Roy turned, annoyance clear on his face. "Yeah, maybe, who are you?"

Gus thought ole Dusty could have taken lessons from this guy about how to be cocky. "Names Gus. I was just admiring the wall. It looks solid as a Snakewood tree."

"Hell yeah it's solid. My Dad designed it himself and I oversaw building it. It'll keep zombies out, you can count on that, old man." Roy flicked the butt of the cigarette he had been smoking at Gus's feet.

His comments rose the ire in Gus, but he decided to humor Roy and play a little cat and mouse with him.

"They use to say the only two things you can count on is death and taxes. Nowadays, you can't even count on those," Gus said, playing with Roy.

Roy wasn't amused. "It will keep your ass safe. I'm busy, you need anything important or are you just bored?"

"No. I'll be moseying along now I reckon. Nice to meet ya, though."

Roy grunted and turned back to the wall lighting another cigarette. Gus could hear him softly mumbling.

Gus took another look up and across the structure. Whoever came here first, they picked a great spot. Only having two access points and those points both having narrow entrance ways between the rocky sides of the mountains. Smart.

Hannah was right about one thing, Roy wasn't a pleasant person. He hoped he never got stuck working with the guy. His distaste in just that first meeting was enough for Gus to watch Roy when he could. If things didn't change, he would have lots of free time on his hands anyways.

Gus walked back through town, meandering this way and that. He wondered just how many people were here. Eighty? A few hundred? Gus guessed from what he saw at dinner time if it was more than two hundred, he would eat his hat. That the number was even that high surprised him. Maybe a lot of them were people who originally lived here?

As he passed through the downtown area, looking through the windows as he passed, he could tell this was a tourist town. Food joints, souvenir shirt shops, gift shops and outdoor sporting goods sellers lined the street, looking both quaint and tacky at the same time.

There wasn't much in the way of property damage. Most windows were intact. The mass carnage he had seen in most of the places they had come across wasn't evident here. Yeah, they were either locals or tourists Gus decided. Lucking out it was the off season when the Outbreak started.

On a bluff overlooking the downtown district was the casino and hotel. Gus looked up at it, shielding his eyes. In front of it was a McDonald's, its golden arches breaking the beautiful architecture of the casino behind it. Gus wondered if Dr. Childs just spent most of his time up there, looking out over a town he hoped to lord over. Or did he even care about the people below? Gus shrugged his shoulders.

At the end of the block the door was open to some kind of an art store. There were many majestic pictures of mountains and wildlife lining its walls. Gus ducked inside to sit down. He was feeling winded and light headed again. It was taking longer than he liked for his body to get use to the mountain air.

It was so quiet he could hear the gurgling of the stream that ran through town, behind the buildings. There was a park back there, along with a couple of wooden bridges that crossed the stream. Earlier he had seen a sign in the park announcing the twenty seventh annual duck races coming this spring.

It was sad to think about how that never happened. The duck races were canceled indefinitely. His mind wanted to go to thoughts about where those kids were now. He cut it off. It was just depressing and pointless. Like this whole town. Spooky as well. The silence all around him when there should be hustle and bustle.

Oh well. That was enough stewing in that particular pot. He got up, his cracking knees sounding like someone breaking celery, damn old age. He left the gallery.

Gus turned the corner and a man coming the other way just about dumped him on his old, not paying attention ass.

"Sorry," the man said, reaching out to steady Gus. He had some accent Gus couldn't pin down. He sure wasn't from around here. "I'm new here and seem to have gotten turned around. Do you know where Dr. Childs is?"

Once Gus was steady, the man dusted off and straightened out the grey peacoat he was wearing. Gus hadn't heard about anyone new had come into town. Then again, it wasn't like he was Mayor McCheese around here. Gus looked the man up and down.

"You sick mister? You look okay to me."

"Oh, I'm fine. I'm just acquainting myself with all of the important places, in case I do need to visit him sooner or later."

The man looked well. Well fed and well groomed. His black goatee and black hair were clean and neatly trimmed. It was hard to tell since everyone went around in heavy coats but he did look fit as a fiddle.

"Well welcome to our little slice of old America. I didn't catch your name. Mine is Gus." His hand went out.

The man gave it a perfunctory shake. "Do you know the answer to my question?"

Alarm bells began going off in Gus's head. The man could have a legitimate reason for not wanting to get too personal right away. Maybe. Gus was going to point the man in the direction of both the clinic and the casino but changed his mind. He didn't see how pointing out the clinic could be harmful in any way.

"Mister, he spends most of his time at the clinic. It's down this main street, turn right and go one block. It use to be an outdoor clothing and camping supply store."

"Thank you, sir," the man said. He clumped off without another word.

That was strange, Gus had to admit. He would have to ask Linda tonight if she had heard about any new people in town. Or what she thought of the man, as she should meet him when he got to the clinic.

His thoughts turned back to JT and Hannah the rest of the way home. About how much he should mettle in their affairs or if he should at all. Also about Roy and if he was up to something, what could it possibly be? By the time he made it back home and Linda came back from the clinic, Gus had forgotten about his run in with the man.

WHO CAN IT BE NOW

Roy glanced around like a frantic chipmunk, licking his lips all the while. With each passing second, his heartbeat seemed to speed up. Just like his plan, which he had moved up after that fuck Gus came nosing around. He knew Gus was friends with that bitch Hannah. He didn't think she could possibly know anything. Still there was Gus, not long after Hannah almost discovered him talking to Gerard's guy. He was too far along though to take any chances now.

It took some persuading and a pack of his smokes to get him on guard duty tonight. Fucking people, they took this shit way to seriously. Like zombie packs were going to attack them at any moment out of nowhere. Even if they did, they wouldn't get in. They could pick them off at their leisure. Not that anyone ever listened to him. Or his Dad anymore.

Why the people here were so loyal to that shithead Childs he didn't understand. They had walls because of his Dad. Protection, electricity, food. They owed it all to him. Yet he was thrown aside and forgotten just because Childs came in and could fix some boo boos. Fucking pussies.

He sat in the little box, shivering and gripping his rifle tight. Peering out through the peephole, waiting for that cocksucker Gerard to show up, Roy went through his plan again and again.

Gerard would take Dr. Childs with him back to their camp. He would claim being knocked out by Gerard's gang.

The people here would boo hoo and act butthurt but his Dad would set them straight and get things going again. Then he would be made second in charge, which is what he deserved. He could see no flaw in the plan, as long as Gerard showed up.

Roy stopped looking long enough to light a cigarette and take some puffs. He looked back out and saw four shadowy shapes stealthily approaching the gate. Gerard had told him he would be alone, the douche.

Roy undid the locks and opened the door. The four men crept in. Dressed all in black, with black ski masks, Roy couldn't tell who was who.

"Alright Gerard," he hissed when they were inside. He shut the door behind them but didn't lock it. It was a tight squeeze, the place wasn't built for this many people. "You said you would be by yourself. What the fuck is going on?"

Gerard pulled up his mask and looked intensely at Roy. Roy held his gaze but then had to look away.

"Just brought a few of my mates. I changed my mind and realized I could use some help."

"Whatever," Roy tried to sound cool and tough. "I'll be glad when that dick Childs is gone. You think he's going to help you?"

"I will be persuasive."

Roy grinned at that. "What do you need him for anyhow? You sick?"

Gerard gave him a look like he had just found something disgusting in his food. Roy was beginning to think this guy was just as much of a prick as Childs. The two would be chummy together.

"Forget I asked."

"Nah, what the hell. We got time to blabber, right? When all this went down I had a crew of fifty strong. By the end of summer, it was down to thirty two. Now it's eighteen. I don't want to lose any more. He'll be our insurance plan. Any more stupid questions or can we get this over with?"

Roy glared then glanced out the window nervously. He didn't like the guy's attitude but he did have a point.

"Go on around the back way. Follow the map I gave you. Make it quick. Just don't forget our deal."

Roy opened the door to the shack, exposing the town. He still felt their eyes watching him. He turned to face them and was slammed up against the wall. He felt a warm and sharp pain on his left side. It suddenly became hard to breath.

"Thanks, mate," the masked man breathed inches away from Roy's face. "Now just stay nice and quiet and we'll fulfill our part of the bargain."

Roy felt a pulling and tearing sensation in the same area below his chest. He seemed to have no strength left in his legs. He slid down the wall holding his stomach, which now was filled with pain. He felt something wet soak his gloves. What the hell? My Dad was going to be in charge again. I'd be the second in command. This wasn't supposed to happen. I was making everything right again. He watched the four men file past until his vision faded to black. His final thought was the irony that he had literally just been stabbed in the back, that he needed Childs' help, and these guys were here to take him.

TAKEN

It was the sound of a barking dog that woke Hannah up. She was just going to roll over and ignore it when another one started up. She had gotten so use to sleeping in her regular clothes she did it all the time. So she only had to slip on her boots, hat, and coat. She grabbed her hunting rifle, a M48 TGR, with a rifle bullet band wrapped around the stock. She had traded one of the assault rifles they had found at the army base for it. She had been practicing with it every day and liked it so much better. It was much more precise.

The first dog quieted but Hannah had a feeling something was wrong. She went down the street, trying to minimize the crunching of snow under her steps. Besides the soft glow of a fire shining through a window of a house here or there, it was almost black. Then a flash of light to her left caused her to freeze.

She was sure it had to have been a flashlight. She crept that way. She turned the corner and saw figures in black who almost blended into the darkness. She saw them because one was using a light. That was dumb of them. She counted four people and to her it looked like they were headed to the casino.

She knelt on one knee, raised up her rifle, and peered through the scope. She had one person in sight and began to put pressure on the trigger. She stopped. Hannah was pretty sure they were up to no good but what if there was more going on she didn't know about. She didn't just want to kill them in cold blood. She didn't want any more death on her hands if she could help it. Instead of taking the shot she followed them.

They arrived at Wild Pines Casino and Hotel. Here they flicked off the light. She could see them fool with the door and then it opened. They went in single file. She counted to thirty and then ran up to the entrance. She flattened herself against the side of the door and leaned to peek inside, just to see the last person go into the stairwell. Hannah counted to thirty before she went inside. She ducked from gambling table to slot machine. At the bottom of the stairs Hannah figured there was only one reason they would be here. It would be for Dr. Childs.

When she reached the top of the stairs, the four intruders were outside the suite's door. Childs' two bodyguards were lying face down on the carpet. One of the attackers kicked in the door and three of them stormed the place. The left one at the doorway as lookout.

She leaned her body around the corner and before he even knew she was there Hannah shot him right in the leg. He cried out as he went down. She crouch-ran down the hallway.

"Shut up or it will be your head next," she hissed at the masked figure as he rolled around on the ground. The crying stopped. He whimpered like dog.

Hannah flattened herself against the wall. She expected the other three to storm back out after hearing her shot and their friend crying out. Instead she heard shouting from inside. There were several lanterns on all around the suite. Thankful for some light, she looked to make sure the room was clear. Still crouched she went in and ducked behind the wet bar, peeping out her head for a few seconds. They had to have heard the heard the shot and the screaming but if they were too busy with what they were doing, maybe she could catch a break.

Patiently she continued to crouched down behind the wet bar counter. Footsteps rapidly approached. Two figures appeared with Childs in between them. His head hung limply and it looked like blood was running down the side of his face. Hannah shot both men in the back of the knees after they passed her position. They collapsed and Childs fell too. They all landed in a big heap.

Another figure whipped around the opposite corner of the bar. Hannah was startled and fell backwards. Her rifle fell between her legs and bounced away. She reached for it but the man kicked it away. It went skittering out of reach. The man yanked on a chain he was carrying. A body attached to the end flew around the corner and thumped into the wall. Hannah scooted on her butt in horror. It was Childs' zombie kid. They must have picked it up sometime before she had woken up.

It had what looked like a collar around its neck. It snarled mutely, pulling at what was holding it back with its dead hands. The stench of death caused Hannah's stomach to flip flop.

"Girl, you shouldn't have gotten involved," the man said, towering over her, letting out the slack on the detained zombie. "Roy told us about Childs locking up this diseased thing. I thought it might come in handy. Looks like I was right."

The man dropped the chain. He picked up Childs by putting an arm over his shoulder and half dragged him out. Hannah went still. The other three men she shot earlier were still thrashing around, hollering.

"Gerard, you can't leave us," one was screaming out the open door.

The zombie turned from Hannah to the commotion the men were making. It scrambled over. The men saw it and tried to crawl away. It grabbed at the leg of the closest person to it and bit into his calf.

Hannah used this opportunity to get up and sprint for her rifle. She got it, ejected the spent casings, and loaded fresh bullets. Her hands were shaking and she almost dropped them. You have plenty of time. The zombies got plenty of fresh meat.

It was a sickening thought she pushed aside. Then she allowed herself to slow down. Ready to go again, she calmly walked back into the living room area. She aimed and fired, taking down the zombie in the back of the head while it chewed on raw human flesh. The man the zombie had ripped it from was quiet. Hannah guessed he must have passed out from the pain and shock. Good for her, it made what she had to do easier. She put a bullet into his brain too.

She went out the door and down the stairs two at a time. She moved her head from side to side as she went, blinking rapidly. The light in Child's suite had ruined her night vision. Outside, she tried to pick out what tracks in the snow could be the man who took Childs. Gerard they had called him.

All she saw were footprints heading towards the casino. Then she thought maybe Gerard was stepping in the same prints, going back the same way he came. The man was clever enough to get in and make it this far without anyone knowing. If it wasn't for the fortunate wake up call from the dogs, no one would even know the doctor was missing until the morning.

She went back the way she came. Her night eyes hadn't returned enough to tell if the prints were only going one way but she couldn't think of what else to do. She had gone about two blocks before she saw what looked like a drag mark in the snow next to some random footprints. That had to be Gerard with the doctor, a struggle perhaps.

She went a little faster now, turning left and then right. Some people were stumbling out of their homes. She could hear whispered conversations as people wondered what was going on. More dogs were barking in the distance. It was normally so quiet at night they probably heard the commotion. She ignored them all. She was close to the front gate now. She turned the next corner and could see the torchlights burning by the wide open gate. Someone's dead body lay in the snow to her right. Gerard was just about outside.

"Stop!" Hannah shouted, dropping to one knee and bringing her rifle up.

Gerard didn't even hesitate. He kept right on going. Hannah fired a warning shot. She was afraid of hitting Dr. Childs. The shot splintered some wood from the wall over Gerard's head. That caused him to stop and turn. Hannah hoped this commotion would bring someone else to help her.

"You might be good at picking off slow stupid zombies girl, but I'm going to be a lot tougher," Gerard snarled. In his anger his British accent was even thicker. "I'm leaving with the doctor and you will let me if you still want your life."

"I've got the drop on you. I could blow your head off before you even knew I pulled the trigger."

"Then do it already. Unless you are not as good as you claim to be. Unless you are worried about hitting the doctor here. I'm done here."

Gerard began walking backwards, the feet of the doctor dragging in the snow beside him. He reached to his waist with his free hand and pulled a gun. He was just about at the gate. Once he was on the other side who knew what would happen. He could have a whole group of people out there.

"What's going on Hannah," a voice slurring his words came from behind her.

"Shit," Hannah said, putting light pressure on her trigger. She didn't dare turn, even though it sounded like JT.

"Answer me Hannah." JT crossed in front of her.

Gerard lazily raised up his arm and fired a few shots. Hannah swore and bounded up, knocking the still clueless JT down into the snow. She rolled off his prone body, searching to get Gerard back into her sights.

Something blurred past her and pounced at Gerard. Gerard dropped the doctor in the snow and ran. A dog landed mere inches from Gerard, barking and growling furiously.

Hannah took a shot and missed. Cursing she ran to the gate. She flung herself back behind the barrier when she saw Gerard had stopped with his gun pointed right at her. He began firing again. Wood chipped around her, the metal sang with ricochets. Her anger rose up, the anger of all that had happened to her backed this new anger. It grew into a rage she had never felt before. Hannah flung herself around the gate when the hail of bullets stopped. She hit the snow hard, puffs of whiteness erupted around her. She rolled, got up, and hauled it to the nearest tree. Making herself flat against it, she peered around the tree. She could see Gerard dimly, the husky dog chasing him.

Gerard paused to line up a shot on the dog. Hannah tracked him and pulled the trigger. She felt a rush of excitement as she saw the figure in her scope fall down. She pumped her rifle in the air with one hand.

She ran across the white field to Gerard. The dog was pulling and tearing at his pants. A whistle, sharp and high, came from behind Hannah. The dog perked up its ears and ran back.

Hannah looked the prone figure over. He was lying on his stomach, his back to her. She rolled him over and saw the spreading stain on his chest making his black, skin tight shirt even darker.

People were rushing out to her. Many with lights. One was Lindsay, her husky dog bounding along beside her. A piece of fabric still hung from its mouth. JT was behind Lindsay. She didn't want to think what that might imply. A big, wooly man looked down at Childs and then grabbed hold of Hannah's shoulders.

"What the hell is going on here?" he demanded while some of the other people lifted Dr. Childs up by his arms and legs and carried him away.

"Something woke me up. I followed the sounds and found this guy along with his friends back at the casino, trying to kidnap Childs. I stopped them." Hannah slung her rifle over her shoulder, a satisfied grin on her face. She had done good work.

"Henry," a townsperson called out. "I think you better come over here." They sounded very disturbed.

Henry went over to the body lying face down by the gate. Hannah followed him back. The body was slumped and some dark stain was smeared against the wall behind it. The person raised the corpse's head and Hannah could see it was Roy. Henry could too. He dropped to his knees and put his dead son's head in his hands.

"Roy, Roy," Henry's voice wavered. "You...I...it can't..."

Henry sprung up and grabbed Hannah again, a little more violently this time.

"What happened," Henry said, getting right into her face. "Did you do this? Why is my son fucking dead?"

JT tackled Henry before Hannah could reply. JT and Henry tussled on the ground, rolling in the snow. JT gained some leverage and was striking Henry as best he could. Hannah noticed red splotches here and there where the two landed. There was also a trail of red a few feet back.

"Alright, alright let's break this up!" Gus was shouting, coming over to the two men.

JT stood up and Hannah could see the top of his shirt was soaked with blood. She rushed over to him. "My God! JT, what happened to you?"

"What do you mean what happened to me?" JT swayed on his feet. He didn't look to be all there. "Henry didn't even land a blow, did he?"

"JT, buddy. It looks like you've been shot!" Gus said, joining them. "I'll go get Linda." Gus took off.

"Huzza," was JT's reply, then he sat down hard in the snow.

Hannah knelt down beside him. "Shouldn't we be doing something, like applying pressure to the wound?"

Josh and Lindsay both came over and helped Hannah get him to his feet. JT felt like dead weight, wasn't able to stand.

"Let's just get him to the clinic," Josh said.

The people who had gathered all around in a semi-circle opened up to let them through.

"Don't all you dipshits just stand there," Lindsay scolded as she past. "Go help Steve and Henry."

"Steve," JT was saying, like it was the funniest word he had ever heard. "Doc Childs is named Steve. Ha. Now, why is my shoulder hurting again?"

Linda met them on the way. Together they guided JT to the clinic. They got him onto a bed. The three stayed with JT as Linda worked on him. Hannah was praying it wasn't worse than it looked. Linda cut off his shirt. There was a small hole pumping out blood in weak spurts in his left shoulder area.

"There's a bigger exit wound on the back," Linda said after examining him.

She bandaged him up and put a blanket over him.

"It looks to me like he is lucky the bullet passed clean through and that it didn't hit anything vital. We'll have Childs look at him when he can."

Just then some people carried in Dr. Childs. Linda directed them to put him on the bed next to JT. She examined him.

"Looks like a blow to the head. Knocked him unconscious. I don't think JT is in any immediate danger, I've stopped the bleeding, so we'll let Childs rest until he wakes up on his own."

"Is it sleepy time, Linda? My arm still feels funny." JT still sounded out of it.

"I'll give JT some pain medication, watch his vitals, and give him some fluids. That man was firing at you too Hannah, you need me to check you out?"

Gus looked to Hannah. "That's probably a good idea darlin'."

"No I'm good. I'll just run and get a pillow and blanket. I'll be staying the night here." She was shocked how suddenly concerned she was about JT. Like the thought of losing him clenched her throat shut. At the moment she couldn't even remember why they hadn't been talking to each other.

Linda took Hannah's hand. "He will be fine, Hannah. After all that just happened, you need rest."

"I know he will," Hannah said, smiling and truly believing it. "I'm staying here tonight, the end."

DEAD OF WINTER

PARADISE LOST

Dr. Childs awoke first, before the morning light. He complained of grogginess and being lightheaded. Hannah watched Linda help him to a sitting position and check his vitals. After finishing, Linda filled Childs in on what had happened to him as well as the other events of the night before.

"The last thing I remember is hearing some noise downstairs and then tremendous pain. My arm aches, too." Childs said.

"That's where one of them were dragging you along," Hannah said, from across the room.

She was sitting and holding JT's hand. She had spent the night watching the rise and fall of his chest. She didn't sleep, as every time she closed her eyes she pictured he had stopped breathing and would jerk awake.

Childs rotated his arm around and flexed it a few times. He winced with each movement. "Seems I owe you an apology Hannah. I thought that dumbass was all bark, no balls. Henry and I will have to have a serious talk about what to do about punishing the idiot-"

"Doctor, you may want to take a moment to think. Think about what you're saying," Linda tried to interrupt.

"Childs, you shut your mouth about my boy," Henry hollered from across the room. He was standing next to a table where a body laid with a white sheet over it.

"Henry. I didn't know you were already here? Roy get hurt to? Serves him right. Kidnapping, what-"

Henry came flying across the room. He grabbed up Childs by his shirt and flung him to the floor. Linda tried to intervene but was pushed to the side by Henry. She glanced off of the bed JT was lying in. Hannah sprung up.

"STOP!" she yelled, putting all of the weight of command into her voice she could.

Henry reared back his leg, ready to give the prone Dr. Childs a boot full of his anger. Hannah rushed over, trying to get between the two men.

"What in the holy hell of horseshoes and handgrenades is going on in here?" Gus yelled, storming into the room.

Henry turned for just a second, distracted, giving Hannah enough time to close the distance, push hard, and dump Henry on his ass. The two men looked almost comical on the floor, with Hannah standing over them.

Linda was rubbing her hip. Gus hurried over to her. "If they hurt you, I can go get my gun and blow them away."

"No, no. Don't think there is a need for that..." Linda gave the two men, who were getting to their feet, a stern look. Like a teacher to misbehaving students. "Yet."

"Let's try to act civilized here," Hannah said, escorting Henry back across the room.

"Childs, the figure under the sheet. That's Roy. He's dead." Linda put a hand on Dr. Childs shoulder, gently forcing him to sit back down.

"I think the attackers killed him, after Roy let them in," Hannah said.

Childs blinked a few times before sitting down on the edge of the bed. "Geez Henry. Sorry. That's tough. I'm not responsible for killing him. You gotta see that."

How lame and weak that consolation sounded to Hannah. She carefully watched Henry. His mouth twitched, his shoulder scrunched up. He looked like a dormant volcano now suddenly ready to blow. He stood.

"Shove your apology up your ass. I'll be back." Henry left, taking most of the tension in the room with him.

Childs sat staring at the white sheet for a long while. "Roy, that son of a bitch. Anything else I should know before I go spouting off about anyone else?"

"I killed all of the attackers, along with your zombie pet. They freed it and sicked it on me like an attack dog. Your guards, Bobby and Joe, are also dead. They almost killed JT."

Hannah was back at JT's side now. All the noise must have woken him. She smiled down at him and he smiled back. Linda must have given him some pain pills, his eyes looked clearer.

"He has a gunshot wound," Linda said. "If you are feeling up to it doctor, can you take a look?"

"Oh yeah? JT took a bullet? Let me have a look at him." With an effort Childs tore his eyes away from Roy's dead body. He held his hand up to his head for a few moments, rose, and came over to JT.

"Is it my birthday?" JT said looking around. Hannah, Linda, Gus and Dr. Childs were now standing around him.

"Hey bud, I know I'm your hero," Gus said. "But you don't have to do everything I do." He patted at his belly where he had been stabbed.

"I can't let you take all the glory, Gus," JT smiled weakly. "Except I wasn't doing anything heroic when I got hurt. I don't exactly remember what happened. I was blitzed I can remember"

"JT, you big dumb dumb," Hannah said, not cruelly. "I told you to stay inside. The kidnapper, Gerard was his name, was trying to shoot me. If it makes you feel better, you can pretend you took a bullet for me."

"Just call me Kevin Costner and I'll call you Whitney." He weakly joked.

Childs examined him while they were talking. "Wound looks good. Strong pulse. Nice blood pressure. It's too bad we can't give you a blood transfusion but I don't think it will hinder your recovery much. If we keep this clear of infection, you will be healed in no time. Except for a scar you won't even know you were shot. Let me just sew up your wound."

"That's great," JT said, then closed his eyes. "It doesn't hurt a bit. I'm just tired."

Childs turned to Linda as he finished up JT's sutures. "Linda, I gotta say, the wound looks well taken care of." He seemed to struggle with the next part. "Hannah, Linda, you are both good additions to my team. I need to ask a favor of you Linda. Can you to watch over things here so I can go address the town? I'm sure everyone's freaked out. I'm sure as fuck am."

"Sure thing, everyone out," Linda said, waving her arms to shoo them out. "You too doctor, you need rest as well. I believe you were spared a concussion. Normally I wouldn't recommend self diagnosis but who are you going to go see."

Childs actually chuckled. "You gotta point there Linda. I feel good enough. Just a little sore."

"Gus, I'll be home later. Make sure some coffee is ready, I'll need it."

"Sure thing sweet cheeks." Gus gave her a peck on the lips.

Hannah looked down at JT. "Don't do another stupid thing, like try to get out of here before you are ready. I know how you push yourself." She gave his hand a squeeze before turning.

"Hannah," JT called out. She turned back around. "I just wanted to tell you, good job out there. You don't need me to protect you anymore." With that JT closed his eyes.

They all went out front together. Before they left, Hannah stopped Childs.

"It was just dumb luck I woke up when I did and decided to check things out, instead of rolling over and going back to sleep."

"I've already thanked you." Childs was blandly dismissive.

"I don't want your thanks, jerk. I just want you to listen to me," Hannah gave Childs a penetrating stare. "Once this group finds out Gerard is dead, the rest may come back. This time to take you and kill the rest of us."

"Why would they do something stupid like that?" Dr. Childs kept on talking to her like she was a dumb kid. It was infuriating her.

"Loyalty. Revenge. Maybe just their backs are to the wall. Regular civilization is gone. I've seen people do extreme things to survive out there. To go through all this trouble to get you, someone might be very ill. Or all of them."

Childs rubbed the side of his face. "Not only did I sustain a head injury, I think I'm in shock. It's just so unbelievable. I tell you what. We can talk about this later. When I have time to appease your fantasy?"

"Think about all the people here, counting on you. Later may be too late." Hannah grabbed his arm but Childs just shook it off. He walked out the door. Hannah looked over at Gus. Gus looked back at her and shrugged his shoulders.

"So much for paradise, welcome back to the jungle." Gus shook his head.

ENEMY OF MY ENEMY

As they were walking out, they bumped into Lindsay, who was walking in. Today the hair spilling out of her puff ball hat was an almost eyeball searing shade of red.

"I got here as soon as I could. I had to take over guard duty after, you know, what happened to Roy. So how's JT?"

"Mr. Hardwired To Self Destruct? He's fine," Gus said when Hannah didn't answer. "He's tough, like these old mountains."

"Yeah you probably know he's as hard as stone," Hannah said, then she instantly wanted to take it back. She was appalled to find herself shooting off her mouth in such a childish manner.

Lindsay didn't look angry. In fact she giggled. "Why Hannah my dear, you always seemed so innocent. Maybe I 've misjudged you."

Hannah told herself to stop it. Jealousy and cattiness weren't her style. She wasn't going to accomplish anything by acting this way. In fact, she could use Lindsay's help she realized. Seemed like Childs still wasn't going to listen to her.

"Dr. Childs stitched up his bullet wound. We were all ordered to go, so JT could sleep. He'll be fine, no thanks to himself."

Lindsay let out a yawn. "Okay. That is so good to hear. It was stressful, sitting up at the shack, not able to find out. I could definitely use some sleep too. Let Parka out to go potty. I need to get her a dog treat or something special. She deserves it after last night."

"Before you go, can I ask you something?" Hannah nervously asked.

"I'll leave you ladies to your girly gossip. Sleep always sounds good to me. Catch you on the flip side," Gus said and walked away.

"I can tell you while we walk to your place if that's okay." Hannah stated.

The two walked away from the clinic. Hannah glanced back at it once more, sending up a small silent prayer for JT to be okay.

"Go ahead, ask me." Lindsay clearly wasn't interested in beating around any bushes.

"Okay. So you know, I haven't talk to anyone about this yet except for Gus and Linda. Childs knows because he was there. I warned him about this. I told him I ran into Roy acting all strange and he could be up to something since he couldn't stop talking about how much Dr. Childs sucked and how his Dad was the best."

"Roy's been saying that crap since Childs got here." Lindsay interjected.

"That's pretty much how Childs brushed me off and look what happened."

"You got a point. Continue."

"Gerald was the guy who almost got away and seemed to be in charge. I've got a hunch once his friends or followers or whoever find out we killed him, they will come for us. Except his time it will be a war. They will avenge his death and they will get the doctor."

"Whoa. That's quite the leap, isn't it? Anyway what's that got to do with me?" Lindsay seemed unconvinced.

"You live here, don't you? Sorry, sorry that came out wrong." Hannah found herself trying to play defense now. Why was everyone here so dismissive of her? Was it because they had been sheltered from what it was like out there now, beyond those walls?

Lindsay just shook her head. "You know, I told JT I basically thought you were stuck up. I can see now you're not. Not exactly. You got a good head on your shoulders."

"Thanks, I guess. I'm sorry it's a lot to throw on someone who is basically a stranger to me. Please, will you help me? "

"Let me ask you something first. Why don't you just leave?"

Oh, JT has been running his mouth. And you, you would like it if I left. Hannah clamped down on her anger. She wasn't going to be a hypocrite and judge JT for his outburst then have one of her own. Besides, she didn't need to justify her change in mind to this woman. Hannah decided Lindsay was a dead end. She turned to leave.

"Sorry," Lindsay called out to her back. "Now what I wanted to say didn't turn out right. I think you're right. I was just wondering why you care. Is it something with JT? You got some issues still going on between you two, don't you?"

"I don't think it's any of your business and if it was, now isn't the time to talk about it." Hannah chewed her lower lip.

"Fair enough. You know what, you've convinced me it's a possibility. What do you want me to do?"

"Get as much guard duty as Childs will let you. Anything suspicious at all, you let me know. If you think we should leave, because there seems to be no getting through to Childs, you will tell me. Can I trust you to do that?"

"Alright but if things are going sideways, I'll want to leave myself." Lindsay put her hands on her hips.

"You do your part well, you're welcome to go."

Satisfied Lindsay was on her side Hannah was about to leave. She had one more thing to say. "I don't know what is going on between you and JT and I don't want to know. He is still my friend though and I don't want anything to happen to him. Underneath that new exterior is still the JT I first met. He saved my best friend and me when the Outbreak started, like a knight in shining armor."

"Funny, that's close to the same thing he said about you," Lindsay gave her a friendly smile. "I'll see you later, oh and Hannah, I'm glad we talked."

Hannah stood there watching her unnatural red ponytails bounce away.

Hannah was sitting in the overstuffed brown chair by the window, sipping her hot cocoa. Her Bible laid open on her lap but for the moment she was entranced and staring out the window. She had on her mind the events of the last couple of days since Roy was killed. She blinked when she heard the now very familiar sound of gunfire. Something she had only heard before the Outbreak in a movie or a video game was now a common real life occurrence. Calmly she set down her book and cup, went to the door, and pulled on her winter coat.

She opened the door, alert to any immediate attack. The biting cold smacked her in the face. She grabbed her rifle and scouted her immediate area. Not seeing any attackers or anything out of the ordinary, she stepped out on to her porch.

The whole street to the south of her house was chaotic. People were running here and there. She rushed down her porch steps onto the compacted snow and was nearly ran over by three men riding horseback.

Not only was the sound of the gunfire now increasing, but the sound of an explosion echoed through the valley. Hannah thought it sounded as if it had come from the front gate.

She wondered if the day had come. Lindsay had been feeding her regular updates but didn't have much to report each day. She thought it likely that it was happening now without warning. Much as she feared. She had said as much until she was called a nag. No extra precautions had been taken. It's was unfortunate for all of the townspeople that Henry and Childs wouldn't listen.

JT emerged out from between two buildings down by the corner from her house. He was sloven and disheveled. He didn't even have a weapon in his hand. It hurt her heart to see him fall apart so badly. After the gunshot wound she thought he would clean up his act. Instead he still drank but had more bouts of sobriety than not. This didn't look like one of them. Another explosion sounded off, a little closer this time.

"JT! Come on! Get inside!" Hannah ran over to him and guided him by his hand back to her house and ushered him in.

"What's going on?" JT said, his speech slightly slurred.

"If I had to guess, Gerard's people. Stay inside and out of sight. I'll come back for you here when I can."

She was going to go to the front gate. Along the way she would gather up as many people as she could to fight. She ran down the street without a glance back. Without warning she found herself with her ass in the snow, looking up at the clear blue sky. An explosion had rocked the ground, causing her to lose her footing. She scrambled up, mad her pants were now wet. She took off again towards the front gate. She rounded a corner in time to see a dump truck plow through the constructed wall like a child's toy crashing through a wall made out of toothpicks. Debris went flying everywhere. A few people along with it.

Hannah ducked down behind a pine tree, the only close cover. She took some shots at the dump truck. Bullets pinged off its metal side. Two small objects flew out of the back and then explosions went off around her.

"Holy shit!" she yelled out.

Bullets whined around her. She made herself as small as she could behind the tree. Snow was hanging in the area, obscuring a clear view around her. Damn these guys, why couldn't they just have left us alone.

That's all she wanted anymore. To be left alone. She let out a cry, ran from the tree to the closest building, firing shots until she was dry. She bared her teeth in a brutal grin as she saw one of the attackers go down.

"This looks like the post-post-apocalypse." Said a voice beside her. She spun to see JT, grinning like it was Christmas morning. He had one of the army bases assault rifles held against his chest.

"Jesus JT, you scared the shit out of me! That's a good way to get shot again. I thought I told you to stay back and wait for me!"

"Who are you my mom?" JT was practically dancing on the balls of his feet. JT popped around the corner, fired some shots, and popped back.

"Can you believe this shit?" he said.

Snow puffed up where JT had just been. Crystals danced in the air, sparking sunlight into tiny rainbows.

Hannah sighed. "JT, if we are going to do this, let's get focused. We have to take these bastards down before they kill all of us."

JT's exuberance went down a notch. "Shit, they've already got some of our people?"

Hannah nodded solemnly. Another explosion shook the area.

"We have to stop the dump truck first. It's the biggest threat."

"Hannah, I have a crazy idea. I'm sure you could pull off the shot. I'm going to get their attention. You flank them and get the driver."

"And get yourself killed, you maniac? What has gotten into you?"

"I'd do anything to protect you Hannah, you know that. It's just too bad we didn't find any bullet proof vests anywhere along the way. Now go!"

JT lept awkwardly across some snow drifts up to his knees, before making it into the clearer shoveled part. He fired his rifle the entire time, taking out two ski masked men who rounded the truck at the wrong time. "Wolverines!" he shouted.

Hannah's heart felt like it was going to hammer right out of her chest. All the attacker's attention went to JT. A few of the townspeople arrived and were following in JT's direction.

The truck backed up, crunching snow and debris in its wake. It straddled the road sideways now, giving Hannah a clearer shot into the cab. She didn't waste any time as she knelt, braced herself, aimed, and fired. Glass exploded and a bright red fountain squirted out of the driver's head, painting the cab's interior. The truck stopped. A grenade came flying in her direction. Hannah rolled, hugging her rifle tight to her body, praying to escape the blast. It landed far away from where she was, deep in a snow pile. A muffled bang and then a geyser of white powder rained down on her.

Taking rapid and shallow breaths, Hannah got back to her feet. She had lost her hat somewhere along the way and her ears now had a cold, burning sensation. She scanned the battle.

In the time it had taken her to get up, JT had pushed the former driver out and was now rocking the truck forward and backwards. Hannah saw a grenade fly up and fall back into the bed.

"JT!" she screamed, even though she knew she was too far away for him to hear. Seconds stretched out and then the grenade went off.

The whole entire back end of the truck lifted up into the air as the fuel ignited from the blast. Pieces of the truck went flying in multiple directions and rained down across attackers and defenders alike. Black smoke, thick as fog, rolled out in waves.

Hannah's eyes stung but now was not the time for tears. She raced to where the stunned forces of the town were regrouping outside a little local hotel. She found Josh in the group.

"That blast probably didn't get all of them. Are more people coming?"

Josh coughed and then moaned. He had nicks and scratches along his face and neck. "Child's got his guards with him so I think this is about it. I don't know why I came. I don't know what I expected myself to do down here."

Hannah spotted Gus. He must have seen her at the same time.He waved over to her and then pointed in the sky. Flying up from the acidic, sooty cloud was a bright red light.

"What you reckon that means?" Gus said, after he made his way to her side.

"Nothing good."

Figures came stumbling out of the smoke. Three, then four, then six. Two were standing near each other. One turned, shot the other then ran with a limp down the shoveled road into town.

"That's got to be JT!" Hannah shouted, incredulous. "Let's get out there and cover him!"

Hannah was already at a sprint, not waiting to see if she was followed. The others started shooting and Hannah fired back. One attacker fell, then another. She reached JT and took put his arm around her shoulder. Lindsay was right behind her and took the other. They pulled JT back while the others provided cover fire.

The first building they came to they had to stop to catch their breath.

"Damn it, JT. Scaring me again," Hannah said, punching him in the shoulder. "How did you make it out of there?"

JT was grinning again, like he hadn't almost gotten blown up. "I heard one of them say 'oh shit' right after slamming on the brakes, so I dove out the door and ran to the other side of the wall. I still about got shish kabobed by a piece of a muffler."

The tremendous sound of metal screeching against metal and the collision of large objects caused the three of them to turn in unison.

"You've got to be shitting me," Lindsay said, agasp. "They got another dump truck up here?"

It had backed in at what must have been its top speed. It splintered off more of the makeshift wall and broke the other smoldering dump truck in two. What had been a cacophony of chaos had fallen to a hush stillness as the town defenders wondered what was coming next. There was a whine and the dump truck's bed rose. It tipped up, spilling out its contents onto the now red and white snow.

Hannah inhaled sharply through her open mouth. "Am I seeing what I think I'm seeing?"

What the truck had dumped out were squirming and twisting to their collective feet.

"Guess we should be lucky it was only a medium sized dump truck or there would be even more zombies." JT said, sounding more sober.

The dump truck rolled forward, leaving its deadly cargo behind. A quick count by Hannah totaled about thirty zombies. There were eleven of them in the streets. She had fought with worse odds. The fortunate thing was there was distance between them. Then an idea occurred to her. What if they had done the same thing at the other end of town? Damn, they needed some way to communicate. She hated the thought of splitting her team up. Hated the thought of getting bitten in the back even more.

"Lindsay, take four people with you and check the other gate. Make sure they didn't pour some out there. If it's clear, you fly back here. We'll need you."

Lindsay said nothing. She nodded and crossed the street. She spoke to four others and they raced off through town.

RUMBLE

Hannah turned her attention to the remaining five people: Josh, JT, Gus and two others whom she didn't know.

"I'm guessing we have all had experience with these things so if we are careful, we will make it through this. We have space and they are slow. Let's team up in twos. JT, you wild man, you're with me."

"Ohhh, JT is in trouble," Gus teased. "He has to go sit by the teacher."

"I don't mind," JT gave a suggestive smile.

"Men, can't live with them, can't feed them to the zombies," Hannah said, straight faced.

"Hey," Gus said, indignant. "That's my catchphrase."

"We going to keep doing the comedy routine until we are bitten or are we going to kill some zombies?" Josh interrupted. "I'll try to help. I'm going to need a weapon."

Gus pulled out his hatchet and handed it over to Josh. "Like a good boy scout I'm always prepared." Josh looked at it was a sick grimace.

"Hey buddy," JT said. "It's okay. You won't even have to do anything unless we screw up and they get close. Just make sure none of them get us."

Gus gave Josh a slap on the back. Josh wrapped both hands around the handle and tried to look tough.

Hannah got serious again. "Two left, two right, two down the center, you guys hang back. Let's try not to have any friendly fire. Not sure how we are on ammunition, so make these shots count. Go!"

Hannah sped off with JT limping along beside her, keeping up as best he could. The silent mob ahead steadily came down the main street. The tall snow piles on either side was like fencing and it kept the zombies pinned in, herding them along like cows. That gave Hannah an idea.

"JT, speed's not your thing. See if you can get up on one of those snow piles. Should give you clearer shots at range."

"I will rain down death upon them, my captain." JT saluted.

Hannah sprinted and then ducked down in the front of an abandoned car not far from where the pack was forming up. She knelt, thinking how this place was lucky they had come here. Gerard's people probably thought this ploy would kill anyone remaining. Little did they know the experience a few of them had with zombies.

Reminding herself not to get to prideful, she took a deep breath, cleared her mind. She looked down the sight and pulled on the trigger in a smooth motion. The crack sounded and a zombie's head exploded. It's now motionless body dropped. The zombies behind it walked over the body like it wasn't even there.

Hannah felt creeped out by the zombies again. She could see there mouths working like always yet no sound came out. Then a Runner broke from the pack, straight towards her. The sound had attracted it, of course, her rifle had boomed in the enclosed space.

She heard firing from her left. Snow puffs danced around the Runners feet. She tried tracking it from her position. It moved, now booking down the cleared road. She scrambled to her feet.

Come on JT. Get it.

She started to jog backwards. Again a shot fired from her left. Again a miss. It was lunging at her now. Clumsily she jumped backwards, not that it would help much. This one could run faster than she could.

The Runner was about on top of her at a full speed charge. Then its body slammed to the right. It crashed into the side of a brick wall. JT had gotten it. It wasn't a head shot though. Hannah could see the star shaped hole in its side. One that didn't bleed. The zombie pushed off, stumbling. Hannah took three steps back and fired. There was no missing at that range.

During the fight with the Runner, the rest of the pack had advanced on JT's position. JT's must have missed several of his shots by the number of zombies still standing. The sound of him firing over and over again had attracted the zombies towards him.

Hannah wondered where the hell the others were. They should have been attacking the zombies flank by now. Then a horrible thought occurred to her. What if some of the wounded on both sides had gotten bit? Even now the zombies ranks could be swelling. The other two groups having to fight them off on the way to the main street. There wasn't much she could do right now. She prayed everyone would be okay.

Mindlessly the remaining zombies began pawing at the wall of snow in front of where JT was perched. JT scooted, trying to slide off the backside. Without warning the snow pack began to collapse. Hannah watched in horror as a jumble of snow, zombies, and JT spilled out into the street with a rumble and a scream of surprise.

Hannah cursed herself for not having a close combat weapon and rushed up the street. She didn't dare just start firing. She saw the other two teams rushing on her position, there was still four of them and they all looked okay. She had to bite her tongue from shouting out finally.

Instead she bellowed. "JT is in the middle of this mess. Go!"

Still a tumbling mass of white, with arms and legs sticking out of it, Hannah could not make out JT's position. She shot open the trunk of the next car she past, a Mazda 6. She rummaged inside for something, anything. She found one of those crappy jack handles that came with most newer cars. She decided it would have to do. Slinging her rifle on her back, she grabbed the handle with two hands, pointy side out and charged into the fray.

The sounds of battle surrounded her. Gus was yelling for JT. Lots of zombies now spread out instead of clumped together were getting to their feet. What some of them had left for feet anyway. She took the first two she came across by japing them point first through the eye with all her strength. When they dropped she took a quick look around. There was a small clump, rolling around on the ground directly to her right. She saw the flash of a blue coat. That had to be JT.

One zombie went flying up and crashing back down to the pavement. JT struggled up, a zombie on either side gnashing and clawing at him. One he smashed in the face with his rifle butt. It went down, jaw hanging by a few strands of muscle fiber now. JT spun and his attempts to hit the other zombie failed. The one he had thrown was getting back up.

It limped towards him. JT must have broken some bones in its back. JT's partner engaged it, kicking it in the face. The man slipped in the snow pile. The zombie he kicked got back up.

Hannah rushed the broken back zombie from behind. She gripped the handle of her rifle like a bat and swung hard. She sheared the rifle across the top portion of the zombies head. It went to one knee and two more whacks knocked its head wide open.

More zombies were encircling JT. He jammed his weapon right into the mouth of the one he missed earlier and pulled the trigger. Nothing happened. She had been afraid to fire into the mass earlier, unsure of where JT was. Now though, while the zombie was held still, Hannah took a shot. Brain matter flew through the air, some landing on JT's coat.

"You could have warned me," JT said. disgusted, when Hannah closed the distance between them.He wiped his face with his coat sleeve. His gun then went click click. "I'm out."

Zombies were still everywhere.

"Guess we do this the old fashioned way." Hannah handed over her tire iron and put her back to his.

They walked in a sidestep crab like way. Down the street, away from the other two teams. Hannah wanted to give them room to fire without worrying. Her and JT never initiated a fight. Instead they only took on any zombies that attacked them first.

A little girl zombie thing in a yellow sundress so faded it was almost white approached. Hannah took it out with one well placed shot. She then sent up a prayer, the child was with God now.

A middle aged man. Tall, bald with the skin on his scalp flapping open and closed with each step emerged out of the snow and was met with two whacks from JT's makeshift weapon.

Lindsay, her red hair a dead give away, was pounding pavement towards them, her dog Parka by her side. She took up a firing position at the end of downtown. She was yelling at them.

"The other wall was good. Guys get moving. I'll take out any that follow."

Hannah looked at JT. The zombies were thinning out around them.

"You going to be able to sprint? We need to get out of here before we accidently get shot."

"That far? Should be. Afterwords, I'll be lucky if I can walk."

Hannah broke off, putting all her energy into making her legs work as fast as possible. She figured it would be more helpful covering JT than trying to pull him along with her.

Hannah slid down in the snow when she reach Lindsay. She was back up in a kneeling position, tracking JT. Hannah squinted as the sun glinted off the ice and snow, the glare blocking some of her vision. He was hobbling and grimacing, pulling to the right as he ran.

He was clear within a few heartbeats. The remaining undead had turned towards the other two firing groups, who were dropping them quickly. A few minutes later, it was over. JT sat with his back to the hotel's wall, panting. He had his hands cupped around his knee.

"No more forty yard dashes for me." he hissed.

Hannah helped JT and the other others check among the people lying on the ground in the aftermath of the attack. JT was really limping. Hannah tried to talk him into sitting down but he refused until the job was done.

They were making sure the zombies were really dead and if any of the townspeople were hurt. Josh had found one of the townspeople, lying under some rubble of a collapsed wall with a faint heartbeat. Josh and a man named Colin made a makeshift carrier out of some bedsheets and took the wounded woman to the clinic. A man, the one who had been teamed up with Josh in the last battle, was holding the top of his arm. Blood was turning his light green coat a weird black color. He stumbled off towards the clinic as well. Hannah hoped he didn't have a zombie bite. She'd find out from Linda later.

She had sent Lindsay up to the hotel to check on Dr. Childs. She reported back that Dr. Childs was quite alright. No one had made an attempt to abduct him again during the confusion.

"Now maybe he can stop being useless." Was how Lindsay had put it.

Hannah thought Childs was going to have plenty to do for the next few days. There were lots of wounded at the main gate and wall. She prayed all of them could be healed and their suffering wouldn't last long. Satisfied she had done all she could where she was, Hannah broke away from them and walked to the wall.

The burning wreckage of the dump truck was still fouling the air. Its metal skeleton make Hannah think of a dinosaur exhibit. There were bodies everywhere. She began checking them. She could see the trauma from gunshot wounds, shrapnel and the evidence of being attacked by a zombie. She felt this was her responsibility.

Gus joined her."Some had been bitten and turned," Gus said, his mouth pulled when giving her the news.

She picked her way from the wall back towards town. Each body she checked was truly dead. She sent up a silent wish that the town could bounce back from this. Those who died, she prayed for any family or loved ones who would grieve for them. They were in a better place now, she was sure. All you had to do was look around to see the truth.

Closer to town, Hannah came across a woman who at first looked alive. She wiggled on the ground, with some nasty looking shrapnel protruding from her leg. She was flat on her back, looking up at Hannah. Hannah looked back gazing into her whited over eyes. Dead eyes.

The shrapnel wound had stopped bleeding. So did the ripped out chunk of her throat, where clearly a zombie had been at her. Hannah put her rifle to its head. She asked for God to welcome his child home and pulled the trigger.

She had no more tears left for the people she barely knew who had died in the attack. Her grieving of Tyrone,

Dusty, Alan and especially her Mom and Ashley, had burned them out. At least for the time being. She knew they would easily flow again if something were to happen to JT or Gus, even Linda. She continued across the town which had become an open grave.

Later, as drained and exhausted as she had ever felt, she sat on the couch in her home with JT. Her head was against his chest. She could hear his heart through the thick sweatshirt he was wearing. She was thinking about Ashley now and how JT was right, they were buried in the ground. It was wrong to bury them from our thoughts and feelings as well. All the death they had been a part of wasn't their fault. They were not bad people. They deserved to live and be happy. They owed it to the people they lost.

"You know, if Ashley was here, we would never hear the end of her whining. She was a summer girl, through and through. We spent just about every day of summer together growing up. This one time we were at the first summer camp I attended after my dad had died. Ashley never even knew her dad. He skipped out on her mom as soon as he found out she was pregnant. Her mom had boyfriends as Ashley got older, none ever stuck around. Anyway we were silly girls, teenagers. We would talk about our crushes. Ashley's big one was Jesse McCartney. Guess I had a thing for older guys even then as I loved Leo. Something else we would talk about, in secret whispers...we would talk about who we would want as our new dads."

"Who's your Daddy?" JT interjected with a terribly put on accent.

Hannah gave him a sour look. "JT, I'm trying to be serious here. I've never told anyone this before."

"Sorry, sorry," he said, looking like he genuinely meant it. "It's a reflex. People set them up, I knock them down. Go ahead, I'm listening."

"Ok. Even though, now that I'm saying it out loud, it sounds pathetic."

"No, I can understand it. Your dad sounded like a cool guy. Ashley, well that's too bad of course. Girl didn't have an easy life and a hell of a death but at least she had you."

Hannah smiled up before continuing. "I use to always pick Danny Tanner. My Dad was a listener like him, even though he could be a lot tougher at times. Ashley would flop between Dan from Roseanne or Sandy Cohen from the OC. She would either want a friend Dad or one who would tell her the right thing to do. I would tease her about it all the time. Even if Sandy told her, she wouldn't do it. She would do the opposite. Kind of mean now that I think back. We were like sisters though."

JT didn't reply, he just held her. She was happy being there. She didn't know how long they sat. She watched the fire crackle across the room. The flames doing a hypnotic dance. She twitched a small amount when JT spoke up again.

"What do you think will happen now?"

Hannah reflected on the question. "There is a good thing going on here. I see that now. I think we help rebuild. Whoever attacked us, we spanked them good...twice. I don't think they will be back. Isn't it nuts they followed us all the way up here in the first place?"

"Sure would have been back in the old world. Now?" She felt JT shrug. "So you do think it's a good thing, this group?"

To Hannah it sounded like a charged question. She sat back up. There was a knock at the door before she could ask him what he meant. It was Josh standing on her porch.

"Oh, JT is here," Josh's eyes opened wide and he adjusted his glasses up. "Dr. Childs wants you two to come up to the clinic tomorrow. He was surprised you didn't come straight there, after, you know."

"Why?" JT asked, coming up behind her. "We were a little tired after, you know, saving his ass."

Hannah gave him a soft elbow to the ribs. "Josh, what does he want?"

"He just told me he would like to check you both over. Make sure you are okay. A complete physical. Since JT is here, I guess I don't have to go over to his house now."

Josh left without another word, turning around once to give Hannah what she couldn't mistake as a look of longing mixed with anger. She hoped JT didn't see it. He was calm now, the anger didn't need to be stirred over nothing. After the day she had, she certainly didn't want to have to deal with two guys puffing out their chests at each other on her front porch.

"Well, I guess I better take off too," JT said, sliding by her. "It was nice tonight Hannah, just sitting and talking. I missed more than I realized. And I missed you. We need to start hanging out again. See you around tomorrow?"

Hannah watched JT lurch down the stairs favoring his knee and closed the door amid a flurry of second thoughts. Those thoughts quickly got the better of her as she opened the door back up. She was surprised to see JT standing there still seemingly staring up into the starry night sky.

"Did you forget where you live?" She joked.

"Nope, just taking a moment and thinking about Red Dawn and Randall." JT was straight with his answer. He pulled a DVD case out of his coat pocket and twirled it.

Hannah let out a giggle at his reply, unsure of what it even meant. Must have been some inside joke. She didn't think JT and Randall even got along.

"The Sheriff was right about a lot of things, some I didn't even give him credit for. But, I'm realizing it now." JT seemed self assured in his comment.

"Well how about you come back, I can make us coffee or cocoa and we can talk about it if you want, I will even rub your knee for you." Hannah said smiling.

"Well that is an amazing offer but I don't think I would be able to walk home after a knee rub so may..." JT didn't get to finish as he was interrupted by Hannah.

"Well then it's a good thing I don't want you to leave tonight." Hannah said trying to conceal the smile she felt as she opened the door wide and JT came back in and hugged her.

BREAK THE CHAIN

Hannah was the first to awake early the next morning. Even she had to admit to herself it felt good to wake up in JT's arms. So why did a creeping feeling of regret waiting to sneak back in?

Even though nothing more than cuddling happened she felt like maybe she was leading JT on too soon or worse, that he was playing on her emotions to reignite the feelings they once seemed to feel for each other.

After letting herself dwell long enough Hannah opted to slip out before JT woke and eased herself from the warm embrace of his arms. JT groggily protested before falling back asleep long enough for Hannah to dress and sneak out to go check on how things were around town in the daylight. It was crazy to think about the attack. What happened to people since The Outbreak? Or did the virus kill most of the decent people, leaving the crazies to inherit the Earth? Hannah didn't know so she just said her morning prayers and left it up to God.

Hannah ran into Lindsay a short ways down the road, she was out taking Parka for a walk.

"So, I heard you and JT might've spent the night together." Lindsay smirked at Hannah.

"And how did you hear that news? Is this the small town gossip cliche in action?" Hannah was more amused than anything. "I'm sure our night was less entertaining than the one you spent at his house." Hannah reminded herself to turn down the anger level.

"Whoa! Hey babe, don't get me wrong, after everything you guys have been through I'm sure you need any release you can get." Lindsay said, brushing off the rising tension with a smile. "TTFN!" She led her dog Parka off.

Hannah had to admit Lindsay was pretty cool. She could tell at that moment she was going to like her. As Hannah walked on towards where the main street massacre occurred she kept thinking back and forth about JT and all of the what ifs and what could be. Her mind studied the details of all the people and situations that had got them to this point and more importantly kept them alive.

WRECKAGE

JT was a little sore in the feelings department after waking up alone in Hannah's bed. He felt almost as bad now as he half heartedly picked through the wreckage. It was the only way to describe how the front of the town looked now after the bombing. Wreckage. The wall was all but gone, along with most of the houses near it.

JT towed some charred wood behind him as he debated with himself about what to do next with Hannah, with the town. And what the hell was he going to do about Lindsay?

Damn, maybe Dusty was right all along. Every time we meet up with or joined someone, tried to make a stand in one place, terrible shit happened. Still same shit different day.

Between his body aching this morning along with confusing thoughts of Hannah after yesterday, he felt the nagging need for a drink.

Damn! No, no, no. He kind of sang the words in his head as a distraction.

He toiled a long time. He felt the dull ache still in his shoulder area from being shot, along with the never ceasing pain in his knee, both irritating, constant reminders of what a few drinks could erase.

Yet even with these distractions he still came back to his mixed feelings for Hannah. After getting home from her place that morning he poured himself a drink. Then he would think about how nice it was to hold her. To listen to her voice, softer than he had heard it in months, tell him about her past. To trust him. Then the drink went down the sink. He must have done it five times. After the last time, he threw the bottle across the room where it shattered, stalked out the door, and walked a couple laps around town before stepping in to help with the clean up process.

Lindsay came bounding over as he threw the wood into the back of a truck. Her red hair, in dual ponytails again today, stood out against the white snow. It was like watching a rose bloom in winter. She stood out in a pleasant way, unlike all the blood and body parts smeared and scattered amidst the stained snow. Not that you could tell the horrific aftermath of the battle had effected Lindsay in the slightest.

"JT," She called out cheerfully. "I've been looking everywhere for you."

"Why's that?" JT grunted, throwing the last of the buildings remains into the truck. He clapped his black gloved hands to clear off the ash and dirt.

"I wanted to make sure you were okay, silly."

"I'm still alive," JT said, trudging back over to the blast site. Someone passed him going the other way, a wheelbarrow full of debris. JT threw him a jealous glare. *I need to get me one of those.*

"So am I, thanks for noticing," Lindsay said as she followed him. "Shit aren't you the Grinch this morning."

"Look around." JT waved his hands dramatically.

"Yeah but we're okay, aren't we?"

Not answering, JT looked around for where he could pitch in next. He happened to notice Hannah rounding the corner with Josh and their eyes locked. She shook her head, her mouth down turned and went back to work.

"My head's not in a good place right now Lindsay, maybe we can talk some other time."

"I guess so. If you want to cheer up, come over when you are done here. I have a sexy little number I wouldn't mind showing you." She grinned and then walked away. More like slinked away. JT appreciated the attempt but felt nothing. It was strange to be so empty. He was use to his head being like a swarm of bees.

He worked away until his muscles trembled and ached. His eyes stung. It was a struggle to keep them open. He was thinking of headed back to his place, open up the Pinot Noir he had found in the wreckage, and just go to sleep. Forget Hannah, forget Lindsay, forget life for now. As dusk came the others peeled away until it was just JT and Josh.

"Hey man, I'm knocking off." JT raised a hand to Josh.

Josh shot him a salute. "Thanks for the help."

That Josh seems like a cool cat. Any jealousy he might have felt towards Josh wasn't there anymore. JT shuffled through the streets, bottle in hand, towards his house. *Seems I can't give this shit up after all. How pathetic.*

He stopped, not even waiting to get home. He screwed the top off the wine and took a big swig. He let the bottle drop to the snow when it was half empty. He reached into his coat pocket.

JT stared at the *Red Dawn* DVD in his hands. How many more chances would he be given to realize he was on a path of self destruction?

He listed a little as he took his next step. As he righted himself he heard a noise. It was a thump from the alleyway to his right. He looked, blurry eyed. A zombie bounced off a brick wall and trundled towards him. JT was sure he recognized him as one of the townspeople. He had a moment to think *not again* and tried to back pedal. The street slipped beneath his shoes. The zombie slammed into him. That's all it took to dump him on his ass.

The ice slicked snow skidded him a few feet away from the zombies biting teeth. His DVD slid out of his hands. He tried to scramble away. The zombie, a full grown and athletic man in his life, scrambled after him. It grabbed JT's boot. JT kicked at it. His boot glanced off its shoulder. With a lunge the zombie man landed on JT's legs. Fear burned away his buzz. He reached out for something, anything, to help him. His hand fumbled with something slick. For a split second he turned his hand to look at it. It was the DVD he dropped. Letting out a war cry, JT jammed the case with all his might into the zombie's open mouth.

The case shattered and broken bits of black and silver poked through the zombies gums and lips. JT was sure it let out a silent roar. With only a second to act JT willed his aching legs to push up. He got the zombie turned over and kneed it in the chest. His knee sank into its chest cavity. JT felt the wetness soak into his pants and his stomach churned. Able to push up into a standing position, JT stood over the squirming zombie man. It reached out its hands up to the sky. JT brought down his boot. The sickening crunch brought a twisted smile to his face. He stomped until what was its head became an indiscernible brown and red smear.

JT stopped. He put his hands on his knees, panting. Plumes of steam rose past his eyes. *That was way to close.* He could see the torn cover of *Red Dawn* flapping in the breeze under the zombie's leg.

"Wolverines bitch," he said, breathless. "Fucking Randall." JT howled with laughter until he got a stitch in his side.

He was done getting wasted. If he thought he had a death wish, he saw now he was mistaken. The path he was on, it wasn't going to help Tyrone. It sure wasn't helping to repair his relationship with Hannah. In fact if he died it would devastate her.

Instead of heading straight home, he pushed himself to go over to Gus's place. Enough was enough. It was time for some help. He knocked on Gus's door. It was a few moments before it was answered.

"Well, it's JT," Gus said. "Come inside, you look like a frozen turd."

"Gus."

JT stepped inside, peeled off his winter gear, and hung it up. JT thought Gus was looking the best he had since they first met. Staying here had helped him recover.

"JT, all I ever see you with anymore is a long face. Even when you have Lindsay following you around like a lost puppy. That would put a smile on most men's faces."

"Well..." JT started. "I'm here to talk-"

"Sit down, JT. I'm gonna guess you're not asking advice about what to do in the sack to make a woman scream. This is going to be serious."

JT just launched right into it.

"How do you do it, Gus?"

"TMA remember? I just got it."

"See, that's what I mean," JT was looking down at his lap, picking at the grime on his pants. "Is it possible that I'm broken?"

"You mean gone off the deep end? Nuttier than a Chippendale review? Nah, I don't think so. Damn it, between you and Hannah I don't know who throws themselves on the sword more. We goof about the old man stuff even though I'm only in my fifties, I've seen more than you two put together. Been through a lot of shit. I think you just got to stick to who you are. Who you are, got it?" Gus jabbed him in the chest for effect. "The rest, what others think you should be, I laugh that nonsense off. From what I've seen it doesn't pay to be too serious. Look where acting like we're all the king dingalings got us."

JT admitted what he feared and could only get it out in a whisper. "What if I don't like who I am? I've done some fucked up things..."

Gus seemed to mull it over before answering. "If we are getting down to brass tacks, then let's. What is this really about? Killing zombies? The accident with the little girl? Harold? Albright? Hannah?"

"Yeah," said JT, speaking a little louder now. "All of it. I blame them, then I blame Hannah, then I blame myself. Because I realize it's all my fault. I was in charge. They listened to me. Then, for it to be over between me and Hannah, before it could even start. I don't know, listen to me."

"Whew son, no wonder you've picked up the bottle. This is heavy. Since you came to me though, I know there is hope for you yet. Are you a good person? Look at what you are doing to yourself. Look at what you are asking me. I think you are but I can't tell you that in a way you'll believe. Neither can Hannah or Lindsay for that matter. Do I think you are flawed as shit? Of course. Aren't we all. I have seen you change even if you haven't. Some good ways and other ways not so much. You have also been pushed farther than most men will in their lives, in the span of what ten months?"

"Doctor Gus," JT joked.

"Put me up there with Dr. Ruth and Dr. Phil," Gus reached over and clapped JT on the top of the shoulder. "JT, set it all down. That's as deep as I get. Honestly, I would have thought getting shot would have woke you up."

"Gus, you know I'm not the sharpest tool in the shed." He gave Gus a crooked grin. "Thanks. I mean that. I feel a little better."

"Just wait until you see my bill young squire. Now get the hell outta here, before you drive me to drinkin."

RECONCILIATION

Hannah was going over some proposals she was going to give to the townspeople tomorrow. Funny how in such a short time she went from wanting nothing to do with anybody outside her little group of four, to joining and being responsible for a whole town. The cowardly absence of Childs had somehow elected her to be in charge. Even though Childs was holed up somewhere and he still held meetings with Henry. Henry wasn't allowed to give his location until Childs decided to come out of his hiding place. Hannah was surprised that Henry was working alongside both of them trying to find ways not only to fix things but to improve them. He was a much better man than his son. That fact made her feel even more sorry for him.

She found it funny this new responsibility gave her a feeling of peace. One that she had been searching for. A deep settling of acceptance had come over her, letting her work through her guilt. The past was the past and she was now on the right path. It was a feeling that was fleeting and fragile in the days after the town was attacked. Now it was a solid foundation.

She had found real, true safety in herself. Along with personal forgiveness. She felt God already had forgiven her. She worked through her feelings about Ashley, Albright. Tyrone was the sticking point for her. Sometimes she awoke from nightmares about being pushed down stairs or from buildings. She was often the one being pushed but once in awhile she would be the one doing the pushing and would awake from those with a startled cry.

Still, here she was, maybe a week after the big attack, helping to run Beaver Creek. Several people had demanded it in the aftermath. Apparently she was considered a hero. There was even her nickname some wise ass, probably Gus, had started. Hannah the Hero. JT often joked when he saw her, "Coming up next on Disney, Hannah The Hero!"

After she was elected, she guessed you could call it that, everyone got busy with clean up. Morale was recovering as those people with losses buried their dead and the grieving began. One of her first acts was to hold a prayer vigil at the little church in town. It had been full, a turn out that surprised her. Even more surprising was that fact that JT was there to support her. Calm is how she would describe the towns mood now. Just like hers.

A knock at her door caused her to spring from her kitchen table. "JT," she said, surprised.

She had seen him around of course, after the night they had spent together at her place. After the attack, he had thrown himself full steam ahead into the clean up. He looked good, happy, every time she saw him working. He would always give her a smile and go right back at it, not waiting to see what her reply would be. He looked sober now, standing in the doorway. He stood tall, he had even trimmed his beard and mustache. A little smile played at his lips. His hair waved in the breeze, which was now down past his collar in the back.

"You're looking better," Hannah said, and she meant it. "I've seen you around, working hard. Thanks for pitching in."

JT laughed. "I didn't come to see Hannah the councilwoman or Hannah the Hero. Can I come inside?"

She pitched her door open wide and he came in. She couldn't help herself, she took a deep breath of him as he passed. He smelled clean. She hoped it wasn't obvious what she was doing. She knew his pride was prickly. She invited him to sit down at the kitchen table, where she had been working.

"Hannah the politician," JT teased, glancing over the scattered papers. "Nothing top secret I shouldn't look at in there?"

"JT, always joking around," Hannah said, settling in across from him.

"I haven't seen much of you lately. This running the place stuff must be keeping you busy."

"Yes, it does. Who would have thought, huh? It's not like I was in school for anything like this. My major was in Athletic Training."

"It doesn't surprise me. Not after all you've done," JT said, a cheesy smile spread across his face. "Not easy though is it?"

Hannah felt a little warmness spread across her cheeks.

JT got serious now. "What do you do, for strength? For the pain caused of bad decisions?"

"Prayer," she answered without hesitation.

"Prayer," JT gave a little ha deep in his throat. "Guess that's healthier than what I've been doing."

There was silence for a long moment as JT studied her. She gazed back, wondering where this conversation was heading.

"I thought things might start working between us. After I got shot. Except for a small one here and there, that is when I pretty much stopped drinking. I honestly think now it was going to get me killed. I didn't stop thinking about it all the time though. Not even then. Now, I have. I'm sorry about what I put you through."

Hannah cocked her head to the side. "You have come to find me, now that you're sober." A smile played on her lips.

"Just like that song." Again he let out a small deep throated laugh. "I'm sure Tyrone would sing it to us, if he was here."

"I'm sure," she agreed in a small voice.

"We should talk about him. We should talk about all of them. Dusty, Ashley, Alan, Randall. I've done nothing but think once I stopped shutting down the voices in my head. That's when I decided I should stop treating them like things, like mistakes. They were people. I did the best I could and neither one of us were to blame. We should celebrate their lives, not their deaths. That is what gave me strength.

What gives it to me now. And not wanting to waste any more time with you." JT was struggling to hold his composure now.

"Excuse me?" Hannah shot back.

"Damn that came out wrong. You know what I mean. "

She watched him squirm, trying not to enjoy it too much, then let him off the hook.

"Yes I do. I find myself at odd times thinking about you. How we first met, the few times I felt safe after the Outbreak were mostly with you. I've been able to move on from most of what happened as well. It wasn't easy."

"No, it sure isn't. Working myself to exhaustion helped the first week. Made myself too tired to even want to do anything but go straight to bed. Guess I have the dickweeds who attacked us to thank for that."

Hannah rubbed her hands together and rubbed them on her pants down the top of her thighs.

"So what is it you have in mind, JT? Wait, before that, what about Lindsay?"

"Lindsay by her own admission isn't looking for anything serious from anyone. Look, she is fun, smart, pretty but she's not you. I haven't seen her in two weeks if that tells you anything. I'll tell her no more...well you know. She might not be happy about it but I don't think there will be any drama. What about you. I've seen you hanging around with Josh a lot."

"He might want to but I've been very clear with him, we're just friends."

JT pursed his lips, then continued. "Okay. You're other question, what do I have in mind? How about we try officially dating?"

Hannah burst out laughing. "Officially dating? As in you will pick me up in your car at six and we will go have dinner then go to the movies?"

"How about on horseback then we can go have Spam from a can by candlelight. From there we can go straight into frisky time."

They both had a good long laugh at the thought.

"JT, seriously, if we were going to try being a normal couple, I think we can skip the dating with all we've been through. I don't know though, we have both said some pretty hurtful things to each other."

"With my big mouth, probably won't be the last time either," JT said squinting his eyes. "I'm going to try to be more honest going forward."

Hannah sat there, pondering it. Her feelings never went away completely. She couldn't deny it.

"You know, I'm so proud you've worked through this thing, with the drinking. I will give you all the support I can, even if we end up just friends because you know, I can't fix you."

"I know that now." JT was humble in his reply.

Hannah chewed at her bottom lip. What if she did something again he hated her for? She didn't want to be vulnerable again. She was frightened by how she felt as she watched him, bleeding, on that hospital bed. The thought of losing him had been tremendous.

"Let me think about it?" Hannah timidly asked.

She saw a flash in his eyes that looked as if he wanted to say more. She braced herself as if a sudden storm was brewing. Instead he calmly stood up.

"Me springing this on you, that's fair." JT swallowed hard and took a deep breath. His body shook a little bit. "No matter what Hannah, I love you." Hannah could see his cheeks flush with the words.

He turned and walked to the door. He reached for it when she called out to him.

"JT. Wait."

She rushed over to him, put her hands over his shoulders, clasped them at the back of his neck and kissed him deep. He was tight, in shock at first, then eased.

"Nice." he said when they parted.

"That's my answer," she said, standing up on her tiptoes to reach for his lips again. There was no surprise in his reaction this time as the sparks flew and JT flashed back to their first kiss back at Harold's.

When they broke their embrace JT couldn't wipe the smile from his face as he backed onto the porch then stopped.

"So just to be clear, was that a yes or a no?" He mocked Hannah as she jumped in his arms for one long kiss goodnight before JT made his way off the porch and into the night.

BREAKING UP IS HARD TO DO

It was tough to cool his jets once Hannah was kissing him but he did eventually leave. It went a lot better than he could have thought. It was like a boulder had been rolled off of his chest. He didn't know now if he wanted to go see Gus, see Lindsay or just go home. He didn't have to decide as he ran into Gus.

"You look like you're floating inches above the ground boy. You get lucky with Lindsay?" Gus said.

"No," JT chuckled. "It's Hannah. Gus, I got to thank you again. I had my head up my ass for too long. Hannah and I just had the best moment in months."

"No it was stuck at the bottom of a bottle you dipshit," Gus was playfully angry. "Nice to see you looking forward instead of behind you at your ass. So when's the wedding?" Gus cackled and held his belly. JT just shook his head.

"Why do I even try," JT said, grinning broadly.

"Hell, you know I'm happy for your buddy. I'm here for you too. There is no need to go all John Wayne and keep all that shit to yourself. Next time you're feeling sorry for yourself, come my way. I'll slap some sense into you. Or the bottle outta your hand."

"Sure you don't want to open a practice, Gus?"

"There is only one thing I like to open." Gus made a gesture like he was parting something and then stuck out his tongue like he was licking an ice cream cone.

"You're disgusting."

"That's not what she said. It was more like 'oh, don't stop'."

They both were wailing now. Someone walked by and looked at them like they were crazy. Maybe they were. When they stopped JT's face hurt. He realized then what he had been missing out on. How good he could feel. He was lucky to be alive he realized, he should enjoy it.

"I'm happy for you boy. I always thought you and Hannah should be together. Don't screw it up this time, either of you. I don't think my old heart could take it. Guess that means your fun days with Lindsay are done for."

"Yes, sir. I'll tell her tonight. Not that I've seen much of her lately anyway."

"Be straight and be nice about it. Lindsay, I like her too. I better get my butt in gear. Linda gave me a honey do list. You know we're back on the brink of civilization now. The women are back in charge again."

Gus continued on his way. JT thought he might as well track Lindsay down now and get it over with. He liked her lots, she was a cool person, and hoped this wouldn't hurt her too bad.

After looking around and asking a couple of people, he found her at the makeshift guard shack, build quickly while repairs were being made on the front gate. The dump truck still sat where it was left right after the attacks, on the other side of the hole it had made. She looked bored as she sat there, staring off, absently petting her husky who was at her side. She brightened up when she saw JT. JT had a sudden bubbling in his stomach.

Several people were up on ladders of varying heights, hammering away at the wall even this late with such little light. Their work ethic didn't seem to even quiver. Henry was there as well, walking back and forth, inspecting it. JT hoped he could get Lindsay away from the crowd.

"JT, come to relieve me?" Lindsay said, a little breathy.

JT smiled. "I was wondering, if you could get away from here for a few minutes. I wanted to talk to you, with some more privacy than this." He had to speak up over the noise.

"With this many people here, I'm not even sure why the hell I'm here. Come on, Parka."

They walked off, the frozen snow crunching under their footsteps. Parka bounded along beside Lindsay, tongue hanging out the side.

"Let me guess, it's bad news," Lindsay started before JT could even begin.

"Why do you say that?"

"I've seen enough chick flicks to know a guy only comes to a woman like you just did for two reasons. I don't see you getting down on one knee and whipping out a ring."

JT sighed. "You're right. I'll just come right out. Hannah and I are getting back together."

Lindsay side glanced at JT then looked down at her dog. "I kinda guessed that's what it was going to be. I haven't seen such a bounce in your step since the first night we hooked up. JT you're a good guy. We had some fun. I wasn't looking for anything, yet I was starting to feel like maybe you were the person I would change my mind for. Oh well, I guess it's not meant to be."

"I'm sorry," JT said, feeling lame for saying such an empty statement. What the hell was he supposed to say?

"JT, don't start being lame now," Lindsay said, mockingly. "If you start saying things like' I'm a wonderful girl' or 'some guy will be lucky someday', I'm going to take this rifle and shoot you. You remember what that feels like right?"

JT put his hands up in a gesture of surrender. "Okay, okay, I got it. Friends?"

"You tell your princess I expect to hang with you still, jealousy free. No drama."

JT nodded. "No drama."

"I better get back. Good luck with Hannah...but JT if things don't work out, come find me."

She turned and headed back. JT stood there until she rounded out of sight. He could tell she tried to mask wiping at her face. Still, he thought things would be okay between them.

Feeling drained, JT headed for home. For the first time in awhile he didn't feel like he needed a drink. Or to vent some deep rage. He felt like he was back in the driver's seat of his own vices.

JT happened by the clinic after another busy day of restoration duties. He wanted to visit with Gus and let him know how things had gone with Lindsay. As he neared the front of the clinic he saw Linda outside, she gave him the friendliest wave JT could recall her ever giving him.

"I seem to of heard some good news about you and Hannah, Mr. JT." Linda said with a proud mama like smile.

"Gus has been spreading the news has he? That old man gossips like an old woman!" JT found his own comment hilarious.

"No sir, not Gus this time. Hannah herself, she's inside with Gus now visiting."

JT became sheepish with embarrassment.

"Well don't blush now," Linda said, "get in there and see your girl."

JT entered to find Gus and Hannah sitting in rocking chairs near the fireplace.

"Well hello, Romeo!" Gus called out with an over zealous tip of his hat. "Pull yourself up a chair."

Before JT had a chance to react Hannah stood to greet him with a kiss.

"Awe shucks, aren't you two just sweeter than my MeMe's strawberry pie." Gus ribbed.

"Gustafson Theodore Wright! You best not be poking fun at these two kids of yours or you will be going to bed tonight without your supper!" Linda jokingly barked as she entered the room.

"Gustafson!?" Hannah teased.

"Theodore!?" JT chimed in on the action.

"Well would you look at that. We can embarrass Gus!" Hannah continued as Gus tried to hide his now red face behind his hand.

"Well in my defense please take note of my perfect last name. You can all feel free to call me Mr. Wright whenever you would like." Gus's comeback brought the whole room into uproarious laughter.

From there the four of them sat and chatted about a little bit of everything. Mainly about the big town council meeting coming tomorrow. It wasn't long before Hannah announced she needed to go home and get some things in order and then hopefully relax a little before the meeting tomorrow, which promised to take up most of her day.

JT offered to walk her home and she gladly accepted, they said their goodbyes and left holding hands the entire way to Hannah's.

Back at Hannah's, JT mostly kept her company while she worked on preparing things for the next day. At one point he forced her to take break and made her a simple dinner of rice and beans over the fire. He even gave her a much needed shoulder massage before she convinced him to let her get back to work.

JT sat across from Hannah now. Out of the blue he got up and went into the kitchen. When he returned he threw a dried bean at her. She looked up at him with a tempting stare and went back to writing on her notes. JT threw another.

"JT!" Was her only reaction.

On his third attempt to get her attention he threw an entire handful of beans at her.

"Oh my God, that's it!" Hannah shouted as she jumped to her feet.

JT took off running around the house, tossing more beans from his other hand at her as she chased him. She cornered him in the bedroom. He tried to jump over the bed and hit his shin on the protruding footboard. Hannah pounced on her injured prey and the two started wrestling around the bed, tickling and playfully hitting each other. When Hannah attempted to give him a wet willie he grabbed her hands, spun around on top of her, and pinned them to the bed.

Feeling overcome he dove down and kissed her, there was no resistance from Hannah whatsoever. JT left her lips and began kissing her neck, his hands found the hem of her hoodie and he slid his hand under her shirt with no protest. JT felt like maybe he was getting too carried away as they had never been this far before and pulled back.

"Wait, what? What's wrong, JT?" Hannah breathlessly asked.

"I just didn't want to be too aggressive or anything because-."

"Don't finish that sentence." Hannah was stern. She responded by grabbing the bottom of his shirt and helping him guide it over his head before taking hers off in turn.

JT was stunned at how good she looked laying there topless and returned to kissing her, their hands wandering all over each others bodies. JT shivered with anticipation as his hands began to work down her purple leggings. Hannah now completely naked under JT pushed at the waist of his sweats, JT stood up and pulled down his sweats and boxers exposing his now rigid self to her.

Neither of them could deny the electricity between them and their naked bodies making out in the middle of the bed. JT could feel Hannah's readiness as she arched her hips to allow him to enter her.

Hannah couldn't believe her self confidence or how good it felt with every thrust JT gave her, right now it was her and him, no zombies, no cabins, no churches, no anything but the two of them and it felt incredible.

The next morning Hannah woke up feeling better than she had in what felt like years. She had never had sex like the kind her and JT had last night, it was probably a culmination of massive amounts of stress but the release was indescribable. She felt like she was walking on sunshine.

Hannah was in the living room when JT awoke. She was fumbling with some papers, stacking them up neatly wearing only JT's shirt. When JT entered the room and saw her he felt like seeing his shirt on her was like seeing your armies flag on a conquered castle.

He couldn't stifle his excitement as he walked over and wrapped his arms around Hannah from behind, spinning her around to kiss her before carrying her back to the bedroom and making love to her again, this time just as fiery as their previous encounter.

After round two Hannah had to convince JT to let her get up and get ready for the council meeting. He eventually agreed and helped her prepare before he ran to his place and grabbed his bag of clothes to bring back go Hannah's before heading to the meeting himself.

DEAD OF WINTER

AVALANCHE

"We're getting deep into the winter season now but we need to start thinking ahead to spring." Henry was standing at the end of the rectangular brown table. At the other end sat Dr. Childs, who had emerged from hiding when he wasn't at the clinic, surrounded by at least ten armed people. In between the two, all on one side of the table, were Hannah, Josh, and Bruce.

They were inside one of the conference rooms of the casino. This is where they always held their council meetings. Henry didn't want to run the power in the casino for this, so several battery powered lamps were lined down the table, casting harsh shadows on the wall.

"Our stores will last until then by my calculations, as long as we get no sudden influx of a large group of people," Henry continued.

"I wouldn't put money on that happening. By now all the roads have got to be nearly impassable," Bruce spoke in his squeaky voice. He was a small, round man with a tiny nose and tiny lips.

"Let's not count on it thought," Hannah interrupted. "We've been surprised before. If people are desperate enough, they will find a way to get things done."

Childs glared at her but she ignored it. Childs had become increasingly belligerent towards her as the meeting went on. It had to be jealousy, since she had become so revered by the town. He acted like that way to most of them, but she got the brunt of it. She had no desire to be the head of this place but she did want to help.

It was funny, this talk of spring. The snows had been coming on strong in the past week. Eight inches had just been dumped on them yesterday. Cold, sub zero temperatures, too. She thought two degrees above absolute zero was about right. It was hard to even imagine spring coming.

"Henry, I didn't know you were in charge of agriculture as well," Dr. Childs said, in a reproachful way.

"I have been checking in on every part of the town's functions. As I would have thought any of us would be." Henry sounded as hard as iron.

Dr. Childs rubbed his eyes. "I've been a little busy these past few weeks. I didn't think training farmers and planting crops was a high priority right now. Not when I still have patients in the clinic who may never walk or have use of their arms again. On top of that, a nasty cold virus is going around."

"Don't think we aren't grateful for all you have done, Doctor," Josh said.

"I was just bringing up a point that should be on the horizon," Henry said. Hannah could still tell there was animosity there, even though Childs wasn't responsible for what happened to his son. "Food and shelter is up there in importance with health. No food, then you won't have any patients, Doc."

"What are you suggesting Henry?" Josh said, trying to soothe the bickering. "Planting would have to wait, if we can find anyone who even knows how to do it. There's like a foot of snow right now. How about hunting? We can do that. We have one of the finest shots in town right here." He thumbed towards Hannah. She blushed.

"Meat will be the first thing to go bad," Henry nodded in agreeance. "Even in cold storage I wouldn't trust what we have much longer. That would be a good idea. Hannah, you think you could find a few people and lead some hunts. Maybe even combine hunting with the exploration teams?"

"JT and myself, we could do it. We're about the only ones who drill ourselves everyday." She smiled. She was beyond happy JT and her were together now. She felt like this goofy smile was never far from her face now."I could find another one or two people."

"Good," Henry said. "We will let you know when we decide to go that route. We will need a team to go get some canned fruits and vegetables as soon as there is a break in the weather."

"Can we move on to something else now please? Like our medical supply situation, which is important too you know. A party will have to go out soon. Weather be damned. I am running low on some important meds. Those ignorant fucks with the dump truck really screwed my clinic up."

Hannah found herself rubbing her temples again. In the first few days after the attack, the community had come together. Childs was so busy treating the wounded and then hiding that he missed several meetings. When he was at work, he was fine. Outside of the clinic he acted more whiney and jealous, like he was now. Now that the threat was over, the people were falling into their old patterns again. She had heard from Josh that Childs and Henry butted heads all the time before she got here.

She questioned if it was a good idea to even be on this council. She thought it would be a way to have some control over what happened to her. If she couldn't leave now then at least she would have some say. That was not how things were working out though. What would happened as the community got even bigger? Someone calling her name snapped her out of her thoughts.

"Hannah, are you with us?" Henry asked.

Hannah shook her head dramatically. "Oh sorry, spaced off there. What were you asking me?"

"Update on the repairs and security?"

"I would say two days then the front gate area will be done. Unless weather turns even worse. Won't hold off anyone with a dump truck," she joked, trying to lighten the mood. She got nothing but stony faces staring back at her. "That reminds me. I've had several people ask me if they can take from houses or businesses that no one is living in right now to fix up their homes. I told them all that would be a council decision."

"Good for you," Bruce complimented her. "We can't have people just taking things apart without some direction or set of rules. What do you think, Henry?"

It went on, back and forth between them. Hannah tried to pay attention. She would have fail a test of what was said. At the end of the discussion, nothing was resolved. "Hannah, for any who ask, tell them to hold tight," Henry said. "When the council decides how to handle it, they'll be informed."

There were a few others things and then the gavel dropped. She got up, stretched, and then put on her parka over the hoodie she was already wearing, over the top of the two layers of clothes beneath. When she was all bundled up, she said her goodbyes and left.

"Hannah," Josh called out to her, stopping her at the casino main entrance. "You doing anything now. Would you like to come over, have some coffee?"

"That's sweet, Josh. I'm going to have to say no, I have plans. Thanks for asking. See you around."

Josh seemed clipped by her answer even though he knew JT and her were together. She had told him and word had been circling around town that her and JT had been spending steamy nights together. *Small town gossip,* she laughed to herself. *People will be people.*

She didn't want to be mean to Josh. They could still be friends. She turned before going out into the winter wonderland. "Lunch tomorrow, though?"

Josh smiled and gave her a thumbs up.

The shoveling crews couldn't keep up with the snows of the past week. It was one huge storm after another, so Henry had them implement something like the emergency route system. Only the area around the casino, and the main road through town down to the front and back gates had a path cleared through them. She followed the path home. The packs were so high around her, she could imagine herself walking through ice tunnels, like something out of a fairy tale.

When she got home, JT was already there. He had a roaring fire going. It looked like heaven to her. She stripped down to her regular clothes, flopped on the couch, and curled her feet up under her. She sighed as the heat washed over her.

She was enjoying her and JT shacking up together. It was a blessing coming home to him instead of an empty house. She had started having these strange feelings, like she was a ghost, haunting this place that wasn't hers. It got so bad, at one point she had taken all the pictures and decorations of the previous owners and packed them all up. They were boxed up in the garage now. She tried not to look at them as she had done it. The smiling faces of the family looking back at her had hurt her heart too much. Turning her thoughts from that tangent, she wondered what JT was up to.

"Hey JT, where are you?" she called out.

JT popped around the corner. "I didn't hear you. I was just making some hot chocolate. I just about froze my twig and berries off, working on the wall all day. Want one?"

Hannah nodded. "You're the best."

JT came in with two mugs steaming. He sat down beside her. She sipped it and watched the marshmallows bob on top.

"Look at us, pretending to play house," she said.

JT spoke deep, like some husband from a lame sitcom. "How was your day, dear?" He couldn't keep it together and cracked up near the end.

"More of the same. Mucho blah, blah, blah. Just like my mom would complain about with the government, we don't get much done."

"Mmmmm."

"That 'hum' sounds fishy. What's up, JT?"

"I've just been thinking the past few days."

"You've been thinking? We're all in trouble now," Hannah hid her smile behind her mug.

"Screw you, I'm going home." JT made motions of getting up off the couch and heading for the door.

"You are home. Go on, I'll be quiet." JT gave her a look. "Okay I promise to try."

"Things have been going so well with you, me, us together. I was thinking, maybe you were right before, maybe we should leave." JT took a sip, watching her over the rim of his mug.

Her face crinkled. " Why? What's sparked this thought?"

"You've done great here. I'm proud of you. I've seen you try your best but I don't think you're happy. You're guard has come down some but you haven't made new friends here. Even though I know Josh has tried." JT raised his eyebrows up and down. Hannah mock slapped him. "You're still hanging around with me, Gus, and Linda. Then that got me to thinking. What if we did starting getting close to most of the people here? The more we are here the more attached you get to the them. On the council you are making decisions that affect them. Right now they are just figures and statistics but what will happen when they are names and faces? What happens to you if there is another attack by people or zombies and some of them get hurt or die? I've seen what that pressure does to you and you've seen what it does to me. I've come around to thinking Dusty was right. We should just stick together and keep on moving."

"You and me or are you talking about the Fab Four?" Hannah was serious with her question.

JT smiled. "I haven't brought it up to Gus and Linda. I will of course if it comes to that. I saw Linda on the way home today. I was feeling like I was coming down with something.

Wanted to see if they had any cold medicine. She gave me some Advil, told me to drink water and rest."

Hannah gave him an over the top disgusted look. "If you are getting sick, you're sleeping in the spare bedroom, mister. I don't want that crap."

JT rolled his eyes before continuing. "Poor woman, she is being worked ragged. Said she hardly even sees Childs anymore. It's like she is the one in charge. When he is there, he just gives the patients the bare minimum of a check over and then he is back with the zombies."

Hannah shivered. During cleanup, it was the second worse thing after having to bury the townspeople who died. Disposing of the zombies. It took all of her will but she made herself be a part of it. While they were piling them up outside the fence to burn, Childs came and said he wanted five of the most preserved. For research. Hannah wanted to protest but the look on his face said that was useless. Picking the zombies, she had no part of.

"Linda's got such a good heart, it's too bad she has to put up with Childs. She will though, she isn't going to let those people suffer."

"Right," JT said, half as a question. "Childs keeps telling her his theory, it's true. From what he's discovered, the zombies bodies really are breaking down. Just as any corpse would, but at a reduced rate. I almost made me blurt out my idea of leaving to her right there. Because, if what Childs is saying is true, think about the possibilities."

JT left his pregnant question floating in the air. Hannah wanted to act surprised at what he was suggesting. The positive impact it could have on a decision to leave. She couldn't deny though some of the same thoughts had crossed her mind. Just on the way home after the useless meetings in fact. Even before then, when she had been moving the undead bodies and recognized some as people she had seen around town. She had a gut feeling since the attack that JT was thinking about leaving as well. He had been restless, even after moving in with her.

It was a good thing here. For the first time since the Outbreak. It was safe, as safe as you could get now. True safety seemed to be an illusion. The town had achieved order out of chaos. Hard work had bought and paid for it.

There was another point, one JT didn't bring up. Who knew if there was another Roy, or Albright, or Harold in town. If not now, then maybe arriving with the next group of survivors. She wouldn't, couldn't fathom the belief of how terrible that world could be, back in what was her sheltered life. Living on those suburban streets and that college campus. That seemed like a different person in a different world now.

"With you is where I want to be JT. We both know I've been thinking about it off and on since we got here. But we can't be rash, let's sleep on it tonight and tomorrow we can get into discussing the logistical possibilities of it."

THE WORLD I KNOW

That night sleep escaped both Hannah and JT. They both decided to get up as the sun began to rise. Gus was an early riser anyhow so they opted to try and catch him before he left his house, along with Linda too.

The two of them commented on how peaceful things seemed early in the morning as they walked hand in hand the three blocks over to where Gus and Linda stayed. They both wore smiles as they saw Gus and Linda embracing while looking out their front window. When Gus saw them approaching his smile came to life as well as he made his way over to their front door and opened it inviting them in.

"Honey, the kids are home!" Gus poked fun as Hannah and JT entered.

The group idly chatted for a few minutes while Linda made fresh coffee. When it was ready they settled around the fire where JT decided it was time to get down to business.

"Gus, Linda we have some serious things to discuss with you guys." JT started.

"Well I didn't figure this visit was for a casual breakfast, let's get down to brass tacks kids, what's eating away at ya?" Gus seemed uncharacteristically concerned.

"Well Hannah and I have been giving things a lot of thought lately. We realize how comfortable things can be here but were still discussing leaving. Possibly soon, before any of us get more attached to anything here."

Gus and Linda shot worried looks at each other before Hannah continued where JT left off.

"I don't think I'm cut out to help save this place. I like most the people here, I have enjoyed pitching in to help out. Its even restored a little bit of my faith that maybe the world can go back to the way it once was but I don't think I want to become anymore involved here." Hannah was solemn in her seriousness.

"So what is it you are proposing here? That we just up and leave like thieves in the night?" Linda could tell they were being sold on the idea already.

"No, not like that at all." Hannah continued, "we will take a few days, plan things out, help where we can in the meantime. Give us all time to gather what we need, say our goodbyes. With any luck Child's or Henry will have someone give us a lift down the mountain or let us take one of the snow vehicles with us. JT had the idea, maybe we can find a place with an RV, so we can avoid having to find shelter while staying on the move."

Gus stood up and leaned on the mantle of the fireplace, resting his head on folded arms momentarily before turning to face them again.

"Well, maybe I can be the one to drive you down the mountain, help you find what you need." Gus said the words while his eyes welled up and he shoved his hands deep down into his pockets. JT couldn't find the strength to look at Gus like that, he felt like they had just broken his heart and he buried his chin in his chest focusing hard on the floor.

"Gus, no..." Hannah trailed off, unable to finish her sentence before getting choked up herself. Linda slid close to her wrapping her arm around her shoulders.

"I can't, I just can't keep up anymore, I'd only slow you kids down. I'm not trying to dissuade you in the slightest. If that's what you two want then I understand. But I need you both to promise this old man you will take care of each other, no more bullshit choices from the either of you." Gus was fighting back his emotions hard as his voice wavered.

The three of them stood, all embraced in a group hug around Gus as tears were shed. Linda joined them and to Hannah she felt that completed her decision.

The four of them spent the next couple of months together making plans and allowing winter to run its final most brutal course. JT found two old calendars from one of the shops in town and decided they would start marking days off until they got to thirty.

JT and Hannah arrived at Gus' house on the twenty ninth night. They were going to have one last night together. Hannah wanted a perfect last night together, because it was going to be hard for her.

"You ready for this?" JT asked as they stood outside the front door.

"No, but I'll survive." She squeezed JT's hand hard. Then she knocked.

Gus opened the door. "If it ain't Bonnie and Clyde. You two get your asses in here." Once inside and coats were off, Gus gave them both bear hugs.

They ate and joked all through the night. When Gus brought out a small battery operated boom box with a handful of CDs JT laughed. It was all old country music but still they all danced and goofed around until the wee hours of the morning.

When they had to say goodbye Hannah couldn't hold it in any longer. She began to cry. "Gus, I'm going to miss your sorry ass so much. Linda, it's been so nice to get to know you."

"Stop missie, before you get my waterworks aflowin'. You know I'm taken you down the mountain tomorrow. When you know you can't see perfection anymore, then you can cry."

Gus gave her another embrace that made her think of her father.

"JT, you make sure you both come back and check on me and Linda. Make sure she hasn't gotten tired of my old ass and poisoned me or something. Being a nurse, she probably knows twenty sneaky was to kill a man."

"It's twenty five, dear. So you best behave," Linda corrected.

JT chuckled but Hannah could also hear the thickness in his voice. "We sure will. See you bright and early in the morning?"

"With tinkerbells on." Gus said. He shut the door on them

"It feels like an end of an era," JT said to Hannah on the way back home.

THE WORLD I KNEW

This is going to be a lot rougher than I thought.

JT could already feel the lump in his throat and a welling in his eyes. Next to him Hannah was already crying, tears glowing in the cold winter sun. Her breath steamed in the frosty air.

They had come down out of the mountains into Colorado Springs. JT and Hannah had fallen into a familiar groove through the months before they left. They had spent the last of the winter slowly withdrawing from life in the town. Hannah gave up her council seat. She nominated Gus in her place. He bitched about it all the time, but JT thought he secretly enjoyed it. They took less and less work, which Dr. Childs bitched at them about. Saying they weren't pulling their weight, even threatening to stop feeding them. Then Henry or Josh would interfere on their behalf and it would stop for a little while and start over again.

Hannah had told him Josh had tried to convince her to stay multiple times, each time grasping at more desperate reasons. He had seen how Josh followed Hannah around like a sorry puppy. He would have been angry before. Not now though, he actually felt bad for the guy.

All that drama just confirmed in JT's mind they were better off on their own. This town was the best they were going to find and it still wasn't for them. Quietly they put together their survival kits, made plans, and they had actually had some luck on their side.

The weather had hit a warm patch lately and most of the snow on the roads melted away. The small streams had turned into rushing rivers. The white covered ground became clearer and clearer as they lost altitude. Early in the morning, they had said goodbye to Linda again. It was a short affair, she said she didn't want it to get sappy. They hadn't known her long but JT thought she was a genuinely good person and was glad Gus had her in his life. She was a rarity these days for sure.

They kept to the outskirts of the Colorado Springs area, keeping a watchful eye for both zombies and what they were looking for. They were in luck again, as it didn't take long to find. Surveying the area first and finding it clear, they drove onto the lot of a place called All Seasons Recreations. JT and Gus loaded the supplies out of the truck Henry had loaned them into the largest RV on the lot. The most difficult part of this part of their plan was prying the key lock box open inside the sales area. The place looked dusty but completely intact, apparently no one had thought to check out these kind of places after the Outbreak.

"Sure you don't want to come with us, old timer?" JT asked, trying to hold back the emotion from his voice as the time neared for them to leave. It was happening.

Gus smiled at him. "I've had enough running around kid, enough killing, and sure as damn well enough of those zombies. It's time for this old man to go into retirement. I'll stay and help rebuild where I can. Besides, I think me and Linda could make a go of it. I don't think there's a woman on the planet that could make a honest man out of me though." They both forced an awkward chuckle.

"Well Gus, it sure was nice meeting you," JT said, holding out his hand. "I would have had a worse life if our paths hadn't crossed."

"Come over here you big dumb galoot," Gus said, grabbing his hand and pulling JT in close for a hug. He gave JT three large pats on the back. "I'm going to miss you reminding me how old I am. You take damn good care of my little darlin' there."

JT sniffled and nodded as he pulled away. He took a few steps back to the RV and made a terrible act of checking the tires as tears flowed. He stood back up once he was in control.

"Hannah, haven't we had enough tears?" Gus asked, putting his gloved hands over hers. "Let me ask you. Are you sure you want to do this?"

"We're done with groups. If the Doctor is right, we just have to ride this out for a few more years," Hannah looked down at the ground. "I'm going to miss you so much though Gus. Without you, I don't....think I could go...."

"You were my sunshine, in this shitty ass world," Gus said, holding Hannah close to him. "I'm going to have to insist that if you ever drive anywhere near here, six months time or not, you're goin' stop in."

"Of course we will Gus," Hannah said, pulling back and wiping her red nose with her gloved hand.

"Also, if JT ends up playing hide the salami with you and you have a boy, you gotta name him Gus." Gus then gave JT a lurid wink.

"Gus!" Hannah cried incredulous, giving him a playful slap on the chest.

"Hey! I don't want to burden my child with a loser name like Gus," JT said.

Gus gave him the finger, then dramatically cleared his throat.

"This rarely happens but I'm serious when I say I wish you kids all the best. I love you guys like you're my own, hell maybe I will even see you on the flip side. If Dr. Childs doesn't change his looking down his nose act, I'll be rearranging it. Then we'll get kicked out and I'll have to come looking for you."

Gus took a quick swipe at his reddened eyes. "I better get back or Linda will worry I've fallen off the damn mountainside."

They all hugged goodbye one more time, Hannah and JT teaming up to give Gus a big kiss on each cheek as their best friend wept but Gus being Gus he still mockingly wiped his cheeks off.

JT and Hannah climbed into the RV. JT started it up. Gus drove his truck past the front, honking his horn. JT waved through the huge windshield, honking his two times in response. JT watched as Gus drove out of the parking lot waving out the window until he was out of sight.

Hannah was sitting in the passenger seat, trying hard to dry up her tears. JT reached over and put a hand on her shoulder. She looked at him, a strained smile on her face.

"Well little lady," JT said in a terrible cowboy accent. "Where are we riding off in the sunset to?"

"How about someplace warm and likely empty, like New Mexico. Out in the desert. Then, after the winter is totally over, we can drive up to Oregon. I've always wanted to go there."

"Alrighty, sounds good to me." He dropped the act. "Are you sure you're ready?"

Hannah squeezed his hand and nodded yes. JT put the RV into drive.

This is it, JT thought, as he pulled out of the lot. *It will just be me and Hannah now. Avoiding both zombies and people as much as we can. With a whole lot of luck, the zombies will just rot away and die, like Dr Childs believed. Then, maybe, there will be a chance of Hannah and I having a regular life.*

They rode in silence for the first few miles as thoughts of their fallen friends were heavy on his heart. Hannah still dabbed at an occasional tear with the sleeve of her shirt.

"Hey Hannah," JT broke the silence as he reached out his hand for Hannah to grab. When she did he slowed the vehicle to a crawl, looking directly at her.

"Hannah, I love you and I am here for you, always."

"I love you too JT." Hannah unbuckled her seatbelt to kiss him before returning to her seat.

"If you keep up that kind of talk we will be breaking in the bed back there sooner than tonight." Hannah slyly winked at JT while she twirled her hair.

JT couldn't wipe the smile off of his face as he watched the mountains in his rear view mirror and drove south. Leaving behind all that happened, good and bad, for the hope of a better tomorrow.

JOIN TEAK 6K

Thank you for purchasing Dead of Winter. We hope you enjoyed.

Our newsletter is the best place to get information about upcoming books, special promotions, and any other interesting updates we would like to share with our fans

Plus, would you like a free short story prequel to The Outbreak Series? Sign up for the newsletter and we'll sent it to you as a way to show our appreciation.

Visit **6kpress.com** to fill out the form and by Internet magic you shall receive.

Connect with 6K Press:

FACEBOOK: **facebook.com/6kpress**

TWITTER: **twitter.com/6k_press**

If you have a moment, please review the book on Amazon. Reviews help authors like us in a big way. Good or bad, honest feedback is appreciate. You have our thanks.

ABOUT THE AUTHORS

Thomas lives in a small rural town in Kansas with his wife and son. He probably thinks about how to survive a zombie apocalypse way too much.

Robert live is the Kansas City area, is a husband, and a father of twin boys. He likes post apocalyptic stories, probably a little too much. Somehow he also fits in the time to write.

Made in the USA
Columbia, SC
08 March 2020